THE POISON PUZZLE

EMILY ORGAN

Storm
PUBLISHING

This is a work of fiction. Names, characters, businesses, places, events and incidents are either the products of the author's imagination or used in a fictitious manner. Any resemblance to actual persons, living or dead, or actual events is purely coincidental.

Copyright © Emily Organ, 2025

The moral right of the author has been asserted.

All rights reserved. No part of this book may be reproduced or used in any manner without the prior written permission of the copyright owner. This prohibition includes, but is not limited to, any reproduction or use for the purpose of training artificial intelligence technologies or systems.

To request permissions, contact the publisher at rights@stormpublishing.co

Ebook ISBN: 978-1-80508-881-3
Paperback ISBN: 978-1-80508-883-7

Cover design: Ghost
Cover images: Shutterstock, Adobe Stock

Published by Storm Publishing.
For further information, visit:
www.stormpublishing.co

ALSO BY EMILY ORGAN

Emma Langley Victorian Mysteries
The Whitechapel Widow

Penny Green Series
Limelight
The Rookery
The Maid's Secret
The Inventor
Curse of the Poppy
The Bermondsey Poisoner
An Unwelcome Guest
Death at the Workhouse
The Gang of St Bride's
Murder in Ratcliffe
The Egyptian Mystery
The Camden Spiritualist

Augusta Peel Series
Death in Soho
Murder in the Air
The Bloomsbury Murder
The Tower Bridge Murder
Death in Westminster
Murder on the Thames

The Baker Street Murders

Death in Kensington

Churchill & Pemberley Series

Tragedy at Piddleton Hotel

Murder in Cold Mud

Puzzle in Poppleford Wood

Trouble in the Churchyard

Wheels of Peril

The Poisoned Peer

Fiasco at the Jam Factory

Disaster at the Christmas Dinner

Christmas Calamity at the Vicarage (novella)

Writing as Martha Bond

Lottie Sprigg Travels Mystery Series

Murder in Venice

Murder in Paris

Murder in Cairo

Murder in Monaco

Murder in Vienna

Lottie Sprigg Country House Mystery Series

Murder in the Library

Murder in the Grotto

Murder in the Maze

Murder in the Bay

ONE

January 1889

The dull brass plaque beside the door bore a sinister symbol: a watchful eye set within a key. Emma Langley's fingers trembled as she traced the familiar design – the same one she'd found in her late husband's diary.

The house stood in darkness while lights glimmered from the smart Kensington townhouses either side of it. Ivy crawled around the porch and a layer of grime coated the dark windows. Emma wondered what the neighbours thought of the ramshackle building which disrupted the elegant uniformity of the street. Who lived here?

It was tempting to knock on someone's door and ask. But she felt too timid to do so. For now, she was content to find the house and discover what it looked like. No one was at home but she felt a sensation of being watched. The skin prickled on her arms and the back of her neck.

She'd found the address in the back of her husband's diary: number seventeen, Stanford Road. The house had no visible name or number, but it stood between numbers fifteen and nineteen so she assumed it was the right place.

A cold January wind whirled around the neglected patch of garden at the front of the house and pulled at her skirts. The rusty iron gate squealed on its hinges and Emma winced at the sound.

She stepped back to get a better view of the house in the early evening gloom, avoiding the deep shadow cast by a gnarled tree. The building was three storeys high and topped by a steep gable. A turret to the side of the roof gave the house an odd, lop-sided appearance. A bent weathervane on the turret's roof pierced the darkening sky along with a cluster of tall chimneys.

What did the symbol on the brass plaque mean? Her husband, William, had drawn it in his diary on the third Thursday of each month, as if marking an appointment.

Movement caught her eye at an upper window.

She caught her breath. Was someone there?

She stopped still, her heart pounding in her ears.

Someone was watching her. She felt sure of it.

A crow flapped out of the tree, startling her. There was something malevolent about this place. Evil even.

Emma turned and hurried along the cracked path to the rusted gate. She'd visited this house at the wrong time of day. It was far creepier in the fading light than she imagined it would be on a bright sunny morning.

She stepped through the gate and briskly made her way to Kensington High Street underground railway station.

Why had William made a note of this address? She'd uncovered so many of his secrets since his death, but it looked like there was one final mystery left to solve.

TWO

Emma met Penny Blakely for lunch the following day. Penny had once been a news reporter on Fleet Street and the pair had become friends after Emma had asked her to help find her husband's murderer. They dined together each Tuesday in the ladies' dining room at Café Monico, Piccadilly Circus. It was a refined yet relaxed place with tall windows, draped velvet curtains and ornate plasterwork.

Penny listened intently as Emma described the house on Stanford Road. 'What a creepy place,' she commented. 'Did you knock on the door?'

'No.' Emma felt embarrassed admitting it.

'You didn't?' Penny raised her eyebrows. 'I would have!'

'I know. I'm not as brave as you.'

'Brave? I don't call it that. It's just being curious. Were you afraid of who might answer?'

Emma shifted in her chair. 'A little bit, I suppose.' She took a sip of water. 'What would I have said to them?'

'Asked for Mr Smith.'

'Who's he?'

'I don't know. But you could have pretended to be looking

for him. It's an easy way to explain why you're there. And if you're lucky, the person who answers the door offers you some information about themselves or the house. The worst that can happen is they tell you to go away. And most people aren't that rude.'

'I wish I'd thought of that,' said Emma. Sometimes she envied Penny's quick thinking and confidence. She had to remind herself Penny had experience. She was thirteen years her senior and had worked for ten years as a news reporter.

The waiter approached their table and gave a courteous bow. 'Would you like to order your usual, ladies?'

'Yes please,' said Emma.

'Consommé au riz followed by saumon grillé?' He enjoyed enunciating the French words.

'Thank you,' replied Penny.

They resumed their conversation once he'd left. 'So the house has a plaque with the same symbol that we found in William's diary?' asked Penny.

'Yes. And in his diary, the symbol marks the third Thursday of each month.'

'Do you remember William going to a meeting on that day each month?'

'Yes, he told me it was a committee meeting he had to attend.' Emma's throat tightened as she recalled the extent of her husband's deceit.

'Your husband was secretive and this monthly meeting was so clandestine that he didn't write the name in his diary,' said Penny. 'I guess it must be the meeting of a society.'

'I suppose so. But he never mentioned it to me. I just...' She trailed off as she felt a surge of emotion in her chest.

Penny patiently waited for her to continue.

Emma took in a breath and tried to calm herself. 'I just feel like I'm being made a fool of all over again. Even though he's dead!'

Penny reached out and took her hand. 'You're not a fool, Emma. You had every right to trust your husband and he broke that trust. He deliberately deceived you. He was a liar and a cheat.' She paused and took a sip of water. 'I'm sorry if my words about him are strong. I never met him, but I've seen what he did to you. You didn't deserve it and it makes me angry.'

Emma smiled. Penny's concern for her was comforting. 'I want to find out what the symbol means,' she said. 'Did my husband go to that house? And if he did, then why?'

'Are you sure you want to find out?'

'Yes. Well... I think I do.' Emma bit her lip as she thought. Was she going to discover something else unpleasant about her husband? Her investigation into his death had revealed he was not the man she'd thought he'd been. But she reasoned it was unlikely any new revelations about his life would sink her opinion of him even lower than it already was.

'If you choose to look into it then I can help,' said Penny. 'And even if you don't, then I want to see that house for myself. Having heard your description of it, I want to see if it really is that creepy!'

'It is,' said Emma. 'And that's what worries me. There's something very unpleasant about the place.'

'Well, then perhaps we should just forget about it. We don't want—'

'I want to do it,' interrupted Emma, feeling resolute. 'Having matched the symbol to that house, I can't ignore it now.'

'Well, if you're sure, then let's go there together.' Penny leaned forward, her eyes alight with an intensity Emma hadn't seen in months. Her fingers drummed excitedly against the table. This was the old Penny – the news reporter who had once chased mysteries through London's darkest corners before motherhood had confined her to home and hearth. Emma could practically see her friend's mind racing with possibilities, already plotting their investigation.

'The third Thursday of this month is the day after tomorrow,' said Emma, her voice dropping to a whisper despite them being alone. 'We could visit the house in the evening and find out if a meeting is being held there.'

'Perfect!' Penny straightened in her chair. 'What time were William's supposed committee meetings?'

'Eight o'clock.'

'Let's get there a little earlier, then we should see who's arriving.'

Emma's heart quickened, a thrill of anticipation coursing through her. 'I wonder who they are. It all seems so puzzling.'

THREE

A misty fog settled over Stanford Road the following Thursday evening. Emma and Penny stood across the road from the mysterious house. It had rained heavily during the day and the fog now trapped the damp and cold. Despite her layers of clothing, Emma shivered, chilled by the frigid air.

A window in the turret began to glow. 'Look!' she whispered. 'A light!' It flickered as though cast by a candle.

'Someone's in there?' said Penny. 'But it was dark a moment ago. How strange. We could knock at the door and see if they answer.'

'I'd rather just see who turns up,' said Emma. She wanted to keep watch for the time being, hoping she'd pick up clues from the people arriving for the meeting. It was possible she'd recognize someone – a friend of her late husband, perhaps.

A horse's hooves and carriage wheels approached and they turned to see the twin lights of a hansom cab.

'Here we go!' whispered Penny excitedly. The two women backed away from the nearest gas lamp to where they could watch unobserved from the shadows.

The cab splashed through the puddles and stopped outside

number seventeen. When it pulled away again, all they could see was the dark silhouette of a person in the doorway. The knocker sounded, and the door opened to admit the arrival into gloomy, flickering gaslight.

'Well, I have no idea who that person was,' said Penny. 'I couldn't even tell if it was a man or a woman.'

'Me neither,' said Emma.

They heard footsteps approach. On the other side of the street, a figure with a dark overcoat, top hat and walking cane emerged from the fog into the pool of muted light beneath a gas lamp. The brim of his hat cast a shadow over his face and masked his features. They watched his dark form turn in through the gate of the mysterious house and knock at the door. He was admitted as quickly and quietly as the previous person.

A four-wheeled carriage pulled up outside the house, then another hansom cab. After a few minutes, Emma and Penny had counted eight arrivals.

A church clock nearby chimed eight o'clock and the two women waited a few minutes more.

'That must be everyone,' said Emma. 'They've all arrived.'

The light in the turret room brightened, as if the curtain had been moved.

Emma startled. 'Someone's watching us!' A dark silhouette appeared at the window.

'But they can't see us,' said Penny. 'It's too dark and foggy out here.'

'Are you sure?'

'Quite sure. They won't be able to see much at all.'

The figure was motionless. Emma sensed the person was staring directly at her. Their gaze felt vindictive and a chill ran down her spine. 'I don't like it.'

'We don't need to stay here for now,' said Penny. 'Let's find somewhere to keep warm for the next hour. Then we can return for when the meeting finishes. It's not much fun in this horrible weather, but I think it could be worth it if we manage to speak to one of the attendees.'

After warming themselves in the coffee room of a nearby hotel, Emma and Penny returned to their observation spot on foggy Stanford Road.

The turret window of number seventeen was still lit but the figure had gone.

They crossed the street to get closer to the house, dodging puddles as they went. Moments later, shadowy figures began to emerge from the building. One climbed into a waiting cab and another walked towards them.

'Someone's coming this way,' whispered Emma. She felt anxious about an interaction, but knew they had to make their long wait in the damp and cold worthwhile.

'I'll speak to him,' said Penny.

Emma's heart thudded as he approached. Would he be friendly?

'Good evening!' said Penny. 'My friend and I were admiring number seventeen, it's an unusual looking building. What's it used for?'

'None of your business,' came the reply as he strode on past.

'Well, that was rather rude,' whispered Emma.

'Maybe he considered my question rude,' said Penny. 'But there was no need to be so dismissive. If anything, his response has only sharpened my curiosity.' She nudged Emma, nodding towards the house. 'Look – someone else is coming our way.'

Emma straightened her shoulders, summoning her courage. 'I'll ask this time.' Her voice was steadier than she felt, but she needed to prove – to herself as much as to Penny – that she wasn't just a passive observer.

Penny's eyebrows rose. 'Are you certain?'

'Of course,' said Emma, clenching and unclenching her gloved hands. 'I can do this.'

Behind her, she heard the wheels and hooves of an approaching carriage. She would have to be quick if the gentleman planned to get into it.

The man drew nearer. 'Good evening!' she said. But no sooner had she spoken, than the cab drove through a puddle and splashed her.

'Oh, goodness me!' said the gentleman, stopping. 'That's quite a soaking. Terrible. These cab drivers are always in a hurry and never looking where they're going. On a foggy night like this, they should be extra cautious. Are you all right?'

'I'm fine,' said Emma, pleasantly surprised by his kindness. 'Just rather wet.'

'You're going to catch a terrible chill. Here, have my coat.' He began to unbutton it.

'Oh no, I couldn't possibly—'

But the gentleman was already removing his overcoat.

He was going to so much trouble that Emma felt it was better to accept. She pulled off her coat and Penny held it for her while she put on the gentleman's coat. The shoulders were too big, and the sleeves came down past her hands. But it was warm and made of good quality wool.

'How's that?' he asked. She could barely see his face in the gloom, but he seemed to be about forty years of age and had a moustache.

'I feel very warm now, thank you,' she said. 'But what about you?'

'Don't worry about me at all. I'm staying at the Imperial Grand nearby. I'll be there in two minutes. Return my coat to me at the hotel tomorrow evening, if you wouldn't mind.'

'Of course.'

'My name's Harpole.' He tipped his hat. 'I shall see you tomorrow.' He slipped away into the fog.

'Oh dear,' said Emma. 'What a disaster. I didn't even ask him about the building.'

'You didn't get a chance,' said Penny.

Emma turned and looked back at number seventeen. The light in the turret had gone. 'I suppose everybody's left now,' she said. 'They all came out at the same time and hurried off.'

'It doesn't matter,' said Penny.

'Doesn't matter? We've been out here all evening! And we're wet and cold and have no answers.'

'But don't you see? We now have a proper opportunity to speak to Mr Harpole tomorrow. He seemed friendly, too. But perhaps a little too friendly, it makes me suspicious.'

Emma felt puzzled. 'Suspicious? Why?'

'I don't know. I just have an odd feeling about it.'

FOUR

Emma met Penny outside the Imperial Grand Hotel on Kensington Road at six o'clock the following evening. The hotel's imposing facade was obscured by fog but the entrance was well-lit by a pair of gas lamps. Emma carried Mr Harpole's coat over her arm.

'I hope we can find out something from him about the house and the meeting there,' said Penny as they stepped into the hotel lobby. Their footsteps echoed on the tiled floor and light from large chandeliers gleamed on the polished carved-wood furnishings. 'I realize it's secret and he's unlikely to tell us much. But he might accidentally let something slip.'

'I can ask him if he knew William,' said Emma. 'I feel sure he must have done.'

One of the liveried doormen was in the centre of the lobby, picking up something from the floor. 'Did you see the lady who just left?' he asked them.

'No.'

'She dropped this,' he said, cradling something in his palm. 'She was in a hurry.'

The object was an ornate cloak pin. He dashed past them to the door.

At the reception desk, Emma asked to speak to Mr Harpole.

'You mean Lord Harpole?' replied the receptionist. He had a sombre face and oiled hair.

'Lord?' Emma exchanged a surprised glance with Penny. 'He told me his name was Harpole, and I assumed he was Mr.'

'He's in room thirty-seven on the third floor.'

Emma and Penny climbed the grand staircase. 'A lord?' whispered Emma. 'I don't know how to speak to a lord.'

'You can speak to him just as you did yesterday evening,' said Penny. 'He's clearly a kind and helpful gentleman.'

On the third floor, the plush carpet muffled their steps in the corridor. Room thirty-seven had a polished oak door and gold numbers. Emma knocked, and they waited.

Everything was silent.

'What do we do if he's not here?' whispered Emma.

'We can leave his coat at the reception desk,' said Penny. 'But it will be disappointing as I'd like to speak to him.'

The thick woollen coat was heavy. Emma rearranged it over her arm. As she did so, something square and silver fell out of a pocket onto the carpet. She stooped down to pick it up. 'His snuff box,' she said.

'Let's knock again,' said Penny, giving the door a sharp rap with her knuckles.

They heard a faint voice from within, but no distinct words. 'Lord Harpole?' Penny called through the door.

The voice murmured something indistinct behind the heavy door.

'I think that means we can go in,' she said, already reaching for the handle with unwavering confidence.

Emma caught her wrist, eyes wide. 'Are you sure?'

Without answering, Penny tried the handle. 'It's not locked.' The statement carried an air of finality.

'Shouldn't we wait for him to come to the door?' Emma whispered, glancing anxiously down the corridor. 'Or for his valet?'

Penny was already pushing the door open. 'We've come this far. Lord Harpole?' said Penny.

There was no answer.

Penny stepped inside and Emma cautiously followed. The dingy room was large and smelled of tobacco and eau de cologne. The only light came from the fire in the grate. Chairs and a table were arranged by the fireplace and Emma could see an enormous four-poster bed in the far corner of the room. Heavy brocade curtains covered the windows.

Lord Harpole sat in a wing-backed leather chair, his head slumped. He wore a waistcoat and his shirt sleeves were rolled up.

Emma felt her stomach contract. Something was wrong.

'Lord Harpole?' said Penny again. He gave a quiet groan, but didn't move. His face was pale and sweaty.

A half-empty bottle of whisky and an empty glass stood on the table next to his chair.

'It looks like he's over-indulged,' said Penny, examining the bottle. 'What's this?' A piece of paper rested on the table. 'Oh, goodness,' she said once she'd read it. 'Look.'

Emma stepped over to the table. The note on the paper was short:

I'm sorry but I couldn't carry on.

Charles

A suicide note. Emma felt a chill run through her.

Two more bottles stood on the table, empty and ominously small next to the whisky. Penny lifted one, turning it to catch the dim light. 'Laudanum,' she said, her voice dropping to a horrified whisper. 'He's drunk this, too. Two entire bottles!' The glass clinked loudly as she set it down and her face drained of colour. She spun back to the slumped figure, urgently grasping his limp hand. 'Lord Harpole? Can you hear me?' Her voice cracked with mounting dread.

'I'll fetch help,' said Emma, flinging the coat over the back of a chair and rushing out of the room. Moments later, she reached the reception desk and told the receptionist Lord Harpole was unwell.

'I'll summon a doctor,' he replied, his face filled with concern.

Back in Lord Harpole's room, Emma found Penny kneeling by his chair, trying to keep him conscious.

'Speak again, Lord Harpole,' she urged, her face inches from his as she searched for any sign of consciousness. Her knuckles whitened as she gripped his hand. 'Tell me what happened.'

Emma hovered anxiously behind her, resting against the table for support. 'Did he say something?' she whispered, her eyes darting between Penny and the dying man's ashen face.

'Just the word "help". But I could barely hear it and he hasn't opened his eyes.'

He moved his head, as if attempting to lift it. Then he groaned. His breath rasped as he managed to speak again. 'Help me.'

'A doctor is on his way,' said Penny. 'He'll help you. Tell me how much whisky you drank.'

His head lolled dangerously to one side, his breathing shallow and irregular.

'Lord Harpole!' Penny clutched his hand between both of hers, her voice rising with urgency. 'Stay with us!' She pressed her fingers against his wrist, frantically searching for a pulse.

The door burst open as the young receptionist rushed in with a bespectacled man carrying a worn leather physician's bag. The doctor immediately pushed past them, kneeling before Lord Harpole with practised efficiency.

'Thank God you're here,' Penny gasped, stumbling backwards on unsteady legs. She pointed to the evidence with a shaking hand. 'Whisky and laudanum. And there's a note – I think he took it deliberately.'

The doctor's weathered face hardened as he assessed the situation. 'I need to work quickly,' he said, snapping open his bag and pulling out instruments. 'You ladies need to leave. Now.'

Emma and Penny waited in the hotel corridor, anxiously awaiting news from the doctor.

Emma paced up and down, recalling Lord Harpole's polite and generous manner the previous evening. What dark desperation had consumed him in less than a day since their meeting?

The receptionist emerged from the room, his shoulders slumped in defeat. He slowly shook his head, not quite meeting their eyes. Emma felt the floor tilt beneath her, a cold void opening in her chest.

'He couldn't be saved?' Penny's voice was barely audible, although they already knew the answer.

'I'm afraid not.' The young man swallowed hard. 'The doctor says it was too late from the moment you found him. The amount he took...' He left the sentence unfinished, backing away. 'I must make arrangements.'

His footsteps echoed hollowly down the corridor as Emma sagged against the wall, the finality of death settling over them like a shroud.

Penny's lips were pursed, and her eyes wide and unblinking. 'We must stay here,' she said. 'We found Lord Harpole and we'll need to tell people what happened. The police will probably turn up, too.'

'Oh, goodness.' Emma leaned against the wall, her knees felt weak. 'We're caught up in this just because we were returning his coat.'

A few minutes later, a group of people advanced towards them along the corridor. Emma felt a sense of trepidation as they approached. She and Penny would be bombarded with questions. They would have to repeat their account of the evening many times over.

The group contained two members of hotel staff, two police constables and a concerned-looking gentleman in a dark suit. Everyone went into the room except for a young, soft-faced constable who stopped with Emma and Penny.

'Did you two ladies know the gentleman in question?' he asked.

'Not very well,' said Emma. 'We met him briefly yesterday evening, and he lent me his coat after I was soaked by a puddle. We came here today to return the coat to him.'

The constable took a notebook from his pocket. 'Can you tell me what happened here this evening, please?'

Emma and Penny gave him their accounts. Once they'd finished, he thanked them and stepped into the room.

'Do you think we can go now?' Emma said to Penny.

'Yes.' Penny took her arm. 'I don't know about you, but I feel exhausted all of a sudden.'

'Here comes someone else,' said Emma.

A short gentleman strode towards them, his arms swinging briskly by his sides. As he reached them, he removed his top hat. He was mousey-haired with a strong jawline, gaunt cheeks and deep-set blue eyes.

'Good evening, ladies.' His smile faded as he noticed the open door and their sombre expressions. 'I'm here to see Harpole. Is everything all right?'

Emma and Penny exchanged a glance, both wary of telling him the bad news.

Penny cleared her throat. 'He was taken unwell.'

His brow furrowed. 'Someone's with him in there?'

'Yes, a doctor,' said Emma. 'And some of the hotel staff.'

'What about Campbell?'

'Campbell?' asked Penny.

'His valet.'

'I saw a man in a dark suit who could have been his valet,' said Emma.

'He's in there?'

Emma nodded.

The gentleman stepped forward but Penny held out a palm to halt him. 'I'm afraid the doctor has just told us that Lord Harpole has died.'

'Died?' His eyes widened and his jaw dropped. 'Charles is dead? How?'

The soft-faced constable, clearly overhearing their conversation, stepped out of the room.

'Who are you, sir?' The constable's hand moved instinctively towards his truncheon.

The man drew himself up, his eyes narrowing with sudden suspicion. 'Rupert Crowfield.' His gaze darted past the constable to the hotel room door. 'I'm here to see my friend Charles.' A muscle twitched in his jaw. 'What's happened? Why are you here?'

Emma and Penny chose that moment to leave.

'What a horrible chain of events,' said Emma as they descended the staircase. 'If that first gentleman we tried to speak to yesterday hadn't ignored us, then we wouldn't have approached Lord Harpole, would we? And if we hadn't approached him, then I wouldn't have been splashed by that hansom cab, and he wouldn't have lent me his coat. We would never have known him at all.'

'And it's all because of a strange symbol in your late husband's diary,' said Penny.

'I wish now that I'd ignored it!'

'But it's too late now,' responded Penny. 'From beyond the grave he's somehow pulled you into another mystery.'

FIVE

'It's all very sad,' said Mrs Solomon, reading the *Morning Express* at the breakfast table the following morning. 'It says here Lord Harpole was engaged to be married to Lady Amelia Somersham, the daughter of the ninth Earl Somersham. Goodness, you can't imagine how that young lady must be feeling at a time like this, can you?'

Emma shook her head and took a small bite of toast. She had little appetite after the previous evening's events.

'Of course it doesn't say here yet that it's...' Her landlady lowered her voice. 'Suicide. I suppose they don't want to report that yet, out of respect for the family. Such a tragedy for those left behind. That poor young woman – to lose her future husband so suddenly! To leave a beautiful young fiancée behind! And he had everything, of course. An enormous stately home in Berkshire. Wickham House, it says here. He inherited it after the death of his father a year ago. It seems Lord Harpole had everything he could have ever wanted in life and he chose to turn his back on it all. More tea?'

'Thank you.'

Mrs Solomon removed the tapestry tea cosy from the teapot. 'It's often the way, of course,' she continued. 'These people rarely know how privileged they are. They're used to it. It's all they've ever known. And so he chose to put an end to it all, just like that.' She clicked her fingers then picked up the teapot. 'Quite astonishing. And it shows you something else, too. It shows that you can have everything you possibly want in the world and it still won't make you happy.' She poured tea into Emma's cup. 'I'll leave you to add your own milk as you like it.'

'Thank you.' Emma rested her half-eaten piece of toast on her plate.

'Oh, you poor thing, Mrs Langley. It must have been such an awful shock for you yesterday. Dreadful to see a gentleman so close to death like that!'

Emma had been trying to remove the image from her mind, but Mrs Solomon's words put it firmly back there. She picked up the milk jug and added milk to her tea until it was a pleasing shade of light brown.

'I suppose you'll be cancelling your lessons today?' asked Mrs Solomon, buttering another slice of toast.

'No, I'll continue with them.' Emma enjoyed teaching the piano. 'They'll take my mind off things.'

'Ah yes. A welcome distraction. Well, good for you, Mrs Langley. Sometimes it can help to put on a brave face and get on with it, can't it? You'll need to eat more of your breakfast, though, to give you strength for the day ahead.'

Emma smiled at her landlady's mothering tone. Although it was sometimes annoying, she liked being looked after occasionally.

She picked up her piece of toast and did her best to finish it. As she ate, her mind turned over the events of the past few days. She'd hoped she would learn more about the mysterious society from Lord Harpole, but his death had put a stop to that idea. Why had he ended his life? And what secrets had he taken with him?

SIX

As Emma readied herself to leave the house for her first lesson of the day, she found something in her handbag which she'd forgotten about.

Lord Harpole's snuff box.

She didn't remember putting it in her bag. She recalled picking it up from the floor of the hotel corridor when it had fallen out of the pocket of the overcoat. She'd been so distracted by the state of Lord Harpole that she'd absent-mindedly pushed the snuff box into her handbag without further thought.

She held it now in her palm. It was a finely crafted item with a scalloped shape and detailed floral engraving. It looked quite valuable and would need to be returned to the Harpole family.

Emma recalled her father and brother taking snuff; she'd never understood the appeal of it. She pushed her thumbnail beneath the lid and carefully opened it to see how much tobacco was left inside.

To her surprise, there was no snuff at all but a piece of folded paper and a small key. Intrigued, she unfolded the paper and saw it was a cloakroom ticket for the left luggage office in

Paddington railway station. It was stamped with the date two days previously: the seventeenth of January. The day when she and Penny had first met Lord Harpole.

Why had he put a cloakroom ticket and a key inside a snuff box?

By the time she'd finished her last lesson of the day, Emma had decided to visit the left luggage office at Paddington station and collect the item which had been left there. She guessed it was a locked case, box or trunk and the key would open it.

Was it wrong to collect the item herself? Emma pondered this as she travelled on the underground railway. By right, it belonged to the Harpole family. But she reasoned that if she passed the ticket to them, then it could be forgotten about amidst their shock and grief. If she collected the item herself, then it would be safely retrieved and there was a possibility it could provide her with a clue about the secret society.

Paddington station echoed with the noise of steam, whistles and porters' trollies. At the left luggage office, Emma fumbled for the ticket in her handbag then handed it to the attendant. She worried he would notice she wasn't the same person who'd dropped the item off. Fortunately he seemed unbothered and returned moments later with a small leather case. The case felt light; whatever was inside weighed very little. She sauntered away with it, acting as if she regularly carried it about. But her hand, which gripped the handle of the case, tingled with anticipation.

Where could she open it? She glanced around her, but there seemed nowhere suitable in the busy railway station. An idea struck her. Penny's home in St John's Wood was only a short journey away. She knew Penny would be keen to look inside the case, too.

. . .

While waiting on the platform in the underground railway station, Emma noticed a man looking at her. Every time she glanced at him, he turned away. He looked about thirty, had brown whiskers and wore a dark overcoat and a bowler hat.

She told herself she was probably imagining it because she was carrying something which didn't belong to her. Even so, she moved a little further down the platform away from him.

When the train arrived, she got into a second-class compartment with two other people. To her dismay, the brown-whiskered man got into the same compartment and sat next to her.

Was it just coincidence? Or was he following her? Her heart thudded against her ribs as the train made its way through the tunnel. Lord Harpole's case rested on her lap. It was a dark shade of brown but appeared well used with scuffed corners and knocks and marks in the leather. She placed a protective hand on it, keen to keep it close.

At Edgware Road station, one of the passengers got off, but the brown-whiskered man remained. Emma planned to get off at the next station, Baker Street. It was a large, busy station and if the man followed her, Emma hoped she could lose him there.

She disembarked at Baker Street and hurried along the crowded platform. She followed the signs for the Metropolitan Railway, glancing over her shoulder as she walked. To her relief, there was no sign of the man. On the platform, she walked to the far end and waited close to the tunnel's entrance. The brown-whiskered man was nowhere to be seen and Emma felt her shoulders relax a little. Perhaps she'd been imagining it after all. Carrying Lord Harpole's case made her anxious and she couldn't wait to reach Penny's home.

St John's Wood was the next station on the line and Emma got there without incident. It was getting dark as she left the station and the gas lamps were being lit. She paused to button her overcoat with one hand, then turned left into the high street, still glancing over her shoulder.

At the top of the high street, Emma turned right into St John's Wood Terrace, then left into Ordnance Road. Just as she was about to cross the road to turn into Henstridge Place, she saw the man again.

She paused. Her stomach knotted. Who was he? And was he dangerous? She didn't want to lead him to Penny's house. What could she do?

Emma took in a breath and calmly walked past Penny's street. Then she turned right into Acacia Road, passing large, semi-detached houses. Could she call at one of them and ask for help? The idea seemed foolish, but she didn't know what else to do. The brown-whiskered man followed her on the other side of the street, as if pretending he wasn't following at all. She kept walking, gripping the case as tightly as she could. If he decided to snatch it from her, she doubted she'd be able to put up much of a fight.

She turned right into Townshend Road, then right again into Henry Street. The man still followed. Did he plan to take the case from her? Or was he just watching her to see where she took it?

Her mouth felt dry and her heart continued to pound in her chest. She didn't feel able to put up with this strain for much longer. She reached the end of the road and found herself on the high street again. She'd walked a complete loop. Glancing behind her, she saw the man loitering by a public house. He appeared to be glancing through the windows, but she knew he was watching her.

She wondered if she should confront the man and ask him who he was. But that risked him snatching the case from her. Perhaps she could report him to the police for causing her a nuisance?

She turned left into the high street, went into a grocer's

shop and asked where the nearest police station was. As she spoke, her breath felt quick and shallow.

'Take the next left, then right,' said the barrel-chested grocer. 'Lower William Street. You can't miss it.'

Relief flooded through Emma when she realized how close the police station was. She hurried forward, the skin between her shoulder blades prickling with the awareness of being watched. The brown-whiskered man maintained his distance across the street, his hands thrust deep in his pockets, his gaze never leaving her.

The blue lamp of the police station glowed like a beacon of safety ahead. Emma quickened her pace, her heart hammering against her ribs. At the station steps, she paused and turned, deliberately meeting her pursuer's gaze. He froze mid-step, his posture suddenly tense.

Their eyes locked for one electric moment before Emma pushed the heavy door.

Through the frosted glass, she caught a glimpse of the brown-whiskered man retreat into the shadows.

SEVEN

'Everything all right, madam?' asked the desk sergeant in the police station.

Emma stood in the wood-panelled waiting area, clutching the case. 'I think someone was following me but he's gone now.'

He frowned. 'Do you know who he was?'

'No.' She felt reluctant to explain more, knowing that the case she was carrying didn't belong to her.

The policeman stepped out from behind his desk, strode over to the door and pushed it open. He glanced up and down the street. 'What did he look like?' he called over his shoulder.

'He had brown whiskers and wore an overcoat and dark hat. He looked about thirty.' She felt keen to be on her way now, worried the policeman might ask her about the case. 'It doesn't matter anymore. I'll go on my way.'

'Are you sure?'

She nodded.

'Very well.' He held the door open for her. 'But if you see him again, come back and let me know.'

'I will. Thank you.'

She stepped out into the street and briskly walked the short distance to Penny's house.

Fortunately, the Blakely family was at home. Penny answered the door with baby Florence in her arms. Her forehead creased with concern as she took in Emma's pale face and trembling hands. 'Are you all right, Emma? You look as though you've seen a ghost.'

'I'm fine.' She forced a smile. 'But someone's been following me.'

Penny's eyes widened behind her spectacles. 'You'll have to tell me all about it! Come in.'

She invited Emma into the sitting room where Thomas, her two-year-old son, was pulling a wheeled wooden dog around the room. Penny's husband, James, greeted Emma warmly. He was still wearing his jacket and Emma guessed he'd just returned home from work.

Penny handed the baby to James and told him she and Emma would talk in the dining room. Once they were there, Emma put the small leather case on the table. 'This belongs to Lord Harpole.'

Penny's eyes grew wider still. 'So that's why someone's been following you?'

Penny listened intently as Emma told her about the cloakroom ticket, the case and the brown-whiskered man.

'Goodness,' said Penny, once she'd finished. 'Your day has been far more interesting than mine. Let's look inside this case.'

Emma took the small key from the snuffbox in her handbag and fitted it into the lock on the case. She turned it and it gave a satisfying click.

A thought struck her. She paused and turned to Penny. 'It might contain something horrible.'

'Like what?'

'I don't know.' The memory of the bloodied knife she'd found in her husband's case returned. 'A weapon,' she said. 'Or something even worse. Like a severed finger.' She shuddered and Penny pulled a grimace.

'Would you like me to look inside first?'

Emma inhaled deeply, squaring her shoulders. She could feel Penny watching her, and she refused to appear cowardly. 'No, it's all right,' she said, her voice steadier than her hands. 'I'll open it myself.'

She lifted the lid. The inside of the case was lined with red felt and a buff-coloured envelope rested inside. Emma took out the envelope. Nothing was written on it and it was closed with a wax seal.

'Perhaps it's Lord Harpole's will,' said Penny, a mixture of excitement and apprehension playing across her features.

Emma sighed. 'In which case, we shouldn't open it. It belongs to his family.'

'That's disappointing.'

A pause followed as Emma and Penny stared at the envelope.

'It might not be his will,' said Emma.

'No, it might not be.'

'It might be something about the secret society.'

'Yes, it might.'

'And it's clearly something important because a man followed me. He must want this case for a reason.'

Penny tapped her chin as she thought. 'It's possible to remove a seal without damaging it. I've done it before.'

Emma's heart lifted. She couldn't bear the thought of not looking inside the envelope. 'And can it be sealed again without anyone noticing?'

'Yes, it's possible.' Penny rose from her seat and fetched a letter opener from a drawer in the sideboard. Her eyes gleamed with animated curiosity.

Penny's hands hovered over the seal for a moment before she began. With surgeon-like precision, she eased the sharp edge of the letter opener beneath the red wax, her breath held. Emma leaned forward, scarcely breathing herself, watching each delicate movement as Penny worked the seal free. The wax resisted, then yielded with a satisfying crack. The seal remained intact.

'Well done!' Emma exhaled in relief.

A triumphant smile spread across Penny's face as she handed over the envelope. 'You found this – you should have the honour.' She pushed her spectacles up her nose. 'Though I'm reasonably confident it contains neither a weapon nor a severed finger.'

Emma's burst of nervous laughter helped steady her hands as she carefully extracted a sheet of thick, rough paper from within. The weight of history – and possibly danger – made the moment feel momentous.

It was a map.

EIGHT

The map was hand drawn in fading black ink. A cross was marked in the centre and lines radiated out from it. Some were marked with names, and the handwriting was cramped and sloped.

Emma turned the map as she tried to read the words. 'Does that say "Ludgate"?' she asked.

Penny peered at the map. 'I think so. And I think another is labelled "Newgate". This must be the St Paul's area.'

'Which you know well because it's close to Fleet Street. Do you think the cross could be St Paul's Cathedral?'

'Yes, I think it could be.'

'And what's this up here?' Emma pointed at some cramped lettering in the top right-hand corner of the map.

'It looks like two words,' said Penny. 'Is that first letter an S?'

'I think so. In fact, both words look like they begin with S.' Emma squinted at the letters, trying to discern their shape. 'I think I've got it,' she said. 'Speak softly.'

'Speak softly?'

'I think so. What could it mean?'

Penny peered at the map again. 'You're right. It says, "Speak softly." And I'm certain St Paul's Cathedral is the location marked with the cross. In fact, it makes sense it's marked with a cross, doesn't it? It's marking a cathedral.'

Emma had an idea. 'When you speak softly, you whisper.'

'So what does that mean?'

A pause followed as they both thought. Then a smile spread across Penny's face. 'St Paul's has the Whispering Gallery.'

'Of course! Why didn't I think of that sooner? I visited the place as a child. The gallery runs around the interior of St Paul's dome, and when you whisper into the curved wall, someone on the other side of the gallery can hear your words.'

'I've no idea how it works, but it does,' said Penny. 'And now we have to understand why a map marking the Whispering Gallery was left in a case in Paddington station.'

'It could have been left there for someone to pick up,' said Emma. 'Either Lord Harpole left it there and planned to give the cloakroom ticket in the snuffbox to someone else, or another person gave him the snuffbox with the cloakroom ticket inside.'

'Maybe the person who followed you after you picked up the case,' said Penny.

'Possibly. But if he had a right to the case, then I think he would have challenged me directly. He didn't. He kept his distance and presumably waited for an opportunity to snatch it from me.'

'Which he didn't get. Why does he want this map?'

'There must be something important in the Whispering Gallery,' said Emma. 'But I can't think what. We shall have to visit and find out.'

NINE

Emma and Penny arrived at St Paul's Cathedral the following day shortly after the morning service had ended. Hundreds of people flowed out of the cathedral doors and down the wide steps. The grand, columned facade rose high above them. Emma felt a crick in her neck as she admired the two ornate towers on either side of it.

'Let's go,' said Penny, as the crowd dispersed. 'We've got a lot of steps to climb.'

Inside, the black-and-white chequered floor stretched along the nave to the magnificent altar in the distance. Towering stone columns supported the arched decorative ceiling high above their heads. Hushed voices echoed in the vast expanse as Emma and Penny walked along the nave. Eventually, they stood beneath the cathedral's magnificent dome. Looking up, Emma and Penny gasped at the elaborate jewelled colours and gleaming gold of the dome's interior.

'It's like an enormous work of art,' marvelled Penny. 'And even though I've been here before, the sight still astonishes me.'

Below the arched windows in the dome, Emma could see

the circular balustrade of the Whispering Gallery. It looked a long way up.

After following signs to the gallery, Emma and Penny climbed the stone spiral staircase. The steps were wide and shallow, but there were over two hundred and fifty of them. Emma was breathing heavily by the time she and Penny reached the top.

The walls of the gallery were surprisingly plain. The dome's intricate interior began at the windows several feet above them. Emma and Penny strolled along the walkway. It was about six feet wide and a stone seat ran around the circumference.

The view down to the nave was dizzyingly breathtaking, but Emma felt despondent. 'What are we looking for now that we're here?' she asked Penny.

'That's a good question.' They glanced about them. The walkway looked the same all the way round.

'Maybe something has somehow been hidden here,' said Emma.

'How?'

Emma paused and ran her gloved hand over the rough stone wall. Then she looked down at the stone beneath her feet. Everything seemed solid and immovable. 'I don't know. There are no obvious hiding places, are there?'

They completed a circuit of the gallery, then began another. Walking slowly, they examined every section of the wall, seat and floor.

'It's no use,' said Penny. 'There's nothing here. And we're running out of time. Another service is starting soon.'

'Perhaps there was something here, but someone who looked at the map before us took it?' suggested Emma.

'That's possible. And when did they take it? In fact, how old is the map? And how many people have seen it?'

The task suddenly felt hopeless. Emma sat down on the

stone seat, and Penny joined her. A long pause followed and Emma felt conscious of time. They wouldn't be permitted to walk around the Whispering Gallery during a service. Emma took the map out of her bag and looked at it again, hoping it would provide a clue.

'We have to remain hopeful,' said Penny after a while. 'This map was being handed over to someone for a reason. And we know at least one other person wants to get hold of it.'

Emma nodded. 'You're right.' An idea formed in her head. 'Something must have been left here, but perhaps not something which can be taken away.'

'What do you mean?'

'A message could have been left here,' Emma whispered, her eyes scanning the ancient stones. 'Not written but carved.'

Penny ran her gloved fingers over the smooth wall, brow furrowed in concentration. 'Carved into the stone?' She tapped experimentally at different points. 'There's nothing here that I can see.'

'Then we need to look elsewhere. It has to be here somewhere.' Emma felt determined to find it.

Penny pushed herself to her feet with a grunt, brushing dust from her skirts. 'We'd better hurry.'

Their footsteps echoed in the circular gallery as they methodically examined every surface, stooping to inspect lower stones, standing on tiptoes for higher ones. The curved walls seemed to mock their efforts, revealing nothing.

As they approached the doorway they'd entered through, Penny's shoulders slumped. 'I despise admitting defeat,' she said, frustration evident in her voice. 'But we've looked everywhere.'

Emma pressed her lips together, disappointment bitter on her tongue. 'Perhaps we've misinterpreted the map entirely. Maybe it's not the Whispering Gallery at all.'

She turned to leave, her gaze dropping in resignation – and

froze. There, partially hidden by shadow in the stone doorframe, was a distinct marking.

'Penny!' she gasped, seizing her friend's arm with sudden ferocity. 'Look!' Her finger trembled as she pointed to her discovery.

A small cross had been carefully carved into the ancient stone, with the letters 'HC' etched beside it. Below them, an intricate line wound around itself in an elaborate pattern.

Penny's eyes widened as she fumbled for her notebook, her movements suddenly urgent. 'What on earth could this mean?' She sketched rapidly, tongue caught between her teeth in concentration, while Emma kept watch for approaching vergers.

'I don't know,' Emma whispered, a mixture of triumph and frustration washing over her. 'But we've found it. The next piece of the puzzle.'

Penny held up her completed sketch for comparison. 'That's it. Now we just need to decipher what it's telling us.' Her eyes sparkled with renewed determination. Let's put our minds to it.'

TEN

Emma and Penny were summoned to attend the inquest into Lord Harpole's death the following day. It was held at the coroner's court in Kensington – a red-brick building in a courtyard just off Kensington High Street. It was accessed through a large arch next to the police station.

Emma's stomach turned as she stepped into the wood-panelled room. She felt nervous about standing up and giving evidence in front of everyone. A panel of jurors sat on one side of the room and the remaining benches were rapidly filling up. Emma recognized the receptionist from the Imperial Grand Hotel and the young soft-faced constable who'd spoken to her and Penny outside Lord Harpole's hotel room. She also noticed Lord Harpole's friend, Rupert Crowfield.

The coroner arrived and began the proceedings. He was a sombre man with a lined angular face and half-moon spectacles.

The police doctor who'd carried out the post-mortem spoke first. He confirmed Lord Harpole's death was caused by opiate poisoning.

'From the laudanum?' asked the coroner.

'That's right, your honour. Two bottles of laudanum combined with a significant amount of whisky.'

Penny was called next. She answered the coroner's questions in a calm, assured manner and didn't seem nervous at all. She gave everyone in the room a clear, concise account of how she and Emma had found Lord Harpole slumped in his chair. When it was Emma's turn to speak, she realized she needn't have been so nervous. All she needed to do was confirm the events had unfolded as Penny had described them.

The bespectacled doctor who'd attended to Lord Harpole then spoke, followed by the constable and the other police officers who'd been present that evening. Then Lord Harpole's valet, Mr Joseph Campbell, was called. He was a lean, pale-faced man and wore a black suit with a black tie.

'Had Lord Harpole made any plans for the evening of Friday the eighteenth of January?' the coroner asked him.

'Yes, your honour. I had reserved a table for him to dine that evening at Verrey's on Regent Street. It's a place he often dined at when staying in London.'

'And when did you last see him that day?'

'I was due to call on my lord at seven to help him dress for dinner. But I last saw him that morning after breakfast. Once my duties were complete that morning, he informed me I wasn't required until the evening.'

'Was that unusual?'

'No, not unusual at all, your honour. During his visits to London, my lord would often carry out errands of a personal nature and my presence wasn't required.'

'What personal errand did he carry out that day, Mr Campbell?'

'He planned to call on Lady Somersham, your honour.' The valet glanced across the room to where a lady sat. She wore a black dress and a little black hat which was pinned onto her fair hair at an artful slant. A black lace veil partially obscured her face, but it was possible to see she was young and pretty. As the eyes in the room turned to her, she brought a black handkerchief to her nose and gave a delicate sniff.

'We shall hear from Lady Somersham shortly,' said the coroner. 'Can you tell me please, Mr Campbell, if your late employer ever expressed any depressive thoughts?'

'No, your honour, he didn't.'

The men in the jury grew a little more interested when Lady Somersham gave her deposition. She was a fine-featured young woman with porcelain skin. Her fashionable black dress had lace trim, a tight-fitting bodice and a large bustle at the back.

'Lady Somersham, you were engaged to be married to Lord Harpole,' said the coroner. 'When did your engagement take place?'

'On New Year's Day,' she said. 'Our wedding day was to be in May.' She sniffed again and dabbed her eyes with her handkerchief. 'We were very much in love.' Her voice cracked with emotion as she told the coroner how excited they'd been about their forthcoming marriage.

'When did you last see Lord Harpole?' asked the coroner.

'On the day he died. He called on me at home.'

'And how was his mood?'

'He was his usual content self. He was happy. I don't understand why he'd do this.' Her voice broke, and a sob engulfed her. The courtroom waited in silence while she composed herself. Emma felt a lump in her throat. Listening to someone's grief was a reminder of her own.

It took some time for Lady Somersham to recover, and a well-dressed older lady eventually came to her aid. Emma wondered if Lord Harpole's fiancée was a little too keen to show everyone how upset she was.

Lord Harpole's brother, Mr Richard Harpole, was summoned next. He was a stocky gentleman with thinning dark hair and a moustache. His posture was stiff and he swallowed nervously. He told the coroner his brother had inherited his title a year previously after their father had died. The family home was in Berkshire and his brother had spent much of his time there, travelling to London once or twice a month to see to his affairs.

'When did you last see your brother?' asked the coroner.

'About a month ago, your honour.'

'And were you close?'

'Not particularly, but we got on well enough.'

'Any disagreements in the family?'

'No, none at all.'

Emma observed how he fixed the coroner's gaze, as if he wished to convince him of his answer.

'Did your brother ever mention to you he had depressive thoughts?' asked the coroner.

'No, he mentioned nothing of the kind to me. But if he had such thoughts, I don't suppose he would have mentioned them. A gentleman's business is his own, your honour.'

'Can you think of any reason he may have had depressive thoughts?'

'My guess is as good as the next man's, I'm afraid.' He rubbed his nose. 'Perhaps he had financial worries.'

'Financial worries?' said the coroner. 'He inherited a sizeable fortune from your father a year ago.'

Richard Harpole rubbed his nose again. 'I'm merely speculating, your honour. As I've said, a gentleman's business is his own.'

The jury didn't take long to consider their verdict. The cause of Lord Harpole's death was given as suicide.

Lady Somersham broke down, sobbing.

People began to quietly file out of the room. As Emma

readied herself, her eyes met those of a brown-whiskered man on the far side of the room.

The man who had followed her.

Her heart gave a jolt. Her face must have registered surprise, for he quickly turned away and headed for the door. A moment later, he was lost in the crowd.

ELEVEN

Outside on Kensington High Street, their breath froze into clouds in the cold air. Emma looked around for the brown-whiskered man, but he was nowhere to be seen.

'The man who followed me was at the inquest!' Emma clutched Penny's arm, her nails digging through layers of fabric. Her eyes darted frantically around the people in the street. 'He was here, but now he's gone!'

'Really?' Penny instantly became alert, scanning the crowd with calculated precision. She gripped Emma's hand reassuringly while her other hand slipped into her pocket – where Emma knew she kept a small hatpin for self-defence. 'Describe him to me again. Every detail.'

'He has brown whiskers and dark eyes. He looks about thirty. He's wearing a dark suit and...' Emma raised herself up on her toes, hoping to peer over the heads of people around her. 'Oh, it's no use. He's gone.'

'That's a shame,' said Penny. 'If he's after the map, it's possible we'll encounter him again.'

Emma felt a shiver. 'I don't like the thought of him following me again.'

'No, it's not nice. Let's hope we can catch up with him soon.'

Richard Harpole and his wife approached. He'd put on a top hat and black frock coat. His wife was a slight, red-haired lady with sharp green eyes. She wore a black velvet hat with black feathers and a fitted black overcoat.

'Thank you for doing what you could to save my brother,' said Mr Harpole. 'It must have been extremely distressing for you.'

'I just wish we'd got there sooner,' said Emma.

'You did what you could,' said Mrs Harpole. 'You couldn't have done anything more.' She gave them a sympathetic smile.

'Please accept our condolences,' said Penny. 'This must be extremely upsetting for your family.'

Mr Harpole drew in a breath. 'Yes, it is. A sudden death is difficult, but when it comes to matters of suicide...' His voice trailed off. 'It's really too dreadful to consider. I'm grateful my poor, dear parents are no longer alive to endure this.'

His wife took his arm and sighed, bowing her head. Emma imagined suicide made grief particularly complicated. It was likely the Harpole family felt anger and shame as well as deep sadness.

Mr Harpole glanced around them. 'I would like to thank the doctor who tried to save him. And the police officers too.'

'I think they've already left, dear,' said his wife.

'That's a shame.' He rubbed his brow. 'They had a tough job that day and I wanted to show them my gratitude.'

'A very tough job,' said Mrs Harpole. 'I would have a fit of hysteria if I was confronted with something like that.' She turned to Emma and Penny. 'You two ladies were extremely brave. To find a man slumped in a chair like that... yet still act sensibly and rationally.'

'I think you'd surprise yourself, Constance,' said her

husband. 'An instinct to save someone can take over at times like that.'

'Oh no, not for me.' She shuddered. 'When you think how dark that room must have been and there, in the chair in front of you, is a dying man! Awful! In fact, I wouldn't have had a fit of hysteria. I would have fainted.'

'That's enough now, Constance,' her husband cut in, his voice sharp. His face had grown ashen, a vein pulsing visibly at his temple. He tugged at his collar as if it were suddenly too tight. 'I don't like to think of it. It's too distressing.'

'Oh, I'm sorry, Richard.' She rested a gloved hand on his arm. 'I spoke thoughtlessly.'

He patted her hand and said nothing.

'I don't suppose you know anything about the society your brother was a member of?' Penny ventured.

'My brother was a member of many clubs and societies. Why do you ask?'

'There's one which appears to have been secretive. Mrs Langley's late husband was also a member and we've been trying to find out more about it.'

His brow furrowed. 'I know nothing about it, I'm afraid. Please excuse us, but my wife and I need to get to our next appointment. It's been a difficult morning and we have a meeting with the family solicitor next.'

'Of course,' said Penny. 'I wish you both well, Mr Harpole.'

They watched the couple walk away. 'Do you think he was being deliberately evasive just then?' Penny asked Emma.

'It's difficult to know. If he genuinely knows nothing about the society, then his reply makes sense. And he seems quite upset.'

'That's true,' said Penny. 'Perhaps I'm judging him a little harshly.'

'He didn't mention the map, did he?' said Emma. 'I wonder if that means he doesn't know about it. And I feel rather guilty that we're holding onto it. Legally, I suppose the map belongs to his family.'

'I suppose it could do,' said Penny. 'But we don't know who left the map at the left luggage office, do we? If Lord Harpole left it there for someone else to collect then, in theory, it no longer belonged to him. I realize I'm trying to come up with a reason for us to keep hold of it for now. But it's logical reasoning, don't you think?'

Emma smiled at Penny's determination. 'Yes, it is. I shall try not to feel too guilty about it.'

'Don't feel any guilt at all. We can trust ourselves to manage it in the right and proper manner. And besides, we're rather stuck with the mysterious symbol at the moment, aren't we?'

Lady Somersham approached, her nose and eyes red behind her black lace veil. 'Thank you both for everything you did,' she said, holding out her hand. She wore black silk gloves.

Emma and Penny shook her hand and gave her their condolences.

'I must go now, I feel so terribly tired,' she said. 'But I would like to invite you both to dine with me soon. I want to thank you properly. And you were the last people to see Charles so I...' Tears welled in her eyes. 'I suppose I would like to talk to someone who was there with him.'

The invitation surprised Emma; surely Lady Somersham wouldn't want to hear too much about her fiancé's final moments?

'Of course,' said Penny gently.

'You must give me your address.'

Penny took out her notebook, wrote her address, tore out the page and handed it over.

'Thank you.' Lady Somersham gave a sad sniff. 'You shall hear from me very soon.'

TWELVE

Emma and Penny dined at a chop house on Kensington High Street. It was a warm, busy place with partitioned seating bays and brass racks above each bench for hats and coats. Drips of condensation ran down the paned windows.

'There's something not right about Lord Harpole's death,' said Penny, leaning across the table, her voice dropping to a conspiratorial whisper. Her fingers drummed restlessly on the tablecloth as she glanced at nearby diners. 'It's been ruled a suicide, and yet everyone says he was in excellent spirits.' Her eyes narrowed, filled with that familiar investigative intensity Emma had come to recognize. 'Happy men planning their wedding don't suddenly poison themselves without reason.'

Emma nodded. 'None of the people who knew him said he expressed unhappy or depressed thoughts. I realize many people keep such thoughts to themselves, but they can still have low moods which people close to them would notice.'

'Perhaps Lord Harpole was good at pretending he was happy,' said Penny. 'But it must be difficult when you feel desperate enough to take your own life. And by all accounts he was looking forward to his wedding in May.'

'And he'd made arrangements to have dinner on the evening of his death,' said Emma. 'Would he really have done so if he'd been planning suicide?'

'It's difficult to say, but it seems unlikely, doesn't it? And Lady Somersham saw him that afternoon and said he was fine.' Penny took off her spectacles and wiped them with her napkin. 'Who was that chap who turned up shortly after Lord Harpole died? Rupert someone.'

'Crowfield,' said Emma.

'Had he arranged to meet Lord Harpole at a certain time?'

'I'm not sure. As I recall it, he turned up and told us he was there to see his friend.'

'If it had been an arranged meeting then why would Lord Harpole drink the whisky and laudanum just before he arrived?'

'Perhaps he was hoping his friend would find him,' said Emma. 'Maybe he didn't intend to die, but he felt desperately unhappy and decided to numb his feelings, knowing a friend would likely find him and get help if needed.'

'Well, that's an interesting idea,' said Penny, putting on her spectacles again. 'Would someone do something like that?'

Emma shrugged. 'I don't know. I wish we knew more.'

A waiter placed two plates of pork chops and potatoes in front of them.

'There was something odd about the scene that evening,' said Penny as they ate.

'What do you mean?'

'There was a half-empty bottle of whisky, an empty glass, two empty bottles of laudanum, and a note on the table next to his chair. But nothing else. Not even the pen used to write the note.'

'So where was the pen?'

'That's what I'm wondering. The location of those items suggests he wrote the note then took the whisky and laudanum as he sat in the chair. But if that's what he did, then you'd expect the pen to be there too.'

'Perhaps it fell onto the floor.'

'Yes, it could have done.' Penny put down her knife and fork as she thought. 'The items on that table were set out in a way that suggests someone wanted them to be discovered there. The note could have been placed anywhere in the room, couldn't it? And so could the whisky bottle and the laudanum bottles. I think someone could have staged it once Lord Harpole was incapacitated.'

Emma's stomach gave a lurch. 'You think he was murdered?'

'Possibly.'

Emma sat back and considered this. It hadn't occurred to her to question the circumstances of Lord Harpole's death, but Penny had an analytical mind and her idea seemed credible too.

'And another thing occurs to me,' said Penny. 'The piece of paper the note was written on looked like it was torn from a notebook. But where was the notebook? I didn't search the room, but I didn't see a notebook lying around. And a hotel like the Imperial Grand usually has letter paper, doesn't it? If Lord Harpole had decided that evening to write a suicide note, then the most obvious paper to use would have been the hotel's notepaper, wouldn't it?'

Emma nodded. 'I suppose so. It's possible there was a notebook in the room and we didn't see it. The note was very brief though.'

'Brief enough for someone to forge,' said Penny. 'Nothing personal was mentioned at all. It would be interesting to find out if it matches his handwriting.'

'If his death has been ruled a suicide then I don't suppose anyone would question who wrote the note,' said Emma. 'Would it have been passed to his family? If so, they would know if it was written in his handwriting. But are you really sure it could be murder? We know Lord Harpole died from the laudanum. How could someone force him to drink it with the whisky?'

'Good question,' said Penny, resuming her meal. 'They pointed a gun at him? Actually, I'm not sure that would work. I think dying swiftly from a gunshot is preferable to dying slowly from poisoning.'

'Unless he thought there was a chance he would survive the poisoning,' said Emma. 'But I can't see it happening that way. Perhaps someone put the laudanum in his whisky without him knowing.'

'Yes!' said Penny, her eyes lighting up. 'And then placed the laudanum bottles on the table once he was incapacitated. That could be it! He never actually knew about the laudanum.'

She pushed her plate away entirely, too consumed by her theory to eat. She leaned forward, her voice dropping to an intense whisper.

'It must have been someone he knew well – someone he trusted enough to share a private drink with.' Her fingers sketched invisible connections in the air between them. 'Someone who could distract him while poisoning his glass right under his nose.' Each word gained momentum as the theory crystallized. Her cheeks flushed with the thrill of deduction. 'Lord Harpole stared death in the face,' she concluded with certainty, 'and it wore the features of a friend.'

Emma sighed. 'Gosh. But his death has just been ruled as a suicide. No one's going to listen to us, are they?'

'No,' said Penny. 'It's going to be quite a task to convince anyone to treat his death as suspicious. And we need evidence to support our theory. We need to look at the hotel room again.'

'But it will have been tidied and cleaned since he stayed there,' said Emma. 'Other people will be staying there now. There won't be any evidence left.'

'You're right. There's probably little use in us trying to

prove anything. It will be a lot of work and we might get nowhere.'

'There's the secret society to consider.'

'Exactly. We were already looking into the secret society, weren't we? And if that's connected to his death then who knows what we might uncover?'

Emma felt a quiver run through her. 'If Lord Harpole was murdered, then we could be caught up in something dangerous.'

'Yes, there's a risk of that,' said Penny.

Emma had hoped she'd be more reassuring.

'But if we believe he was murdered, then we can't do nothing, can we?' continued Penny. 'We have to look into it some more and try and prove it one way or the other. I believe it's the right thing to do. And don't forget the secret society.' Penny's eyes gleamed with determination. 'That symbol in your husband's diary, the map leading to St. Paul's – they're all connected.' She clenched her fist on the table. 'I won't rest until we understand what it all means.'

Emma glanced down at her half-eaten chop; her appetite had left her. Penny seemed keen to investigate but Emma felt wary. What could they be getting themselves into?

THIRTEEN

Stephen Lydney removed the monocle from his eye. His head ached with tiredness. He sat back in his chair, picked up his chalice and took a mouthful of port. Closing his eye, he enjoyed the warmth which the port brought to his throat. He took another sip and was interrupted by a knock at the door.

'Enter!'

Rupert Crowfield stepped into the room. 'Good evening, sir.'

'How was the inquest?'

'The verdict was suicide.'

Lydney gave a nod and placed his chalice back on the table.

Crowfield surveyed the map which Lydney had been examining. 'Have you identified a site for digging yet, sir?'

'Yes. Several, in fact. But we need to establish how we go about it. The land is private. I want to know who lives there. Will you find out for me, Crowfield?'

'I will, sir.'

Lydney fixed him with his eye. 'Do we know what Langley's widow and her friend were doing outside the lodge that night?'

'It wasn't explained at the inquest, sir. But I can make a good guess. I suspect Mrs Langley has discovered her late husband's connection to Inveniam. She must have found the lodge address somewhere.'

'Typical of Langley. He probably mentioned it to her. Didn't I say the man couldn't be trusted?'

'Yes, you did, sir.'

'And what about Mrs Langley's friend?'

'She's Mrs Penny Blakely. At the inquest, she gave her address as Henstridge Place in St John's Wood. I've discovered she's married to Detective Inspector James Blakely of Scotland Yard, and she used to work as a news reporter for the *Morning Express* newspaper.'

Lydney was impressed. 'A lady news reporter?'

'Not anymore,' said Crowfield. 'She's a mother now. From what I've learned, the women share a friendship after Mrs Blakely helped Mrs Langley find her husband's murderer.'

'So the pair of them like to do detective work, do they?' Lydney gave a snort. 'Typical of genteel women who think they're cleverer than they are. And Harpole couldn't resist a bit of chivalry by lending them his coat. Do we know what he said to them?'

'No. But it was merely a brief exchange when he lent them the coat. When they found him in the hotel room, he couldn't say anything to them other than the word "help".'

'And what about the map? What does it show?'

Crowfield shifted from one foot to the other and a weight sank in Lydney's chest as he realized there was a problem. He watched Crowfield without a word, allowing the weight of the silence to increase his discomfort.

'There's, erm...' Crowfield cleared his throat. 'A slight problem, sir. The map is missing.'

Lydney said nothing for a moment. When he eventually

spoke, he kept his voice low and quiet. 'What do you mean it's missing?'

'After Harpole died, I checked the safe to make sure everything was in place. I'm not sure why... Peace of mind, I suppose. I looked in the safe and there was just an empty envelope.'

'And no map?'

'No map. I'm wondering if it was ever in there. I watched Harpole put the envelope in, but perhaps it was empty even then.'

Lydney clenched his jaw. 'You didn't check it?'

'No. I...'

'Trusted him?'

Crowfield swallowed. 'I'm afraid I did, sir.'

'That was your mistake, Crowfield.' He got to his feet and began pacing around the table. 'So where's the map now?'

'I don't know, sir.'

'You don't know?' He slammed his fist onto the table and bored his gaze into Crowfield. He knew the effect was more alarming with one eye.

Crowfield swallowed and looked at the floor.

Lydney sighed and resumed his pacing. 'So Harpole betrayed us.'

'He must have done.'

'Yes. Well done, Crowfield. Have you got anything helpful to say?'

'I, er...'

'Your answer is no, then. That map could be just about anywhere now, and you need to find it. That map was the only reason I asked Harpole to join Inveniam. It has to be found, do you hear me?'

Crowfield nodded. 'Yes, sir.'

'Perhaps you can start with that pair of ladies who think they're detectives. If they get to that map before we do, Crowfield, then you know what you'll have to do, don't you?'

Crowfield paled. 'Yes, sir.'

FOURTEEN

'Murder?' said James after dinner that evening. Penny had just finished telling him about the inquest. 'So you're questioning the coroner's ability to do his job, Penny?'

'No, I'm not. He conducted the inquest according to the evidence he had.'

'And you think there's more evidence which proves Lord Harpole was murdered?'

'I hope there is.'

'Hope?'

'There must be. Emma and I want to go back to the hotel room and see if there are any clues.'

'It was three days ago and the scene will have been tidied. And besides, I'm sure the constables who attended would have noticed if there was anything suspicious at the time.'

'Not necessarily.'

James sighed. 'Penny. Are you convinced the police don't know how to do their job, either?'

'I'm not suggesting anyone doesn't know how to do their job. And the police who attended were uniformed officers, not detectives. They may not have been prepared to treat the incident as suspicious.'

'They're trained officers, they know what to look for. I'm worried you've come up with a theory and you're trying to make the evidence fit into it. Every good detective knows that's not the way to do things.'

Penny felt her jaw clench. 'You appear to have forgotten all the cases I've worked on in the past!'

'No, I haven't. You're a good investigator, Penny. An excellent one, in fact. But sometimes when you've had a bit of success, there's a certain bravado—'

'Bravado?' Penny got to her feet. 'When have I ever displayed bravado?'

James raised a hand, keen to calm her down. 'I chose the wrong word, I'm sorry. It's just a certain...'

'What?'

'Too much confidence, perhaps.'

She scowled. 'What do you mean?'

'Penny, please sit down again. And don't be angry with me.'

'I'm not angry!' She paused, realizing she was losing her temper. She took in a breath. 'I'm annoyed.'

'All right then. But will you sit down again?'

Penny perched on the edge of the armchair, still scowling.

'Perhaps you're right,' said James cautiously. 'Perhaps Lord Harpole's death does need looking at again. But I don't think there's any need to jump to the conclusion yet that he was murdered. Perhaps it's suspicious.'

'It is suspicious.'

'Very well. But proving it will take a lot of work. You don't have—'

'Much spare time,' said Penny, finishing his sentence. 'I realize that. And my priority is always the children. Fortunately, Mrs Tuttle helps to mind them some days.'

'Yes, she does. But...' James scratched his temple. 'This could come to nothing, Penny. You could spend a lot of time looking into Lord Harpole's death and discover it was suicide all along. Your time is precious. And if you want to do something worthwhile, then aren't you better off spending it writing articles again? You told me Mr Fish, the editor of the *Morning Express*, is happy for you to contribute articles to the newspaper.'

This was true. Penny gave it some thought. 'Yes. I have some ideas for articles, actually.'

'Excellent!' James smiled. 'Then perhaps that would be a more worthwhile way to spend your time.'

'I could offer to write an article about Lord Harpole's death.'

'You could. But don't you have other ideas too?'

'Yes. Why don't you agree with me writing about Lord Harpole's death?'

'I don't disagree with it, Penny. I'm just worried it will pull you into something which may come to nothing at all.'

Frustration rose in her chest again. 'But don't you agree his death seems suspicious?'

He stroked his chin, and the time it took him to reply told her his answer. 'To be honest with you, Penny, I don't think it's suspicious. I realize Lord Harpole gave no indication he would do such a thing, but sometimes that can happen, I'm afraid. If he was a private man and pretended to be happy, then no one could possibly guess his true feelings. Not even those closest to him.'

'Very well.' Penny smoothed her skirt and got to her feet. Despite James's misgivings, she still thought Lord Harpole's death seemed suspicious. Was she being foolish? 'I think I might look into it a little bit more.'

James studied her face for a moment, a slow smile spreading across his features. 'I've seen that look before,' he said with affectionate resignation. 'And truthfully, I'm just as curious as you are.' He held out a hand to her and she took hold of it. 'Whatever you uncover, I want to hear every detail.'

FIFTEEN

Penny asked Mrs Tuttle to mind the children for an hour the following morning while she visited the *Morning Express* offices on Fleet Street.

The editor, Edgar Fish, was arguing with a compositor via the speaking tube in his office when she called on him.

'I can see now why Mr Sherman used to get so annoyed,' he said once he'd finished. 'Those men think they know best. If I say something has to go on page two, then it has to go on page two! I do apologise, Mrs Blakely, we're just finishing this morning's second edition. It's lovely to see you again.' He got up from behind his desk and removed a pile of papers from a chair. 'Please take a seat.'

'Thank you, Edgar, I won't keep you long. I know you're busy.'

'Oh, don't worry at all, Mrs Blakely. As long as you don't mind the occasional interruption, you can stay as long as you like. You know what it's like here.' He glanced around the room, looking for somewhere to place his pile of papers. He gave up and put them on the floor next to his desk.

'I read the report on the inquest into Lord Harpole's death

and saw your name mentioned, Mrs Blakely!' He sat down again. 'How did that come about?'

'He lent my friend, Mrs Langley, his coat when she was splashed by a cab in the street. We went to his hotel to return the coat the following day, and that's when we found him unwell.'

'Good gracious. How alarming for you.' Edgar shook his head. 'I suppose he must have had an illness of the mind to do such a thing. Now what brings you here? Do you have some ideas about what you'd like to write for the paper?'

'Yes.' Penny sat a little straighter, clutching her notebook.

'Wonderful!' Edgar slapped his desk enthusiastically. 'Let's hear them.'

'I would like to write a series of articles about the challenges of motherhood.' Penny's voice grew stronger with every word.

Edgar's enthusiastic smile froze, then slowly melted into bewilderment. He blinked several times, as if waiting for the real proposal.

'Yes.' Penny held his gaze steadily. 'Motherhood can be a challenging time.'

'Why?' He looked genuinely perplexed.

Penny's fingers tightened around her notebook. She hadn't expected to defend such an obvious truth. 'It's physically exhausting, for one. Many women spend months – years even – barely sleeping more than an hour or two at a stretch.'

Edgar waved a dismissive hand. 'That's what nursemaids are for, surely.'

'Not everyone has nursemaids, Edgar.' A flush crept up Penny's neck. 'I don't.'

His eyebrows shot up in genuine surprise. 'But you should, Mrs Blakely. A woman of your standing—'

'Most of the *Morning Express*'s female readers can't afford nursemaids,' Penny interrupted, her voice gaining an edge.

'They struggle alone, often while managing households with limited funds.'

'Oh.' Edgar looked momentarily chastened. 'I hadn't considered that.' He stroked his chin thoughtfully. 'I suppose tiredness could be difficult. Although many things are tiring,' he added, gesturing around the chaotic office. 'This job nearly kills me most days.'

Penny bit her tongue, knowing he had no idea of the difference.

A knock at the door interrupted them and a man in print-stained overalls stepped in. Edgar scowled and got to his feet. 'There's no use coming here and complaining about it, Macintyre. I've told you already. Page two.'

'It won't fit.'

'You have to make it fit!'

The compositor left and Edgar was half-lowered to his seat when another knock sounded at the door. 'Oh, what now? Oh hello, Miss Welton. Coffee. Thank you very much.'

The secretary hovered with the coffee tray, unsure where to put it. 'Your desk is rather untidy, sir.'

'Yes, it's one of those days. Just put the tray on top of those papers there.'

'It might slip.'

'It won't. I'll keep an eye on it.'

Miss Welton put down the tray, gave Penny a smile, then left.

'Now where were we?' Edgar sat down. 'Ah yes, the challenges of motherhood. Tiredness, you say?'

'Yes,' said Penny. 'And it's demanding, too. Your baby needs a lot of attention. They need to be kept warm, fed and entertained.'

'Which is why we have nursemaids.'

'I would like to write this for mothers who don't have nursemaids, Edgar.'

'Right.' He steepled his fingers. 'Who will be interested in these articles, Mrs Blakely?'

'Other mothers. Like me.'

'I was hoping you'd say something like that because our gentleman readers aren't going to be interested at all.'

'I'd like to think that some might be. It can be useful for them to understand what daily life is like for their wives when they're looking after babies and young children.'

Edgar wrinkled his nose. 'No, I don't think they'd be interested. Are the wives interested in the daily detail of their husbands' jobs? No. I don't see why it would work in reverse. Here, let me pass you your coffee. Goodness, this tray is going to slip off in a moment. I can't think why Miss Welton put it in the most precarious position possible.'

'Do you remember when Mr Sherman asked me to write a ladies' column?' asked Penny.

'Yes, I remember.'

'Well, my articles on motherhood would be a similar feature. They could even sit next to the ladies' column.'

'Yes, I like that idea, Mrs Blakely. A page for the ladies. Quite a few of them read the newspapers these days. We could even encourage mothers to write in with their questions. How does that sound?'

Penny liked the idea. 'Yes, I think that could work very well indeed.'

'Excellent! Can you write something for Thursday?'

Penny considered this. It was only two days away and she didn't have a lot of spare time. But if she suggested longer, then there was a risk Edgar would lose interest in the idea.

'Yes.' She smiled. 'Thursday is fine.'

'Good. I may not be the best judge of its content, I'm afraid, I'll probably pass it to Mrs Fish to read. Our third child is due to be born next month, so she's the expert on those matters.'

Penny took a sip of coffee. 'It's possible I can write an article about Lord Harpole too, once I can convince the police that his death should be treated as murder.'

'Really?' Edgar raised his eyebrows. 'You haven't changed at all, have you, Mrs Blakely? You always had these wild theories.'

'It's not wild, Edgar. I can explain to you why I think it could be murder.'

'Well, there's no need to explain it all to me. The person you need to speak to is our new ace reporter, Mr Harry Wright.'

'I recall you mentioning him when I last visited.'

'He really is wonderful. I would introduce you to him, but he's out and about at the moment, sniffing for stories. He's got the Harpole story, so if you get wind of anything else about it, then just let him know.'

Penny felt a little disappointed by this; she'd been hoping to write the articles herself. She took another sip of coffee. 'All right then. I shall.'

SIXTEEN

'When can I play with both hands at the same time?' asked Emma's young pupil, Beatrice Montgomery. Emma sat with her at a well-polished baby grand piano in a large, comfortable house in Stoke Newington.

'When you've practised both hands separately,' said Emma.

'I have practised them separately.' Having heard Beatrice play that morning, Emma doubted this was true.

'All right then. Why don't you show me?'

Beatrice bit her lip, then cautiously placed her right hand on the piano keys. Emma listened as her pupil haltingly played the first eight bars of Mozart's 'Minuet in C' while paying no attention to timing or phrasing.

'Well done,' said Emma in a flat voice. 'Can you remember what type of note this is?' She pointed to the opening note with her pencil. 'We practised it in our last lesson.' Beatrice shook her head. 'This is a minim and we hold it for two beats.'

'What's a minim?'

Emma tried to relax her shoulders and forced a smile. Some pupils picked up music quickly, others were destined never to manage it. 'Let's learn about it again, shall we?'

. . .

Emma met Penny outside the Imperial Grand Hotel late that afternoon. It was almost dark, and the gas lanterns above the hotel entrance gave a warm, flickering glow.

Although Emma felt wary about investigating Lord Harpole's death, she also couldn't stop thinking about it. She agreed with Penny that the circumstances were suspicious. She felt anxious, but she knew Penny had investigated similar cases in the past. She had to put her trust in Penny and do her best to help.

As they stepped into the hotel lobby, Emma stopped. 'I've just recalled something,' she said. 'When we were last here, one of the doormen was picking up a cloak pin from the floor. He asked us if we'd seen the lady who'd dropped it.'

'Yes, that's right!' Penny's eyes widened. 'And he said she'd left in a hurry. I wonder why? And I wonder if they ever saw her again to return the cloak pin to her. I realize this is a big hotel with lots of people coming and going, but she could have been with Lord Harpole, couldn't she?'

'Yes, it's something to bear in mind,' said Emma.

At the well-polished reception desk, they found the same sombre-faced receptionist they'd spoken to on the night of Lord Harpole's death.

'Hello again, ladies,' he said. 'How may I help?'

'This is an odd request,' said Penny. 'But I'm wondering if we may have a look in the room which Lord Harpole was staying in. I think I left my gloves there that night.'

'I don't believe the maids found any gloves in the room, madam.'

'That's a shame. They were quite expensive and I miss them at this time of year.' Penny held out her bare hands to demonstrate. 'Would you mind if I check the room myself? They could have ended up beneath a piece of furniture and not been noticed by the maids. There was a lot happening that evening, you know how these things can happen.'

The receptionist's face grew more sombre at the memory. 'Very well.' He stepped over to the rows of hooks behind the desk and retrieved the key for the room.

'Is there anyone staying in there at the moment?' Penny asked.

'No.' He handed her the key. 'The manager thought it best to keep the room empty for a while. Out of respect for the Harpole family.'

'Of course. Thank you very much for your help, we won't be long.'

They climbed the grand staircase and Emma felt a weight of trepidation in her stomach. Although she hoped the hotel room held some clues about Lord Harpole's death, she didn't like the thought of being in a room where a man had died.

On the third floor, they made their way to room thirty-seven. Penny put the key in the lock and opened the door.

The room was dark inside, just as it had been on the night of Lord Harpole's death. But this time, there was no fire in the grate. Penny found the gas lamp and turned it on.

Light flooded the room and Emma's stomach turned. Although everything looked neat and tidy now, she couldn't forget what had happened here. The curtains were drawn and the room was cold. A faint odour of tobacco mingled with the smell of disinfectant.

She struggled to look at the chair which Lord Harpole had sat in that fateful night. The image of him slumped and dying loomed in her mind.

'The table's not next to the chair,' said Penny. 'Look, it's over here with a vase on it.' She picked up the vase and rested it on one of the chairs. Then she lifted the table, moved it out of the way and bent down to examine the floor. 'There are marks from the feet of the table on the floorboards here,' she said. 'I think the table is usually kept here with the vase on it.'

'So on the night Lord Harpole died, the table was placed next to his chair and the bottle, glass and note were put on it,' said Emma.

'Exactly,' said Penny, getting to her feet. 'I think it was staged.' She replaced the table and the vase. 'But that's not enough evidence that someone was behind this. I need to find something that will convince James.' She glanced around the room.

'He doesn't believe you?'

'He's a sceptic. And I suppose that's quite right too, his job requires him to question everything. Let's look around some more.'

Emma opened the drawers in the dressing table and found them empty apart from a small mending kit. On the writing table was a set of hotel writing paper and envelopes. 'Here's a pen,' said Emma. A fountain pen sat proudly in a brass stand. She opened the drawer of the writing desk and saw a pot of ink.

'What colour is the ink?' said Penny.

'Blue. I think Lord Harpole's note was written in black.'

'Yes, it was,' said Penny. 'Is there a pot of black ink anywhere?'

Emma searched. 'I can't see one. And there's no sign of the notepad that the note was torn from.'

'Interesting.' Penny stood in the centre of the room with her hands on her hips. 'So we know the table was moved to be next to the chair. Lord Harpole may have done it himself, but the position of the table conveniently staged the bottles, glass and note. Those are the things a murderer would want people to notice. Lord Harpole may have written the note in his own notebook with his own pen. If so, then where are those items now? They weren't obvious on the evening of his death.'

'His valet must have gathered up his belongings,' said Emma. 'We could ask him.'

'Yes, we could.'

Emma stepped over to the wardrobe and opened the doors. The smell of wood and camphor greeted her and the clothes hangers rattled. There was nothing inside the wardrobe. She closed it and turned to see Penny looking under the bed covers.

'This is all freshly laundered,' she said. 'If anything had been hidden in it, the maids would have found it.' After checking the eiderdown, pillows and mattress, Penny stooped down and peered under the bed. She remained there for a few moments. 'I think I can see something,' she said. Her voice sounded quiet, most of it lost in the cavity beneath the bed. She stretched an arm out. 'I can't reach it,' she said.

'What is it?' asked Emma.

'I don't know. It looks quite small. A container perhaps.'

Emma opened the wardrobe again and took out one of the hangers. 'Here.' She handed it to Penny. 'Maybe you can reach it with this.'

'Thank you.' Penny took the hanger and reached under the bed with it. Straining, she eventually managed to hit the item beneath the bed. Emma heard a clunk, then a glass rolled out slowly from beneath the bed.

She stared at it for a moment, then stooped to pick it up.

Penny got to her feet and pushed her spectacles up her nose. 'A second glass,' she said. 'You know what this could mean, don't you? Someone else was in this room drinking whisky with Lord Harpole.'

'And they hid their glass beneath the bed so everyone would think he'd been alone,' said Emma. She smiled. 'This could be the evidence we're looking for!'

'I hope so!'

. . .

They returned the room key to the hotel reception.

'Found them!' said Penny cheerily. She waved a pair of gloves at the receptionist. They had been hidden in her bag all along. 'They were under the bed.'

'Is that so? Well, I'm pleased you found them, madam.'

'When we were here last time, a lady lost her cloak pin as she was dashing out of the door,' said Penny. 'Did you ever find her?'

'Oh yes, that matter was resolved.' The receptionist's voice remained neutral, but Emma noticed he avoided meeting Penny's gaze. 'A maid came in to collect it on the lady's behalf.'

Penny leaned slightly across the polished counter. 'Did the maid mention whom it belonged to?'

'No, madam.' His fingers idly straightened papers on the desk. 'She didn't say.'

'And this lady, might she have been visiting Lord Harpole?' Penny's tone remained conversational, although Emma recognized the subtle shift in her posture – the same alertness a cat shows before pouncing.

The receptionist's shoulders tensed almost imperceptibly. 'His lordship had several visitors during his stay. That was usual for him.'

'Including Lady Somersham?' Penny pressed, her eyes never leaving his face.

'Yes.' A flicker of something – recognition, perhaps – crossed his features. 'She did call upon him.'

'On the evening in question?' Penny leaned in closer.

'I don't believe so, no.' His gaze flitted briefly to the clock behind them.

'What about other female visitors?' Penny's voice softened disarmingly. 'Anyone that afternoon or evening?'

The receptionist finally met her gaze, his expression carefully composed. 'I can't recall any, madam. May I ask why you're inquiring?'

'Professional curiosity.' Penny smiled warmly. 'I'm wondering who might have been with him before his... unfortunate incident.'

'He was quite alone, madam, I assure you.' His voice carried a note of finality. 'You ladies were the first to discover him.'

'Yes,' said Penny, her smile never wavering as she straightened. 'So it seems. Thank you for your assistance with the key. Most helpful indeed.' She turned away, but not before Emma caught the triumphant gleam in her eye.

SEVENTEEN

'A glass,' said James.

'That's right,' said Penny. 'We found it beneath the bed in the hotel room Lord Harpole stayed in. Have a sniff. You can still smell the whisky.'

Emma watched as James picked up the glass from the dining table and gave it a tentative sniff. 'You're right,' he said.

'Someone drank whisky with Lord Harpole that night then hid the glass under the bed,' said Penny.

James frowned. 'How do you know it wasn't Lord Harpole who drank from this glass? Perhaps he dropped it and it rolled beneath the bed so he fetched another.'

Penny pursed her lips. 'It's possible, I suppose. But there's other evidence too.' She told him about the table which was moved to stage the scene.

Emma then mentioned the ripped-out note written in black ink. 'Lord Harpole's valet, Mr Campbell, would have tidied away his belongings after his death,' she said. 'We need to find out if the notebook and pen with black ink were in the room.'

'We need to speak to him,' said Penny. 'But I imagine he's probably returned to Lord Harpole's home in Berkshire.'

'I can call on him there,' said Emma.

'Are you sure?'

'Yes, I don't mind at all.' Emma liked the idea of leaving London for the day and visiting somewhere new.

'I would accompany you,' said Penny. 'But I haven't seen much of the children over the past few days and I've been asking rather a lot of Mrs Tuttle to mind them.'

'It's fine,' said Emma. 'I'm happy to do it.'

'Thank you, Emma.' Penny turned to James. 'It would be useful to have both the drinking glasses examined by an expert. We're certain the one under the bed contained whisky but I suspect the glass which was left on the table next to Lord Harpole's chair contained whisky and the laudanum. The murderer would have put the laudanum in Lord Harpole's drink. Can you ask someone to examine the two drinking glasses, James?'

Her husband rubbed his chin, his expression troubled. He glanced towards the window, then back at Penny, lowering his voice. 'That's treading into dangerous territory. In an official investigation, yes, we'd have police scientists examine both glasses.' His fingers interlaced, his knuckles whitening slightly. 'But Lord Harpole's death is officially ruled suicide, Penny. The case is closed.' He leaned forward, his eyes conveying more concern than his measured words.

'Isn't there someone you could ask about it? Unofficially?'

Emma noticed Penny push her lower lip out and look up at her husband from beneath her eyelashes. It was clearly an expression which worked.

'All right then,' he sighed. 'I can try. But I don't know where the glass from that night has got to. I'll have to do some asking around.'

EIGHTEEN

Emma took a train from Paddington station the following morning. Grimy clouds hung low over the city but began to lift as the train left the western suburbs. Soon, frost-covered fields and frozen hedgerows rolled past the window. Cows gathered around bales of hay and large birds wheeled in the pale grey sky.

Emma was alone in the carriage compartment, so she lowered the window slightly to let in a rush of cold, clean air. She tightened her scarf, pulled up the collar of her coat and enjoyed the freshness.

She felt anxious about meeting Mr Campbell. Would he be helpful or uncooperative? Although she'd told Penny she was happy to meet with him alone, she didn't have Penny's confidence in dealing with awkward people.

Forty-five minutes later, Emma disembarked at a small station in the village of Pangbourne. The stationmaster told her it was a two-mile walk to Wickham House and much of it was uphill. Fortunately, a pony and trap was available to take her there.

The road followed the River Thames for part of the way

before leaving it and continuing alongside the railway line. The frozen landscape was empty of colour and Emma's nose, feet and hands felt numb. She tucked the knee blanket in tighter and hoped they'd soon arrive at the house.

They turned off the road and through a large stone gateway. The pony then laboured up a steep track to where a large Palladian house stood at the top of the hill.

Emma paid the driver and her feet crunched on the gravelled driveway as she approached the imposing columned facade. She recalled hearing at the inquest that Lord Harpole had recently inherited this estate from his father. He had lived alone here with a company of servants to look after his needs. It was a grand place and Emma imagined Lady Somersham had been looking forward to making it her home.

A grey-haired housekeeper answered the door. She wore a black dress and a stern expression. Emma introduced herself and asked to speak to Mr Campbell.

'May I ask the nature of your business?' said the housekeeper.

'I was one of the ladies who found Lord Harpole and there are a few matters I'd like to discuss with his valet.'

'You found him? I see. Well, you'd better come in and I shall fetch Mr Campbell for you.'

The enormous entrance hall was cold. Black sheets covered the mirrors and the pale faces of Lord Harpole's ancestors stared out from dingy portraits.

Mr Campbell appeared out of the gloom and invited Emma into the library where a fire had been lit. She sat in a chair by the fireside, grateful for the warmth.

'I remember you speaking at the inquest, Mrs Langley,' said the valet, seating himself in the chair opposite. He was impeccably dressed in a smart black suit and maintained the stiff, impassive expression of a man who'd spent many years in service. 'How can I help you today?'

'This will sound like an odd question,' said Emma. 'But I'm wondering if Lord Harpole had a notebook with him while he was staying in London.'

'A notebook? What sort of notebook?'

'The note he left was torn from a notebook,' said Emma. 'I was wondering if you found it when you tidied his room.'

'I don't recall seeing one. Why do you ask?'

'Mrs Blakely and I are wondering where the piece of paper came from...' Emma tailed off. His impassive stare was disconcerting. And how was he going to react when she told him they suspected murder? She took in a breath and continued. 'Do you think Lord Harpole wrote that note himself?' she asked.

'Yes. How could he not have?'

'We wondered if someone else wrote it and put it there.'

His brow furrowed. 'What are you suggesting?'

'I'm suggesting he was poisoned by someone.'

The valet opened then closed his mouth. His gaze wandered to the fire for a moment, then returned to her. The professional mask-like expression hardened. 'No, that's impossible.'

'May I ask why?'

'No one would have harmed him. The nature of his death is particularly distressing to me...' He looked at the fire again. 'But he wasn't poisoned. His mind was troubled by something and he saw no alternative.'

'But you didn't find the notebook the letter was torn from?'

'No, but that doesn't mean anything nefarious happened that evening.'

'And a pen and pot of black ink?'

'What do you mean?'

'Were they among his possessions?' She noticed his jaw tighten.

'I can't recall. I must be frank with you, Mrs Langley. I don't fully understand the purpose of this conversation. If it's little more than salacious speculation, then I want no part of it, I'm afraid. Discussing the death of my esteemed employer... a peer of the realm, nonetheless... I find the matter quite unsavoury. And I won't be drawn into it any further. Now, if there's nothing else you wish to discuss, then I can ask the coachman to take you back to the railway station.'

Emma's shoulders slumped. She'd lost his cooperation. If Penny had been here, she would have managed the conversation far better. Certain that she was about to be asked to leave, she tried one last question. 'Do you know anything about the secret society which Lord Harpole was a member of?'

'Secret society?' He scowled. His contempt for the question caused his mask to slip. 'What secret society? What are you talking about?'

She got to her feet, readying herself to leave. 'Never mind, Mr Campbell. I'm grateful to you for talking to me. Thank you for your time.'

NINETEEN

'I'm going out to do a bit of shopping, Mrs Blakely,' said Mrs Tuttle. 'I'll get some beef from the butcher's and see what's looking fresh in the grocer's shop. I wasn't impressed with his offering yesterday, hopefully he's had a delivery this morning. I won't be too long.'

'Very well, Mrs Tuttle. Take your time,' said Penny.

Florence was asleep and Thomas was playing peacefully with his toy soldiers. Mindful of the short deadline for the article she'd agreed to write for the *Morning Express*, Penny decided she had some time to get it done. She went upstairs to her writing room – a room which had been little used since Thomas had been born. Her typewriter sat on the desk but she wouldn't be able to write up here because she had to watch Thomas. She reasoned she could watch him while writing in the sitting room.

She picked up the typewriter and carried it downstairs. It was heavier than she remembered and her arms ached by the time she reached the foot of the stairs. In the sitting room, she put the typewriter on the table in front of the sofa, fetched her notebook and some paper, and began her work.

The opening sentence was always the most difficult. Penny chewed her thumb and watched Thomas playing as she thought. Then she began to type:

```
Lack of sleep can be the scourge of new
mothers.
```

The clack of the typewriter keys reached Thomas's ears. 'What's that?' He got to his feet and joined her.

'It's a typewriter. I use it to write with.'

'Can I have a go?'

'You can have a go in a little while. I need to get some writing done first.'

'But I want a go now.'

'Yes, I realize that. But you've been playing ever so nicely with your soldiers. Why don't you finish your game first?'

'I've finished it.'

Penny sighed. 'Really? It didn't look like you'd finished when I began this. Why don't the soldiers go on an adventure to the windowsill?'

'They don't want to.'

Penny felt her hopes of getting some writing done rapidly fading. 'Perhaps I can let you have a little go on the typewriter and then, after that, the soldiers can go an adventure somewhere?'

Thomas nodded.

Penny spent some time showing him how to press the keys and make a letter on the paper. It was hard work for his small fingers, but once he'd achieved it, he laughed with delight. Then he discovered how to wind the paper up and down and touched the ink ribbon.

'We'll have to wash your hands now,' said Penny with a sigh.

Once that was done, she hoped Thomas would return to his soldiers. But he fetched one of them and told her the soldier wanted a go. Penny reluctantly agreed to it and then the tin soldier became stuck between the Q and the W keys. No matter what she did, she couldn't prise the soldier out.

'Oh dear.' Twenty minutes had passed since Mrs Tuttle had left and Penny had got nothing done.

Thomas grew upset about the stuck soldier and Penny wondered if she could write her article without using Q or W.

'Perhaps some soap and water might help,' she said, getting up to fetch the soap from the kitchen. She eventually managed to free the soldier with the help of the soapy mixture. Thomas was overjoyed and took the freed soldier to join the others. Finally, he'd lost interest in the typewriter and Penny could get on with her article. She fed a new sheet of paper into the typewriter and re-wrote the first sentence. Disappointingly, the action of the W key wasn't as straight as it had been before.

Then a cry carried down the stairs.

Florence was awake.

'Right,' said Penny, trying to calm herself. She waited a few moments, hoping Florence might go back to sleep. But she knew it was unlikely. As the cries grew louder, Penny went upstairs to fetch her.

Florence beamed at her as she lifted her out of her cot and Penny felt a pang of guilt that she'd been annoyed by her waking up.

When she returned to the sitting room, the soldier was typing again. He was adding a row of random letters after the sentence she'd just typed for the second time.

Penny sank into the sofa, resigned. 'What's the soldier writing?' she asked Thomas.

'A story about cats.'

'I like the sound of that. What happens in it?'

Thomas's voice rose and fell with childish enthusiasm as he narrated his nonsensical tale. Penny nodded and smiled at all the right moments, her heart swelling with love for this small, imaginative being she had created.

Yet beneath her attentive exterior, a familiar ache spread through her chest. She adored her children with a fierceness that sometimes frightened her – they were miracles, precious beyond measure. But in quiet moments like this, the truth crept in: she was disappearing. The woman who had once chased stories through London's darkest corners now struggled to complete a single paragraph without interruption.

Her mind, once consumed with mysteries and investigations, now tracked feeding schedules and laundry needs. The world seemed to expect her gratitude for this narrowing of existence. Other mothers appeared to make this transition effortlessly, surrendering former selves without complaint.

Why couldn't she find that same contentment? The guilt of such thoughts made her pull Thomas closer, as if to physically push away the shameful longing for her former freedom. She kissed the top of his head, breathing in his familiar scent, even as part of her mind remained with the abandoned typewriter.

TWENTY

When Emma returned home, she found Mrs Solomon standing rigid in the parlour, her complexion ashen. A police constable sat with his notebook open, quietly questioning Mr Solomon, whose hands trembled visibly around his teacup.

'What's happened?' Emma's voice caught in her throat as a wave of cold dread washed over her.

Mrs Solomon turned, her usually composed features twisted with distress. 'Someone's been in the house,' she whispered, pressing a handkerchief to her lips. 'We came home from the recital and found...' She gestured helplessly towards the disrupted room behind her.

Emma's heart hammered against her ribs as her gaze took in the scene: drawers pulled out, contents scattered, cabinet doors hanging open. 'Dear God,' she breathed. 'What did they take?'

'That's what's so unnerving,' Mrs Solomon said, her voice breaking. 'Nothing is missing. Not the silver, not my grandmother's china, not even my jewellery.' She clutched Emma's arm with surprising strength. 'They weren't after valuables, Mrs Langley. They were looking for something specific.'

The constable looked up sharply at this exchange. Emma felt the blood drain from her face as understanding dawned.

'You should check your room immediately,' Mrs Solomon urged, her eyes suddenly wide with concern. 'Whatever they wanted – I fear it might have been among your belongings.'

Emma's heart pounded as she dashed up the stairs. She gave a gasp when she saw her room in disarray. Most of her belongings had been thrown onto her bed. The doors of her wardrobe stood open and the trunk on top of the wardrobe had been flung onto the floor. She checked her jewellery box on the chest of drawers and thankfully, none of her precious items had been stolen. This hadn't been someone looking for valuables. They'd been looking for something else. Could it have been the map?

Emma began picking up her clothes from the bed and returned them to the chest of drawers and wardrobe. The thought that someone had been here and gone through her personal belongings sickened her.

Had it been the brown-whiskered man who'd followed her from Paddington station when she'd picked up the case? Was he watching the house?

She returned downstairs, feeling cold and shivery.

'Is anything missing?' the constable asked her.

'No. Everything's there.' She wondered if she should tell him about the man who'd followed her. But there was a chance the intruder was someone else. She didn't want to mislead the police.

'I shouldn't have left the window open in the back room,' said Mrs Solomon. 'I've done it every day for years just to get the air circulating. But I shan't do it anymore. Northampton Square isn't as safe as it used to be.'

The constable scratched his chin with his pencil. 'This intruder was clearly after something specific, Mrs Solomon. Have you really got no idea what it could be?'

'No. I've told you this already.'

'You didn't lend something to someone and forget to return it?'

'No! I would never do that. And even if I did, they would ask for it, wouldn't they? They wouldn't climb in through my window to fetch it. Perhaps they got the wrong house? I think that can be the only possible explanation.'

Laurence, the shaggy cat, strolled through the room with his tail in the air, impervious to the anxious mood.

'Very well.' The constable made a note of something in his notebook. 'It's all very odd,' he said. 'I've never come across a burglary before where nothing has been taken. I'll ask at the other houses in the square, someone may have seen something.' He folded his notebook shut. 'I shall keep you updated.'

The constable left and Mrs Solomon gave a sad sigh. 'I suppose I should get on with the tidying up,' she said.

'I'll help,' said Emma. 'And I'll make some tea first as you've had a nasty shock.'

'Oh well. If you insist. I'm sure Ronald would like one too, he's tidying his study at the moment.'

Once Emma had made the tea, she sat with Mrs Solomon in the parlour. 'I'm afraid this break-in could be my fault,' she said.

'Your fault, Mrs Langley? Of course not. I was the one who left the window open.'

'But I had something which I think this person was after.' Emma told Mrs Solomon about the map and the brown-whiskered man who'd followed her.

Her landlady listened with puzzled interest. 'So you think the man who followed you could be the intruder?'

'Possibly.' Emma nodded. 'Someone wants that map. Fortunately, it's not here. Mrs Blakely has it at her home.'

'Well, if it's the map they're after, then you'd better warn her.'

'I will. I'm so sorry about this, Mrs Solomon. I feel awful. If I'd known that someone would come looking for the map, then I would never have picked up the case from the left luggage office.'

'But you weren't to know, were you? You can't blame yourself. Hopefully now they've realized the map isn't here, they'll leave us alone. But you must be careful, Mrs Langley. What have you got yourself caught up in?'

TWENTY-ONE

'We can't be certain the intruder was after the map,' said Penny later that evening. 'But it seems likely, doesn't it? I'll put it in a deposit box at the bank tomorrow so it can be kept out of harm's way. I'm so sorry you suffered a break-in, that must have been frightening.'

'You need to look out for anyone suspicious near your home,' said Emma.

'There's someone in most of the time so I don't think an intruder would risk it. And my children would probably frighten him away!' Penny laughed, but not for long. Emma could tell she was worried.

They sat in an expensive restaurant in Knightsbridge. The tables were covered with white linen and glittered with silver cutlery and cut glassware. The chairs were narrow and uncomfortable, and Emma felt underdressed in her plain indigo evening frock. The ladies at tables around them wore fashionable gowns and sparkling jewellery.

Penny had removed her spectacles to smarten her appearance, but she had to put them on again whenever she wanted to look at something over three feet away.

They were waiting for Lady Somersham. She'd sent a note to Penny inviting them both to dinner, but she was late.

Emma told Penny about her visit to Wickham House. 'I'm quite certain you would have got somewhere with Mr Campbell,' she added. 'My conversation skills aren't as good as yours.'

'I'm not sure I would have,' said Penny. 'If he was determined to be evasive, then my experience would have been much the same as yours. I think you did extremely well because we've now learned two things.'

'What are they?'

'Lord Harpole didn't have a notebook with him and Mr Campbell has something to hide.'

'But Lord Harpole might have had a notebook with him, his valet couldn't be sure.'

'I think that means he didn't. If Mr Campbell had picked up the notebook in that room, then he would have remembered it. He may even have realized it was the notebook which Lord Harpole's note had come from.'

'So why didn't he tell me he didn't see it in the room?'

'Because he didn't want to consider the theory that someone else wrote the note. Either the thought of his employer being poisoned was too upsetting for him to consider, or he wrote the note himself.'

Emma gasped. 'Of course! I didn't even think of that. If Mr Campbell poisoned Lord Harpole, then it makes sense he was evasive. And what's the other thing we've learned?'

'That Mr Campbell is hiding something,' said Penny. 'It's either the fact he murdered Lord Harpole or it's something else he doesn't want us to know. If he had nothing to hide, then I think he would have been a lot more helpful.'

'Perhaps it's just his character to be unhelpful.'

'Maybe it is. But I think he's suspicious, and you did all you could when you called on him. Oh, look.' She glanced over

Emma's shoulder, then put on her spectacles. 'Here's Lady Somersham.'

The restaurant fell into a momentary hush as Lady Somersham glided between the tables. Even in mourning black, she commanded attention – her silk gown shimmering in the lamplight, the luxurious fur draped artfully across slender shoulders. The dramatic contrast of her pale complexion against the dark fabrics only enhanced her striking beauty. Society gentlemen discreetly watched her pass, while their companions pursed disapproving lips.

Emma and Penny rose as she approached, Emma suddenly aware of her own modest attire.

'I do apologise for my tardiness,' Lady Somersham said, her cultured voice carrying just the right note of contrition. Her gloved fingers arranged the fur with practised precision as she took her seat, the subtle scent of expensive French perfume settling around them like an invisible veil.

'I've just had a terrible disagreement with Mother and Father,' she said as an attentive waiter helped her sit at the table. 'They told me I shouldn't be leaving the house while in mourning and that it's not respectable to visit a restaurant. I'm afraid I ignored them. I'm not a widow! And as Father forbids any discussion at home about Charles's death, I have to leave the house in order to discuss him with anyone. I want to talk about him, you see. It makes me feel closer to him.' Her voice cracked and she dabbed at the corner of one eye with a fingertip.

'I'm sorry to hear it,' said Penny. 'Why won't your father talk about your fiancé?'

'Because of the nature of his death.' She lowered her voice to a whisper. 'Suicide. It's sinful and Father disapproves very strongly. He's worried it will bring shame on our family. And so I'm not allowed to mention Charles's name at all. I'm not allowed to talk about him and yet I'm not allowed to leave the house! It's quite ridiculous. I shall be in terrible trouble with my parents when I return home, but that doesn't matter to me at the moment. I wanted to meet you both again and thank you personally for all that you did for Charles on the night he died. You barely knew him and yet you did what you could to save him.'

'We only called for help,' said Penny.

'Which was very important! And more importantly than that, you were with him.' Her voice cracked again. 'He wasn't alone. You were there.'

Emma's throat tightened. Lord Harpole had suffered a great deal, and there was some consolation he hadn't been on his own when he died.

The waiter took their order. The menu was in French and Lady Somersham pronounced each word perfectly. 'I had a French governess,' she explained once the waiter had left. 'Father insisted on us all being fluent.'

'You speak it very well,' said Penny.

'Thank you.' She moved her fur to one shoulder and stroked it as if it were a pet. 'I sometimes wonder whether I should live in France.'

'Why?' asked Emma.

'Everything here is so miserable now that Charles has gone. And my family is unbearable. I've often thought I should like to live where the climate is so much better than dreary England. They don't have any fog down there. Maybe they have a little now and again but they certainly don't have any filthy, suffocating fog which sits around for days and drives one half-mad because one can't get about in it without risking life and limb.'

'I can see why France might be appealing,' said Penny. 'Especially if you can speak the language too.'

'Oh yes. I plan to get away there sooner rather than later.' Lady Somersham snapped her fingers at a waiter and asked for some bread. 'I'm hungry,' she explained to Emma and Penny. 'I haven't eaten all day.'

Penny asked Lady Somersham how she'd met Lord Harpole.

'We met last year at a ball given by the Duchess of Wellington.' She described how their eyes had met across the room and how they'd danced almost every dance together. When the bread arrived, she broke off small pieces as she spoke and pushed them delicately into her mouth.

Lady Somersham's account gave little away about Lord Harpole's character, but Emma and Penny heard a lot about the other attendees at the ball and their outfits.

When the soup course arrived, Emma was growing weary of the frivolous conversation. She interrupted Lady Somersham with a question. 'I understand my late husband and Lord Harpole were both members of the same society,' she said.

Lady Somersham looked puzzled. 'Which society is that?'

'I don't know the name of it. It appears to be a secretive society and I don't know its purpose either.'

'Charles never mentioned it to me,' said Lady Somersham.

'Did he not tell you he attended a meeting in Kensington the night before his death?'

'Yes, he said he had a meeting. I think it was with his solicitor or someone. That's what he did when he came to London, he had meetings. I don't know what they were about, just business, I suppose. Boring things.' She lifted her soup spoon and gently sipped from it.

'So he never mentioned a society in Kensington?' asked Penny.

'No.'

'The society was the reason we encountered him,' said Penny. She explained to Lady Somersham what she and Emma had been doing the night they met Lord Harpole.

'I wish I could tell you more about the society, but I know

absolutely nothing about it whatsoever.' She bit her lip and looked concerned. 'You don't suppose they could have been up to any trouble, do you?'

'No,' said Emma, keen not to upset her. 'I'm sure there was no trouble at all. As I've explained, my husband was also a member of the society. He never mentioned anything about it when he was alive, so I suppose that must be the rule. You're not supposed to tell anyone you're a member.'

Lady Somersham smiled conspiratorially. 'I suppose gentlemen like doing that sort of thing, don't they? They like secretive clubs and gatherings. Perhaps it's just a dining club or something similar.'

'Perhaps Lord Harpole's friends might know more,' said Penny. 'Do you know Rupert Crowfield?'

'No.' Lady Somersham frowned. 'Who's he?'

'He arrived at the hotel room shortly after Lord Harpole died. He told us he was a friend of his.'

'I've never met him.'

Emma and Penny exchanged a puzzled glance. It seemed odd Lady Somersham hadn't met one of Lord Harpole's friends.

'I would have met him eventually, I'm sure,' she said. But she scowled a little, as if bothered she hadn't known about the mysterious Mr Crowfield.

Emma recalled the woman who'd rushed out of the hotel that night, dropping her cloak pin. 'Did you visit Lord Harpole at his hotel that evening?' she asked.

'No. He called on me at home earlier that day. And we arranged to go to the theatre the following evening. We were going to see a new play at the Opera Comique by Mrs Oscar Beringer. But then he... Oh, why did he do it?' Her face crumpled. 'I just need to know why!'

TWENTY-TWO

'Fascinating,' said Edgar Fish once he'd finished reading Penny's article the following morning. 'I didn't realize babies woke up that often at night-time. It's just as well we have a nursemaid.'

'So you'll print it?'

'Yes, I'll show it to Mrs Fish for her expert review, then I'll publish it next to the ladies' column this Saturday.'

Penny smiled. 'Thank you.' It had been a long time since she'd had an article published.

'Can you write another for next week?'

'Of course. I'd love to.'

'If you could get it to me sooner, that would be marvellous. How about Tuesday?'

'Tuesday is fine.'

'I don't mind what you write about, just so long as it's something motherly. I think the ladies are going to enjoy your series of articles, Mrs Blakely.' He got up from his seat. 'Have you met our new reporter, Harry Wright, yet?'

'No, but you've told me a lot about him.'

'I think he's in the newsroom now, come along.' Penny followed him out of the door.

In the scruffy newsroom, the corpulent parliamentary reporter, Frederick Potter, was speaking to a young man with dark hair and keen hazel eyes.

Edgar introduced Penny to Harry Wright. 'And this is Mrs Penny Blakely, Harry. When she worked here, she was Miss Penny Green.'

The young man's face broke out into a grin. 'Miss Green! I've heard all about you!'

'Really?' Penny felt her face warm up. 'I hope it was complimentary.'

'It was,' said Mr Wright. 'You were the only lady news reporter to work on this newspaper. And it remains that way.'

'Now that's a good point,' Penny turned to Edgar and said pointedly, 'Have you not employed another lady reporter yet, Mr Fish?'

He scratched the back of his neck. 'No. There aren't many of them about, really, are there? And besides, none of them could be as good as you, Mrs Blakely.'

'Now you're just trying to flatter me. I really think you should attempt to find another lady news reporter.'

'So do I,' said Potter. 'It would be nice to have a lady here brightening up the place.'

'Brightening up the place?' said Penny.

'Yes. It can be very dull just having chaps around. Of course, there's Miss Welton, but... she doesn't exactly brighten things up.'

'Miss Welton is the longest-serving staff member on the *Morning Express*,' said Edgar. 'She may not brighten things up, but she keeps everything ticking over. Now as for Mr Wright here, the chap has boundless energy. He will work morning, noon and night to get everything he needs for a story.'

Harry gave a bashful smile and shuffled from one foot to the other.

'Well, that's excellent,' said Penny. 'I wish you well in the job, Mr Wright.'

'I've heard you found Lord Harpole,' he said. 'And there are rumours he was murdered.'

'I think there's something suspicious about his death,' replied Penny. 'But we need to wait for the police to say what they think about it.'

'You're married to a detective from the Yard,' said Harry. 'What does he make of it?'

'He agrees it could be suspicious,' said Penny. 'But don't write about it yet. He's in discussions with T Division about it at the moment.'

'T Division? I could speak to Inspector Trotter there about it.'

'Splendid chap,' said Edgar. 'Keen, isn't he, Mrs Blakely?'

'Yes, but I wouldn't speak to Trotter just yet,' said Penny. She worried Harry was too keen. 'You don't want to antagonize him. You want him to cooperate, so just give him a chance to decide.'

'I want the *Morning Express* to break the story first!' said Harry with a grin.

'I'm sure you do, I recall being like that myself,' said Penny. 'But sometimes it pays to bide your time.'

'All right, Mrs Blakely. You're the expert.'

'Perhaps.' She felt a little embarrassed by the description.

'Although I could have a look around the Imperial Grand Hotel,' said Harry. 'I could disguise myself as a bellboy to get in.'

Penny forced a smile. The young man seemed relentless.

Frederick chuckled. 'Steady on, young man.'

'There's no stopping him, is there, Mrs Blakely?' said Edgar. 'We're certainly getting our money's worth with him. If Lord Harpole was murdered, then I'm sure he'll get to the bottom of it before anyone else!'

TWENTY-THREE

Emma grew bored of staring at an advertisement for Allbright's Artificial Teeth as she travelled home by omnibus after a piano lesson. The traffic was moving slowly along Edgware Road and she could hear the omnibus driver shouting at the carts and carriages around them.

The lady next to her was reading a newspaper and Emma couldn't resist a quick sideways glance. She saw a report that a man had been arrested in Tunis on suspicion of being Jack the Ripper. Almost three months had passed since the last murder in Whitechapel, and there had been many reports the murderer had travelled abroad. Emma had read of attacks in Paris and the West Indies which were being attributed to him.

The lady noticed her reading her newspaper and edged away.

Emma pulled her notebook out of her bag and decided to make some notes on what she and Penny had learned so far about Lord Harpole's suspicious death. She tapped her pencil against her chin and thought about Lady Somersham. Had she spoken honestly at dinner the previous evening? Emma thought she had, but it was possible she'd lied to her and Penny and had called on Lord Harpole that evening. Could she have been the mysterious woman who'd dropped her cloak pin? Emma wrote down her name.

Then there was Mr Campbell to consider. He'd seemed guarded when she'd met him, and also reluctant to help. Penny felt sure he was hiding something and Emma agreed. She wrote his name down too.

Could Richard Harpole have murdered his brother so he could inherit the title of Lord Harpole? The idea was far-fetched, but not impossible. She jotted "Richard Harpole" in her notebook.

And there was the man who'd turned up at the hotel shortly after Lord Harpole's death. Was he really a friend? Lady Somersham hadn't heard of him. She wrote down his name: Rupert Crowfield.

Then there was the man who'd followed her when she'd collected Lord Harpole's case from Paddington station. Who was he? She felt sure he had to be another suspect. She wrote down the words "Mystery Man" and noticed the lady next to her looking over her shoulder. She pursed her lips and closed her notebook.

TWENTY-FOUR

'I called on Inspector Trotter at Kensington T Division today,' said James when Penny arrived home that evening.

'Trotter?' Penny gave a groan.

'Yes, I realize he didn't do a particularly good job when we were investigating Sophia Glenville's murder five years ago,' said James. 'But you'll be pleased to hear he was quite helpful today. I gave him the glass you found under Lord Harpole's bed and he was quite intrigued by the find.'

'He thinks it could be murder, too?' Penny asked hopefully.

'Not quite yet. But he still has the whisky bottle, empty laudanum bottles and the glass at the police station. They were examined by the police doctor who carried out the post-mortem.'

'And what did he find?'

'The empty glass contained traces of whisky and laudanum. It's the doctor's belief that Lord Harpole mixed the laudanum and the whisky together to make it a little more palatable.'

'Or someone else put the laudanum in his whisky without him noticing.'

'That's possible, but Inspector Trotter doesn't believe that was the case. Not yet, anyway.' James pinched the bridge of his nose, his forehead creasing in thought. 'I think he might be willing to consider someone else was involved. I've asked him if the police doctor would be willing to examine the glass which was found under the bed. If that contains traces of whisky and not laudanum, then it could support the theory that someone else was drinking with Lord Harpole and secretly put laudanum in his glass.' He leaned back in his chair, weighing each word. 'On the other hand, it could have been a glass which Harpole had used earlier. He could have accidentally dropped it and then it rolled beneath the bed.'

'I think someone was drinking with him and put laudanum in his whisky without him knowing,' said Penny.

James shook his head sceptically. 'Two bottles' worth? I feel sure he would have tasted it.'

'Perhaps it was well-diluted.' Penny countered, leaning forward.

'That would have to be a lot of whisky.' James's eyebrows rose. 'Both Harpole and the assailant would have been quite drunk.'

Penny gave this some thought. 'I wish now that I'd looked for a jug of water in the room. The murderer could have secretly used it to dilute their drink so they didn't drink too much whisky.'

'The hotel staff will be able to answer that question.'

'The murderer would have presumably wanted Harpole to become quite drunk,' said Penny. 'The more inebriated he was, the less likely he was to notice the laudanum in his whisky.'

'So the murderer must have been someone who was quite persuasive,' said James.

'Yes. Someone he knew who could have cajoled him to drink a lot within a short space of time.'

'Interesting.' James rubbed his chin. 'I think it's feasible, but we need to be careful about making too many assumptions. Even if the police doctor confirms there was no laudanum in the second glass, it doesn't mean Lord Harpole was murdered.'

'And that's why other matters need to be considered too,' said Penny. 'The lady who rushed out of the hotel so quickly that she lost her cloak pin without realizing. And the fact we don't know where the paper the note was written on came from. And the way everything was neatly arranged on the table... I'm convinced someone else did that.'

James rubbed his chin some more. 'You've almost convinced me too, Penny.'

'But not completely?'

'Not yet.'

Penny sighed. 'I shall keep working on it. In the meantime, perhaps you can help me with something.' She took her notebook from her bag and turned to the page with the symbol she had copied from the carving on the doorway in the Whispering Gallery at St Paul's Cathedral. 'Have you any idea what this could be?'

James peered at the drawing. 'What is it? A wriggling worm?'

'That's very helpful, James. Thank you.'

'And what does "HC" stand for?'

'I don't know. I've been trying to come up with ideas for four days now. That's why I'm asking you.'

'I'm afraid I don't know either. What's the cross for?'

'That's another thing I don't know.'

James continued to stare at the symbol. 'It's not a worm or a snake. It's a long line which winds around itself...' He narrowed his eyes and squinted at it. 'Is it a route you have to take?'

'A route?'

'Yes. Perhaps this matches a pattern of streets somewhere. In HC, perhaps, wherever that is. High Court?'

'The streets around the High Court?'

'Possibly. I don't know. Is there a region of London with the initials HC?'

'I've been trying to think of one. Highgate something, Hampstead something...' Penny stared at the drawing again. 'A route... Why would you follow a winding route like that? You'd be walking about in circles and going back on yourself and... it makes no sense to me. Oh!' A sudden thought entered her mind.

'What is it?' asked James.

'A maze. This could be a route through a maze!'

'A maze...' said James.

'Yes! And I think I know what HC stands for now. Not High Court. But Hampton Court.' Penny's heart flipped with excitement. 'Hampton Court Palace! With one of the most famous mazes in the country. I wonder if that's it?'

'There could be other possibilities.'

'No, I think this could be it. I'll write to Emma and let her know. We need to visit it. I could take the children too, it would be a nice day trip for them.'

James frowned. 'Isn't it a bit cold to be taking them around a maze?'

'I'll make sure they're wrapped up warm. I think they'll enjoy it!'

TWENTY-FIVE

'I'd forgotten how big this place is,' said Constance Harpole as the carriage came to a halt outside Wickham House.

'It's big all right,' replied Richard. 'And now it's ours.'

'I'm struggling to believe it.'

A footman opened the carriage door and helped Constance climb out. Richard followed. He paused before they entered the house and cast his gaze over his childhood home. Twenty years had passed since he'd lived here and he'd never imagined he would return as the head of the house. He'd grown up so accustomed to the idea of Charles inheriting it that he'd never considered it would one day be his.

But he'd inherited the house, and he'd inherited the title too. Lord Harpole. Like his older brother and father before him.

'Come along, Richard.' Constance took his arm. 'It's too cold to linger out here.'

The housekeeper had lined up the staff to greet them at the entrance. His family had employed many of them for several years, so he knew most of them. Jones, the butler, had been at the house since Richard was a boy. He recalled being scolded by him when he and his brother had broken a vase in the billiard room. Now Jones was grey-haired and his features lined and sunken with age. But his handshake remained firm and the warm glint in his eye made Richard feel welcomed.

'It's draughty in here,' said Constance as their footsteps echoed on the tiled floor of the vast entrance hall.

'I wish you wouldn't complain quite so much,' he replied sharply. She was Lady Harpole now and was going to live in one of Berkshire's finest stately homes.

'Oh, I'm sorry, dear. I suppose I'm just a little daunted by this.' She glanced around her, eyes wide. 'You're used to it because you grew up here. But to think all this is ours now...'

He took her hand and gave it a comforting squeeze. 'You'll have a lot of responsibilities here as lady of the house. I'll try to be more understanding.'

'Oh, thank you, Richard. I'm sorry if I've been complaining a little too much. I just wasn't prepared for any of this.'

'Of course not, my dear.' He gave her a comforting pat on the shoulder as they stepped into the drawing room. It was furnished in pale blue and gold and its tall windows overlooked a formal octagonal garden. Beyond the formal garden, the grounds sloped down to a valley and a range of rolling hills lay in the distance.

'Oh, it's just so pretty!' said Constance. 'And I remember now how lovely this room is in the summer when the doors can be opened out onto the gardens and the flowers are in bloom.'

'But in January it's certainly chilly.' Richard stepped over to the fireplace and rubbed his palms together. 'I suspect the fire has only just been lit in here.'

Mr Campbell, Charles's former valet, joined them moments later.

'Good afternoon, my lord. How was your journey from London?'

'Very good, thank you, Campbell.' Richard had always

found the valet rather stiff and old-fashioned, but he was good at his job.

They sat in the chairs closest to the fireplace while Campbell told Richard how he had packed away Charles's personal effects. 'The trunks are in the dressing room next to his bedchamber at the present time,' he added. 'I can arrange for them to be removed if you and Lady Harpole would like to use the room imminently. It is one of the nicest in the east wing.'

'Yes, I'm aware,' said Richard. 'However, my intention is to use the room which my parents used because that's a little larger. It will need redecorating, of course, but Lady Harpole will discuss that with the housekeeper.' He glanced at his wife who bit her lip. She was going to be kept busy for the next few months.

'Of course, sir.'

'I understand you did a good job as my brother's valet,' said Richard. 'I don't suppose you'd like to work as valet for me now? I don't actually have one, you see. Constance and I have lived a rather humble existence in our home in Knightsbridge and I've never really felt the need for one. But as I'm now Lord Harpole, I suppose I should begin to follow a lifestyle more suited to my position.'

Campbell bowed his head reverently. 'I'd be more than happy to serve you, my lord.'

'Excellent.' Richard rubbed his hands together. 'Well, it makes sense that you should join us in our home in Knightsbridge for the time being. I intend to spend the next couple of weeks there before making Wickham House my home.'

'Of course, my lord.'

They discussed a few other practical matters before Campbell prepared to leave. 'There's just one other matter, my lord,' he said. 'Two days ago, I received a visit from Mrs Langley. She's one of the two women who—'

'Yes, I remember,' said Richard. He felt surprised to hear she'd visited the house. 'What did she want?'

'I'm not entirely sure, my lord. She asked an odd question about a notebook which the...' He lowered his voice. 'The note was torn from.'

'Note? You mean the note he left?'

'Yes, my lord.' He swallowed, clearly uncomfortable about discussing it. 'I thought it was an impertinent question.'

'What exactly was the question?'

'It was whether the notebook it had come from was among the belongings I retrieved from the hotel room.'

'And was it?'

'I don't believe it was, my lord.'

Richard felt a snap of irritation. It seemed a trivial thing. 'And what does it matter, anyway?'

'I suppose it raises the question of when the note was written.'

'Who knows when it was written? Who knows when or why my brother chose to carry out an act of self-destruction?'

Constance let out a little cry. 'Oh don't! I can't bear to think about it.'

'And neither can I.' He turned back to Campbell. 'What else did this woman ask?'

'She talked about the pen which was used to write it and—'

'And why is that important?'

'I don't think it is, my lord. And she also asked about a secret society which she claimed the late Lord Harpole had been a member of.'

Richard let out a laugh. 'A secret society? My brother? He doesn't seem the type. But if he was a member of one, then I suppose it could only have been the freemasons. Were you aware he was a member of a secret society, Campbell?'

'No, not at all, my lord.'

Richard sat back in his chair and crossed his legs, his jaw

tightening. 'Fancy coming here and asking personal questions about my late brother!' His voice rose sharply as a flush of red crept up his neck. 'It sounds as though Mrs Langley needs her head examining by a doctor.' He turned abruptly to his wife, his fingers drumming impatiently on the armrest. 'What do you think, Constance?'

'I agree it sounds very odd indeed. It's a shame because I found her quite pleasant when we spoke with her.'

'Indeed.' Richard uncrossed his legs and recrossed them the other way. 'Well, let's forget about her for now, we have more important things to be getting on with. Thank you for your time, Campbell.'

The valet got to his feet and gave a slight bow. 'My lord.'

Richard ground his teeth as he watched the valet leave. Despite saying he would forget about Mrs Langley, he couldn't. What did she know?

TWENTY-SIX

Hampton Court Palace was southwest of London and the journey on the train took about half an hour from Waterloo station. Penny's son, Thomas, was excited about the trip. He bounced around on the seats of the carriage compartment while Penny urged him to sit down quietly. She cradled her daughter Florence on her lap. The baby sucked on her mittened hand and made occasional grabs for Penny's spectacles.

Emma had last been to Hampton Court maze the previous summer. She and William had visited the place shortly after their marriage. It was going to feel strange returning there again. She also felt anxious about Penny's children. What if the brown-whiskered man made an appearance? Although she hadn't seen him since the inquest, he could have been following her without her knowledge. And the break-in at the Solomons' home had unnerved her. It felt difficult to relax and enjoy the train journey with these menacing thoughts on her mind.

Penny, on the other hand, seemed untroubled by such thoughts. Emma reasoned age and experience helped her manage them. She told herself Penny's manner was reassuring; perhaps there was no need to worry as much as she was.

Thomas clambered up on the seat next to her and pointed out of the window. 'I can see a train!'

'That's right. That's a train.' They were pulling into busy Clapham Junction railway station.

'And another one!'

'Yes, another train too.'

'And we're on a train!'

'Yes.'

He pointed at her. 'You're on a train and I'm on a train.'

'Yes.'

'Mummy's on a train and Flonce is on a train.'

Emma smiled. 'That's right.'

'And you're called Emma.'

'That's right. I am.'

Their conversation continued for the rest of the journey. She welcomed the distraction.

An icy wind blew as they approached the Tudor palace. Penny pushed the perambulator with Florence inside it and Thomas sitting on a little seat strapped to the top.

The palace was an attractive brick building with crenelations on the roof, ornate chimneys and tall narrow windows edged with stone. The palace had been a residence for King Henry VIII and successive monarchs before opening for public visitors about fifty years ago. Emma felt a lump in her throat as she recalled the tour she and William had taken. Together they'd marvelled at the history of the place and at the opulence of its interior such as the great hall and grand staircase.

William had been a loving, attentive husband then, and she'd had no clue he'd been leading another life. Emma longed to live those days again without her husband's deceitful behaviour. He'd brought her a lot of happiness and, despite everything he'd done, she missed him.

'Emma?'

She realized Penny was talking to her. 'Yes?'

'I said we'll have to be quick. I don't want the children to get cold.'

'Of course. Sorry, I was lost in my own thoughts just then. Let's go straight to the maze.'

They paid their entry fee and made their way through the grounds of the palace. Even though it was a cold January day, there were a few people exploring the maze.

As they approached the entrance, Penny took her notebook from her bag. 'I think the carving in St Paul's shows the route through the maze,' she told Emma. 'I've redrawn it on this page here and made it larger so it's easier to follow. Do you mind guiding us with this drawing while I push the perambulator?'

'Not at all,' said Emma, taking the notebook from her. 'I think you and James did very well to work out what the carving meant.'

'We could be mistaken. And we're about to find out if we are!' Penny smiled, then gripped the handle of the perambulator. 'Right then, let's go!'

They stepped in between the tall hedges.

'We go left first,' said Emma, examining the route.

'All right then.' Penny marched on ahead, apparently keen to move quickly. It wasn't long before they met someone coming the other way.

'What an enormous contraption!' exclaimed a lady in a fur-trimmed hat and coat. She walked arm-in-arm with a young lady who looked like her daughter. She scowled at the perambulator. 'You shouldn't be bringing that in here. It's too big!'

'There's room to pass by,' said Penny.

'Only if I squeeze myself into the hedge.'

Penny nudged the perambulator to the side. 'Do you have more room now?'

'Barely.' The lady gave a huff and walked on past with her nose in the air.

'Some people are very unreasonable,' muttered Penny as they went on their way.

'Right here,' said Emma, pausing at another junction, her finger tracing the path on the paper. 'And right again.'

'Well, this seems to be working so far,' said Penny.

They heard voices on the other side of the hedge. 'Is someone cheating in here?' demanded a man's irritated voice. 'You're supposed to work it out for yourself!'

'Don't make a fuss about it, Walter,' said a lady.

'But I want to make a fuss about it! If you cheat in a maze, then you're ruining all the fun!'

Penny stopped and whispered to Emma. 'You take the lead and I'll follow. We don't want to upset people by reading out the directions.'

Emma smiled and went ahead of her. She could see from the route that the path followed the perimeter of the maze for long sections before reaching junctions where there was a choice of right or left.

'You again!' They came across the lady with the fur-trimmed hat and her daughter.

'How nice to see you again,' said Penny. 'Have we made enough room for you to get past?'

'Only just.' She tutted as she strode past them without too much trouble.

Emma and Penny went on their way and Emma realized they would soon reach the centre of the maze if the route was correct.

'We've already been this way, Margaret,' said a man's voice beyond the hedge.

'No, we haven't.'

'We have! I recognize that corner.'

'All the corners look the same, Walter.'

'So how do you know we haven't come this way before if all the corners look the same?'

Emma and Penny rounded the corner to see Walter and Margaret stopped on the path ahead of them.

'Watch out, Margaret, there's a perambulator.'

'I can see it, thank you.'

Emma greeted them as they squeezed past and they marched on. After a turn to the left and a short walk, they found themselves in the centre of the maze. Two bare-branched trees stood in a small, gravelled quadrant.

'We did it!' said Penny.

'Is this the maze?' asked Thomas.

'Yes, it is,' said Penny. 'And we've got to the middle of it. Emma helped us.' They exchanged a grin.

'How do we get out again?' asked Thomas.

'We'll manage it easily,' said Penny. 'Just wait and see.'

The lady with the fur-trimmed hat and her daughter arrived.

'Oh,' said the lady. 'Is this the middle?'

'I think so,' said her daughter.

'Well done, you did it!' said Penny.

The lady looked her up and down. 'How did you get here before us?'

'I suppose we must be very good at mazes,' replied Penny.

The lady said nothing. Her lips pressed into a thin line of disapproval as she tugged at her gloves with unnecessary force. 'Come along, Joanna, let's find our way out again.'

Once the two women had left, Emma began examining the trunk of the nearest tree. 'There must be another carving somewhere,' she said to Penny. 'What do you think?'

'There must be.' Emma examined the rutted bark, running her gloved fingers over rough patches. 'I can't see anything, though.'

Penny walked over to the other tree. 'There's nothing obvious here, either.'

'We found it, Margaret!' Walter and Margaret arrived.

'Hello,' said Emma. 'Well done for getting here.'

'We did it without cheating,' said Walter. 'I overheard someone cheating earlier. They were saying "right" and "left" and so on.'

'How awful,' said Penny.

'They're only ruining it for themselves,' said Walter. 'We enjoyed it, though, didn't we, Margaret?'

Margaret gave an unconvincing nod.

'Very well.' He tipped his hat. 'We'll race you out of here.'

Once their footsteps faded, Emma and Penny returned to examining the tree trunks. Above them, the sky darkened ominously, shadows deepening across the maze. Thomas shifted restlessly in his perch on the perambulator, his small face growing increasingly fretful. 'I want to go home,' he said. Time was running short.

'All right then,' said Penny. 'We'll leave in two minutes.'

'I want to go now!'

Emma looked up at the upper part of the trunk. Was it possible the carving was too high for her to see? She glanced over at Penny who was frowning as she hurriedly looked for the clue.

'I want to go home,' said Thomas again.

Emma felt sorry for him. 'We should leave,' she said to Penny. 'I can come back here another day and look.'

Penny sighed. 'All right then. It's just frustrating we can't find it. The carving at St Paul's clearly leads here because we had no trouble finding our way through the maze. But now we're stuck again.'

'Perhaps the carving is no longer visible,' said Emma. 'Or maybe the clue lies somewhere else.' She glanced around her, but no other ideas came to mind. 'Whatever it is, I'll come back here.'

'All right then.' Penny walked back to the perambulator. 'Don't worry, Thomas, we're going home now.'

She pushed the perambulator towards the exit, and Emma's gaze caught something at the foot of the tree.

'Wait!' She stooped down to get a closer look. 'There's something here!'

TWENTY-SEVEN

The carving on the tree trunk appeared to have been there for some time. It was the same colour as the bark and was slightly distorted as the tree had grown.

'This has to be it!' said Emma.

Penny stepped over to have a look. 'Well done!'

'I'll copy it down.' Emma hurriedly took her notebook from her bag and sketched what she saw.

There was a small cross next to the letters "YOCC". Beneath was a symbol which was a rough semi-circle with a circle at one end and a short wavy line at the other.

'Are we going home?' said Thomas.

'Yes, we're going now,' said Penny. Emma led the way again and followed the route in reverse to guide them out of the maze.

They met no one else as they walked. Everything was strangely quiet. Low thick cloud rolled in overhead and the gloom deepened. Emma feared fog might be on its way.

She quickened her step and she could hear Penny directly behind her.

Then she heard the scuff of a footstep on the other side of the hedge. It shouldn't have felt like a surprise, but an icy prickle crawled up the back of Emma's neck, raising the fine hairs there. Her heart quickened as she consulted the route with trembling fingers, then hurried forward, desperate to escape the increasingly claustrophobic hedges.

Each turn brought fresh dread. Emma's breath caught in her throat at every corner, her imagination painting the unseen stranger with menacing intent. The rational part of her mind insisted she was merely projecting her fears about the intruder and her mysterious follower, but the primitive part of her brain screamed danger.

The distraction proved costly. After several turns, nothing looked familiar. The exit seemed farther away with each step, not closer. Above them, the sky had transformed to a threatening slate-grey, casting everything in a ghostly half-light. Emma's temples throbbed as the endless twisting paths blurred together, disorienting her completely.

She stopped for a moment to get her breath.

'Is everything all right?' asked Penny.

'I think we're lost.' She looked at Thomas and felt a pang of guilt that he and his sister were out in the cold.

'Oh.' Penny looked unimpressed. 'I thought you were following the route.'

'I was and I've gone wrong somewhere. I'm sorry.'

'Well, never mind. Have you any idea where we are on the route?'

'No.' Emma looked around. 'This looks unfamiliar to me.'

Penny sighed. 'Well, all we can do is keep walking. We're bound to find a place we recognize shortly.'

Emma was about to move when she heard footsteps on the other side of the hedge. Then they came to a stop.

She turned to look at Penny and she could tell from her expression that she'd heard them, too.

They both stared at the hedge they'd heard the footsteps from. Emma held her breath and her heart pounded. It was probably nothing to worry about. But why had the person stopped?

'Hello?' said Penny. The sudden sound of her voice made Emma startle. Her breath was shaky as she listened for a response.

None came.

Penny gave her a nod, and they walked on. Emma guessed the way, blindly making turns through the labyrinth of hedges. Her mouth felt dry and she could feel panic rising in her chest. They were walking through sections of the maze which still looked unfamiliar. It hadn't even seemed that big when they'd first entered it.

The top of the hedge was fading as the fog thickened. The thick layer of cloud above their heads felt suffocating.

Then Emma heard quick footsteps. Someone was running through the maze. Were they searching for them?

Whoever it was, she felt fearful of coming face-to-face with them. She wanted to run, but Penny couldn't move any faster with the large perambulator.

Baby Florence let out a cry. Emma winced. The noise would help the other person find them. Did they know she and Penny had found the next clue? Would they threaten them? She could feel her skin prickling and anxiety filling her chest as her breath became shallow.

Turning left, she then saw a section she remembered. 'I know where we are!' she whispered to Penny. She jogged on ahead and saw the final part of the hedge leading to the entrance. It was hazy in the thickening fog.

Penny lagged behind with the perambulator. Emma paused to wait for her and willed her to move faster.

'We're almost there!' she whispered as Penny caught up. She turned and headed for the gap in the hedge. As she did so, she saw movement on the far side of the gap. Someone was moving towards them.

It was too foggy to see who it was.

'Someone's there!' Emma hissed. She dashed to the gap and could hear the wheels of the perambulator immediately behind her. Penny was managing to run with it.

Emma made the sharp turn right and ran into the gardens. Penny followed. Emma then gripped one side of the perambulator and handle and together they pushed the perambulator towards the vague silhouette of the palace.

Emma didn't want to look behind her; she knew it would slow them down. Soon, they saw a couple on the path up ahead. They slowed to a walk, knowing they were probably safe with other people around.

They recovered their breath. Emma glanced over her shoulder and saw nothing but fog and a faint outline of the gardens and maze.

'They're not there anymore,' she puffed.

'Good,' said Penny. 'Who was it?'

Emma's voice trembled as she glanced back towards the maze, now shrouded in mist. 'Perhaps we didn't need to flee like that. Maybe I overreacted.'

'Maybe,' said Penny softly, but her hand gripped Emma's arm. 'But in my experience, if something doesn't feel right' – her eyes met Emma's with steely certainty – 'it's because it isn't. Trust your instincts. Always.' A shiver passed between them as they hurried away from the shadowy labyrinth, both suddenly eager to return to the safety of crowded streets.

TWENTY-EIGHT

Rupert Crowfield hesitated before the crooked oak door, adjusting his tie with nervous fingers. He smoothed his sleeves, swallowed hard, then raised his hand. The moment stretched as doubts flooded his mind.

Stay calm, he commanded himself silently. Lydney was intimidating, certainly – with that unnerving stare and quiet intensity – but not dangerous. At least, that's what Rupert had convinced himself.

Until Charles Harpole's death. Now, with that blood on someone's hands, Rupert found himself wondering just how far Lydney might go to get what he wanted. The thought sent a cold shiver down his spine as he finally rapped his knuckles against the ancient wood.

Had Lydney had something to do with it? Rupert couldn't be sure.

He took in a breath and knocked on the door.

'Enter!'

The room was lit by candlelight and Lydney sat at his round table poring over maps and old books. He removed his monocle, sat back in his chair, and fixed him with his eye. The other eye socket was red and empty.

'Tell me you've found the map, Crowfield.'

'I'm afraid I haven't, sir.'

Lydney said nothing. He replaced his monocle and turned back to his map and books.

The silence grew. Was he going to say anything at all? An uncomfortable crawling sensation crept over Rupert. An expression of anger or disappointment would be preferable to this. Lydney's lack of response made Rupert feel he wasn't worth bothering about. He felt irrelevant.

'Sir.' He cleared his throat again. 'Have you any—'

'Are you still here?' Lydney didn't look up from his book.

'Yes, I'm er...'

'Find that map, Crowfield. And don't come back here until you have it.'

Rupert opened his mouth to speak. Then he reasoned Lydney had no interest in hearing anything else he had to say. He quietly left the room.

TWENTY-NINE

Emma and Penny met for lunch the following Tuesday at Café Monico, Piccadilly Circus. Polite chatter hummed around them, and a string quartet played on a small stage at the far end of the room.

'I feel rather embarrassed about running away from the maze at Hampton Court,' confessed Emma. 'I became certain someone was following us. And when I saw that person in the fog, my instinct was to get away. It seems so silly now.'

'It's not silly,' said Penny. 'A man followed you recently, and an intruder got into your house. You're being understandably cautious.'

As Emma reflected, she realized the situation had almost been amusing. 'I've no idea what that person must have thought when they saw two ladies running away from them,' she said with a laugh.

'One of them pushing a perambulator!' added Penny. She grinned. 'They were probably quite surprised. Or on the other hand... it was someone following us.'

Emma shuddered at the thought. 'I'm so pleased you were there with me, Penny. If I'd been on my own, I would have been terrified. In fact, I don't think I would have gone into that maze on my own in the first place.'

Penny smiled. 'Everything seems a little easier when there are two of you, doesn't it? And what I'm about to say might seem odd, but... Oh, it doesn't matter.'

'Yes, it does,' said Emma. 'What?'

'Well, it doesn't seem right to say it when you felt so frightened, but I actually enjoyed our visit to the maze. There was something rather thrilling about it. When you spend a lot of time at home with young children, the days can feel rather predictable. Running through a maze with a perambulator was quite fun when I look back at it. It's not the sort of thing I get to do every day!' Penny laughed. 'And it's thanks to you, Emma, that I had the opportunity to do it.'

Emma laughed too. 'You're grateful?'

'Absolutely! It reminded me of what I used to do when I was a news reporter. Without the perambulator, of course.'

'It's quite astonishing when you think of the path we're being led along now,' said Emma. 'And it all started when Lord Harpole lent me his coat.'

'It all started when you found that symbol in William's diary,' replied Penny. 'You could have chosen to ignore it, but here we are trying to puzzle out a series of obscure clues. Who knows where it will lead us?'

'Answers, hopefully,' said Emma. 'I want to find out what William's connection to all of this was.'

Penny nodded. 'We need to understand the purpose of the map. So far, it appears to be leading us from one carved symbol to the next. But what's it all for?'

'I don't know,' said Emma. 'But I have an idea about the latest clue.' She took out her notebook and turned to the page where she'd sketched the symbol from the tree carving in the Hampton Court maze. 'I've been looking at this during the weekend and I think the symbol is a mouse.'

'A mouse? Let's have a look at it.'

Emma showed her the drawing. 'I think the semi-circle is its body,' she said. 'The circle at this end is its ear, and the wiggly line at the other end is the tail.'

'Yes, I see it now!' said Penny. 'And the letters beneath are "YOCC". What could that mean?'

Emma shrugged. 'I wish I could come up with something.'

'And there's the cross again. I wish I knew what that referred to.'

The waiter arrived and placed two bowls of consommé au riz in front of them. 'Enjoy your food, ladies,' he said with a bow.

They thanked him and began to eat. 'We're having to work on two puzzles, aren't we?' said Emma. 'The possibility that Lord Harpole was murdered and the mysterious map and symbols.'

'It's possible the puzzles are connected,' said Penny. 'Lord Harpole could have been murdered for the map. If that's the case, then we should be able to find a link before long.'

'Do you think the map could be connected to the secret society?' said Emma.

'Yes, I suppose it could. It frustrates me that we haven't found out anything more about the society.'

'I asked Mr Campbell about it and he denied all knowledge,' said Emma. 'And we asked Richard Harpole too.'

'And I recall he swiftly changed the subject,' said Penny. 'Which suggests he knows about it but didn't want to answer any questions.'

'And I think Lord Harpole's valet denied knowing about it for the same reason,' said Emma. 'It's annoying when people lie to you.'

Penny gave a knowing smile. 'Yes, it is. Unfortunately, you have to get used to it when you're investigating something.

You'd think everyone would want to be helpful, but some of them only want to protect themselves.'

'I think Mr Campbell could be suspicious,' said Emma. 'I've no idea what his motive could be for murdering his employer, but he seemed defensive when I spoke to him.'

'He had the opportunity to murder his employer, didn't he?' said Penny. 'He was staying in a room close by. He could have spent an hour or two with Harpole and would have prepared their drinks. He could have prepared the drinks somewhere in the room out of Harpole's view and that allowed him to add the laudanum.'

'And Harpole trusted him,' said Emma. 'His valet would have often made his drinks.' She felt her throat tighten as she thought about the betrayal. How could someone be so cold-hearted?

'But what does Campbell have to gain from Lord Harpole's death?' said Penny. 'That's what we need to find out. And there are other suspects to consider too.'

'Richard Harpole has inherited the estate,' said Emma. 'He's benefited more than anyone else.'

'Very true. I'd like to know if he has an alibi for the time of his brother's death. He could have arrived at the hotel unnoticed and encouraged his brother to share a bottle of whisky with him.'

'When he spoke at the inquest, he said he and his brother got on well but weren't close,' said Emma. 'And when the coroner asked him if there'd been any disagreements in the family I felt sure he was lying when he said there weren't.'

'I agree,' said Penny. 'He seemed particularly uncomfortable when he was asked that question.'

The waiter approached their table and frowned. 'Are you unhappy with your food today, ladies?'

Emma looked down at their uneaten consommé au riz. 'Oh no, it's lovely, thank you. We've just been talking too much.'

He gave a half-smile and drifted away.

'Oh dear,' said Penny. 'They get offended here when you allow your food to go cold.' She scooped some spoonfuls into her mouth.

'There's Lady Somersham to think about, too,' said Emma. 'Could she have been the lady who dropped her cloak pin as she rushed out of the hotel?'

'Yes,' said Penny. 'It's a possibility, isn't it? If she dropped her cloak pin, that suggests she was wearing a cloak. A cloak has a hood and perhaps she was wearing the hood so she could conceal her identity. The receptionist knew who she was when we asked him about her so she would have wanted to enter and leave the hotel without being recognized.'

'She was probably aware she'd dropped her cloak pin, but didn't want to go back for it because she knew they would recognize her,' said Emma.

'Yes, so she had to run off and leave it then send a maid there to fetch it later. I'd like to know if she has an alibi for the time of her fiancé's death. The trouble is, what could her motive have been? She was due to marry a lord and would have lived on that beautiful estate in Berkshire. Why would she have denied herself that opportunity?'

'Perhaps their engagement wasn't as harmonious as it seemed,' said Emma. 'Maybe she found out something unpleasant about her husband-to-be.' She gave an inward sigh. A deceitful fiancé was a familiar experience for her. She noticed the waiter wandering towards their table again and quickly finished her food.

The saumon grillé was placed in front of them as soon as their first course had been cleared.

'We've come up with three suspects,' said Penny. 'But we haven't yet considered the possibility someone from the secret society murdered Lord Harpole. I'd like to find out more about that Crowfield character who turned up shortly after Harpole died. Do you think he could be something to do with the society?'

'He could be,' said Emma. 'And he could have murdered Harpole. His arrival in the corridor after his death could have been a ruse to make everyone think he'd had nothing to do with it.'

'Yes, an excellent ruse! It seems a foolproof plan to murder someone, then turn up at the scene a short while later and pretend to be upset about their death. And we have to think about the man who followed you the other day and possibly followed us in the maze. Who's he?'

'I don't know.' Emma gave a shiver. 'I feel there are too many people to think about now. How do we make any progress? And let's not forget no one else is even considering the fact Lord Harpole was murdered. His death is officially a suicide.'

'True,' said Penny. 'But don't get disheartened, Emma. We must persevere. And I think it's about time we find out what's going on in the secret society's building in Kensington.'

'How?'

'We have a look inside it.'

'And how are we going to manage that?'

Penny smiled. 'I have a plan.'

THIRTY

After sharing her plan with Emma, Penny called at the *Morning Express* offices to hand in her next article. She found Edgar Fish busily scribbling on proofs.

'I'm sorry to interrupt you while you're busy,' she said. 'I'll leave this here.' She placed her article on a pile of papers on his desk.

'I'm never too busy for you, Mrs Blakely,' said Edgar. He tucked his pencil behind his ear, sat back in his seat and gestured for her to sit. 'I could do with the break to be honest with you. I swear everybody here drives me half-mad. The compositors constantly argue with me, Potter does next to nothing and Wright is so full of ideas that he can't concentrate on one thing for any length of time. I miss a calm, sensible presence like yours, Mrs Blakely.'

'You have Miss Welton,' said Penny, sitting on a chair with an ink-stained cushion.

'Yes and she's excellent at her job. She's just a little...' He pulled a grimace. 'Sombre. Anyway!' He grabbed the article Penny had just placed on his desk. 'Let's have a read of this, shall we? "It's not unusual these days for women to take part in activities outside the home. These could be charitable works, leisure pursuits or paid work. Such activities are enjoyable and fulfilling and, as we march towards the twentieth century, women are increasingly encouraged in such pursuits." Quite right, Mrs Blakely!' He smiled. 'I think all women should be encouraged to have hobbies and pursuits.' He continued reading. '"When a woman becomes a mother, however, her life must be devoted to her newborn child. This means any activities she previously enjoyed must be put on hold."' He nodded. 'True. "The loss of time to spend on other interests can come as a shock to the new mother. Even simple pleasures such as reading a book or cutting flowers in the garden can become impossible when an infant demands care and attention."' Edgar frowned. 'Is that so? Surely it's not that difficult to read a book or cut a few flowers?'

'It's possible when a new mother has a nursemaid to help,' said Penny. 'But I'm writing this article for mothers who don't have a nursemaid.'

'They may not have a nursemaid but every household has a woman who comes in. Even a charlady can mind an infant for a bit.'

'I don't think many mothers would want to leave their baby with the charlady. And I'm not sure a charlady would wish to do it either.'

'I see. All right then, let's read on. "I was fortunate to be employed as a news reporter on Fleet Street for a decade. It is a profession which is unusual for women and I enjoyed my work immensely. Marrying and becoming a mother has changed my sense of personal identity. No longer an intrepid reporter, I am now just as busy tending to my two young children. I have found it difficult to accustom myself to the change…"' Edgar stopped and laid down the piece of paper. 'I'm not so sure about this article.'

Penny felt a flash of anger. 'Why? What's wrong with it?'

'Well... it's not very jolly is it?'

'Does it have to be jolly?'

'Quite jolly, yes. Your previous article discussed sleep and contained practical tips. This, however, sounds like you're complaining.'

'I'm not complaining, I'm just discussing the challenges of balancing your own interests with the needs of your children. And how, when you become a mother, that's all you are. All your past achievements are forgotten about.'

Edgar narrowed his eyes. 'Is that how you feel, Mrs Blakely?'

Penny's throat tightened and tears felt alarmingly close. 'I suppose I do... Well, yes I do. That's why I wrote it.'

He sensed her upset and glanced away. Penny quickly dabbed at her eyes with a finger.

'I think I understand the sentiment behind it,' he said, after a pause. 'A quick rewrite will smooth it out a bit and make it a little more...'

'Jollier?' suggested Penny, forcing a smile.

'Yes. That's the word, Mrs Blakely.' To her disappointment, he handed the article back to her. 'Take your time with it, we don't have to publish an article every week.'

'I'd like to. If possible.'

'Just see how you go. And I want to say your achievements here at this newspaper have not been forgotten about, Mrs Blakely.'

'No?' She felt fresh tears in her eyes again.

'No. Not at all. I'll never forget how you always got the best stories. And our editor, Mr Sherman, saw to it that you did. He knew what you were capable of. And you still are. Becoming a mother doesn't change that, Mrs Blakely.'

Penny never imagined she would hear such thoughtful and

encouraging words from Edgar Fish. She could only muster a choked reply.

'Thank you, Edgar. That means a lot to me.'

THIRTY-ONE

Once Emma's lessons were over the following day, she met Penny at Stanford Road in Kensington.

Light snow had fallen overnight. It sat in dirty clumps on the pavements and roads, but it lay pristine on the rooftop of number seventeen. Even the gnarled tree looked pretty with its frosted white coating.

No footprints led up to the black front door. 'There have been no recent visitors,' said Emma. 'Hopefully that means no one's inside.'

'Yes, hopefully,' said Penny. 'But we need to make a show of calling at the house before we do anything else.'

'All right then.'

Snow tumbled from the crooked iron gate as they pushed it open. Penny strode up to the door and knocked.

Emma held her breath as they waited. 'No one's there,' she said eventually.

'I'll knock again. Just to be sure.'

The longer they waited, the more anxious Emma felt. If someone finally answered, would they be angry with her and Penny for disturbing them?

Penny gave a sigh. 'You're right, Emma. No one's here. Let's call at the house next door.'

They spoke to the housekeeper at the neighbouring property. 'We need to find someone who can let us into number seventeen,' said Penny. 'My cat is trapped in there.'

The housekeeper raised her eyebrows. 'Your cat?'

'Yes. I live on Merton Road and my house backs onto this street. My cat didn't come home last night. My friend here, Mrs Langley, and I have been walking around trying to find her. We heard meowing coming from number seventeen. Somehow she's got in there.'

'How?'

'Well, that's the question I've been asking myself. But you know what cats are like, they find a way in.'

'Well, if she's found a way in, then I'm sure she'll find a way out again,' said the housekeeper.

'Well, you say that, and I thought the same when she climbed up a tree once. She got up the tree with no problem at all, so I assumed she'd be able to get down again. But she couldn't, and we had to find someone with a ladder to bring her down.'

'Your cat sounds like a lot of trouble.'

'She is,' said Penny. 'She's an absolute nuisance. But I would really like to get into number seventeen and rescue her. Do you know who lives there?'

'A gentleman who's away a lot. I don't know his name. He could do with maintaining the upkeep of the place. It's an eyesore. Your cat has probably got in through a broken window or shutter.'

'Yes, I expect so.'

Emma wondered if they would have to break into the house. She didn't want to get into trouble for doing such a thing.

'You'd best speak to Lewis,' said the housekeeper. 'He's at

five, Kelso Place. He keeps an eye on number seventeen for the gentleman.'

Mr Lewis was a stooped, elderly man with a clay pipe in his mouth. He was also hard of hearing. Penny had to repeat her explanation a few times before he understood it.

'A cat? Maybe it can catch a few rats while it's in there,' he said.

'She might,' said Penny, 'but I don't want her in that building catching rats. I want her home with me.'

'So you want me to go looking for the cat?'

'My friend and I are happy to search the building for the cat. All we ask is that you let us in.'

'They don't like people going in there. It's private.'

'Who's they?'

'Eh?'

'Who owns the building?'

'Mr Lydney.'

'And who's he?'

'The gentleman who owns it.' He disappeared for a moment, then came back with a key. 'I should go in there with you, but I've not been right recently.' He smacked his chest and pushed out a hacking cough. Emma recoiled.

'It sounds like you need to stay by the fire, Mr Lewis,' said Penny, taking the key from him. 'You don't want to catch a chill and make that cough worse.'

'No, I don't. This will probably be my last winter, but if I can see another, then I'll be grateful to the Lord for sparing me.'

'Indeed,' said Penny. 'We'll return this key to you as soon as we've found my cat.'

He nodded and closed the door on them.

'That was easier than I thought,' said Penny with a grin. 'Let's go and look around.'

. . .

The entrance hall of the house was gloomy with wood panelling and a dark tiled floor. A grandfather clock gave a steady, heavy tick and the air smelled musty. Emma and Penny had brought candles and candleholders with them. Once they were lit, they cast a feeble glow in the oppressive gloom.

They explored the large reception rooms on the ground floor. The house had presumably once been a home but now served as an informal gentlemen's club. The velvet curtains were drawn and the furniture was old and heavy. Shabby leather chairs were placed around low round tables. An old newspaper rested on a table and a stale tobacco smell hung in the air. Emma could picture the men sitting here with drinks and socializing. Was this where her late husband had sat too? She could see him now in one of the chairs, talking energetically with a drink in his hand.

Penny opened the doors of a large cabinet. Inside were glasses and bottles of drink.

They climbed the staircase to the next floor.

On the first floor, rooms which had presumably been bedrooms now served as offices and meeting rooms. The largest room had a long table in it and was surrounded by chairs with faded velvet seats. There was a painting on the far wall above the fireplace. They walked over to it and held their candles up so they could see it properly.

'The symbol which was written in William's diary!' said Emma. The painting depicted the key with an eye in its loop and the circle of laurel leaves. Beneath the symbol was a single word.

'"Inveniam",' said Penny. 'Is that Latin?'

'I think so,' said Emma. 'Something to do with finding. "I will find", I think.'

'Find what?'

'Something which a secret map could lead to?'

'Yes, that makes sense. How do you know Latin?'

'I was envious of my brother, Alfred, learning it at school while I studied dull subjects at home with a governess. I made him teach me when he was home for the holidays.'

Penny smiled. 'It sounds like he did a good job! I wish I'd learned Latin too.'

Emma glanced around the room. 'It's strange to think William must have attended meetings here. I still don't understand why.'

They went into a room which appeared to be used as an office. A large desk sat by the window and old books filled the shelves. A map was pinned to the wall. Penny walked over to it. 'This looks like some sort of nautical chart.'

It was a map of the world with lines drawn across the oceans connecting various ports.

'The voyages of Sir Francis Drake,' said Emma.

'How do you know that? Did your brother teach you that too?'

'No. It says so in this corner.'

Penny laughed. 'You shouldn't have given it away.'

'Why would someone be interested in his voyages?' Emma walked over to the desk and held her candle over the many books and papers which covered it. 'There's another map here,' she said. 'And it looks old.'

Penny joined her at the desk. The old map was hand drawn and showed a slightly inaccurate map of the world. It was brightly coloured and rich with illustrations of ships and a small portrait of Sir Francis Drake. The map's description was in French.

'"The heroic circumnavigation of the world by Sir Francis Drake 1577 to 1580",' said Penny. 'There you go. I found my chance to do some translating too.'

'Well done,' said Emma.

'But I expect you know French too, don't you?'

'Yes, my governess taught me French.' Emma turned her attention back to the desk. 'There's a book here about the Knights Templar. What could they have to do with Drake?'

'They were a few hundred years before him,' said Penny, leafing through the book. 'Oh look, there's something here.' She rested her candle on the table and examined a piece of paper which had cramped handwriting on it. 'Someone's been making notes from this book. "Treasures of the King of France",' recited Penny. '"Jewels of the King of England deposited at The Temple in 1204" and "Cressing Temple, Essex" is also written here. What could it mean?'

While Penny examined the notes from the book, Emma stepped over to a wide chest of drawers with three columns of small shallow drawers with little bronze handles. She began pulling them out to look inside. They contained notebooks, small ledgers and administrative paperwork. She came across a leather-bound volume with the word "Subscriptions" embossed on it. Setting her candle on top of the chest of drawers, she leafed through the book, searching for her husband's name.

It wasn't long before she found it. The name William Langley was written next to the sum of ten shillings. Then she found his name again for the same sum. It appeared to be a monthly subscription which he must have used her money to pay for. Ten shillings was a decent weekly wage. Membership of the Inveniam Society wasn't cheap.

Emma kept turning the pages and almost dropped the book when she saw the next sum William had paid. Fifty pounds. It was enough money to rent a modest house for a year. Next to his name was written the word "Investor". William had used her money to invest in the secret society. Why? What had he hoped to gain from it?

A noise sounded downstairs.

Emma froze and stared at Penny. Penny returned her gaze, the candlelight reflected in her spectacles. Then she slowly closed the book she'd been looking at and picked up her candleholder.

THIRTY-TWO

'Perhaps it's Mr Lewis,' whispered Emma. 'He thinks we've been here too long and he's come for the key.' She put the subscriptions ledger back into its drawer and closed it.

Penny bit her lip. 'We didn't lock the door behind us,' she said. 'That was our mistake.'

Emma dared not move, worried her footsteps on the floorboards would alert the person downstairs to her and Penny's presence.

She strained her ears, listening for another noise. The tick of the grandfather clock drifted up the stairs and she felt sure she could hear footsteps, too.

An icy chill lurched in the base of her stomach. 'They'll have seen our footsteps in the snow,' she whispered. 'They must know we're here!'

Penny gave a long exhale and slowly tiptoed across the room to the door. Emma held her breath, terrified one of the floorboards would make a noise.

Fortunately they didn't. Penny stood by the doorway and blew out her candle. In the gloom, Emma could see her peering out of the doorway.

Another noise came from downstairs. It sounded like a cupboard opening or closing.

Was it Mr Lydney? Emma calmed herself as she thought of the explanation they had for being here. They were looking for a cat, but she'd somehow found her way out again.

The footsteps moved onto the stairs. A cold sweat broke out on Emma's face and palms. She blew out her candle and stood frozen to the spot.

The footsteps continued up the stairs; they were heavier than a woman's step. The person was carrying a candle and the light glimmered on the wall beyond the doorway. Penny's silhouette retreated into the room and appeared to hide itself behind the door. Emma's heart thudded as she carefully tiptoed her way across the room to join her. One floorboard gave a small creak, but it wasn't enough for the person on the stairs to hear. She reached Penny just as the person got to the top of the staircase.

Emma stood next to Penny and pushed her back against the wall. She hoped there was a chance they wouldn't be spotted.

Penny's breathing came quick and shallow beside her; Emma could feel her friend's pulse racing where their arms pressed together. What would they do if the intruder entered?

The footsteps veered away – towards the meeting room with its grand table and wall painting. Emma's eyes darted to the door, calculating their chances of escape. Beside her, Penny shifted her weight subtly forward onto the balls of her feet, clearly thinking the same thing.

But the footsteps drew close again and the candlelight reached the doorway. They heard his breath now, regular and deep.

Every muscle in Emma's body tensed as he stepped into the room. He held his candle in front of him as he walked over to the desk. Emma knew they would be spotted in a moment, but for the time being, he was distracted by the books and maps just as they'd been. He was clearly a stranger in this house.

As his head turned a little, she caught sight of his brown whiskers. Her heart gave an extra strong thud when she saw he was the man who'd followed her from Paddington station.

They waited while he looked over the things on the desk. Then he lifted his candle to look at the bookshelves. His arm then traced an arc around the room as he moved his candle. His eyes followed the light and his gaze was almost upon them.

'Waahh!' Emma almost collapsed in fright as Penny sprung forward and headed for him. He let out a yelp of surprise and dropped his candle. It extinguished itself on the floor.

Emma followed, unsure of Penny's plan. Was she going to attack him? She could barely see anything in the darkness. Someone knocked into the chair behind the desk and then came another thud.

'Get off me!' cried out the man. 'I mean no harm!'

'What are you doing here?' said Penny.

'I can explain. Just let me get up off the floor.'

'How can we trust you?'

'Trust me, please!'

Emma stepped over to the window and pulled open the heavy velvet curtains. The fading light from outside cast a grey glow into the room. Emma could see now that Penny had pinned the man beneath the chair.

'You'd better not try anything,' she said as she pulled it off him.

'I won't.' His bowler hat lay on the floor next to him. He picked it up and got to his feet.

'Who are you and what do you want?' Penny asked him sharply.

THIRTY-THREE

'I'm Archibald Maitland,' he said, straightening his posture defensively as recognition flickered in his eyes. 'And I worked for Lord Harpole.'

'You worked for him?' Emma felt her mouth fall open in surprise.

Maitland's eyes darted nervously to the shadows around them. He leaned closer, voice dropping to a whisper as he tugged at his collar. 'I'll tell you more, but not here.' His gaze swept the space behind them. 'There's a risk someone might turn up.'

'I agree,' said Penny. 'And we need to return the key to the caretaker, Mr Lewis, before he gets suspicious.'

They arranged to meet Mr Maitland a short while later in the coffee room at the nearby Langton Hotel.

'He's the man who followed me from Paddington station,' said Emma as they walked to Mr Lewis's home. 'I don't think we can trust him.'

'He's the one?' said Penny. 'Well, it's a relief to find out who he is. And hopefully he can give us a proper explanation when we speak to him.'

'You frightened me half to death when you ran at him with your war cry.'

'I'm sorry,' Penny said, her lips twitching with barely suppressed laughter despite her apologetic tone. Her eyes sparkled with residual excitement as she smoothed her dishevelled hair. 'I didn't know what else to do! I wanted to frighten him before he spotted us, and that horrible noise was all I could think of.' She shrugged, somewhat sheepishly. 'It was reckless, I suppose. He could have been armed or fought back.' Her smile dimmed momentarily at the thought before returning. 'Fortunately, we caught him completely off guard.'

Archibald Maitland was already waiting for them when they arrived at the hotel. The coffee room was warm and well-lit with comfortable blue velvet chairs.

Mr Maitland ran a nervous hand over his wavy hair and gave an awkward smile. His dark eyes had a warmth to them, but Emma couldn't forget how he'd followed her and presumably broken into the Solomons' home. She stared at him coolly, waiting for his explanation.

'I see they have electric lighting here,' he said once they'd made themselves comfortable. 'I like a hotel with electric lighting, it's a remarkable improvement. Gas lighting seems rather primitive by comparison, doesn't it?'

'It does,' said Penny. 'I hope we'll be able to afford electric lights for our homes before long.'

'That could be some years away yet.'

A waiter brought them coffee and Mr Maitland wiped his palms on his knees. 'I suppose I should explain myself,' he said. 'But if I do, will you two ladies offer your explanation too?'

'What have we got to explain?' asked Penny.

'Your involvement in all of this.'

'Very well. Let's hear your explanation first.'

'Yes, indeed. I must say I'm still recovering from the wild banshee attack in the lodge.'

'Banshee?' said Penny.

'Yes.' He smoothed his hair and smiled. 'That's what it seemed like. Anyway, I know you're not a banshee, Mrs Blakely.'

'You know my name?'

'Yes, I saw you... both of you, in fact, speak at the inquest. Anyway, I'm a private investigator and Lord Harpole hired me to find something one of his ancestors is rumoured to have hidden. It's said his ancestor was a friend of Sir Francis Drake. You know who he was, don't you? He was a sailor, privateer and explorer in the days of Queen Elizabeth.'

'Yes, we know who he was,' said Penny. 'And we saw maps of his voyages in the room where we encountered you.'

'Ah yes, I was just looking at those when you... Anyway. You've probably heard Drake plundered ships and settlements in the Caribbean and South America. During his exploits, he captured a Spanish galleon, renamed it the *Golden Hind*, and sailed it around the world. When he returned to Devon, he'd filled his ship with gold and other treasures such as silk and spices. Most of it was taken to London and stored in the Tower of London. But not all of it.' He raised a cautionary finger. 'There are rumours some of the treasure was hidden in secret locations and some was gifted to friends of Drake. Lord Harpole's ancestor, Lord Henry Harpole, was apparently a recipient. He hid his treasure somewhere and, on his deathbed, told his heir where it was. The heir decided to keep it hidden but passed on its location to successive generations until Lord Theobald Harpole drew a map leading to the location of the treasure.'

'A map?' said Emma.

'Yes. A map which I believe you two ladies are in possession of.'

Emma and Penny exchanged a glance. Was it sensible to confirm this?

Mr Maitland continued. 'Lord Harpole left that map in a case for me to collect from the left luggage office of Paddington railway station. He planned to give me the ticket to collect it, but he died before he could do so. I tried collecting the item without a ticket but they refused to let me have it. So what could I do? I watched that office for a few days to see who turned up to collect the case.'

'And I turned up,' said Emma. 'Why didn't you just ask me for the case? Why follow me?'

'I had to keep my work secret. If I'd asked you for the case, then you would have discovered my connection to Lord Harpole. You would have told other people about it and I would have had some explaining to do. However, I overestimated my ability to follow you without arousing your suspicion. I'd hoped I'd be able to catch you unaware and snatch the case from you. Without hurting you, of course, I never meant any harm. But you guarded it too closely and when you went to the police station in St John's Wood, I had to give up.'

'And then you broke into my home.'

His jaw dropped in surprise. 'No, I didn't do that!'

Emma frowned. 'You must have done.'

'No, I can promise you it wasn't me.'

'But if it wasn't you, then who was it?'

He shrugged. 'I don't know.'

Emma sipped her coffee as she gave this some thought.

'Did you follow us in Hampton Court maze last Friday?' Penny asked Mr Maitland.

He ran a hand over his whiskers. 'Yes. That was me, I admit that. I realized you'd probably visited St Paul's Cathedral and got another clue from there. Lord Harpole told me the map identified St Paul's as the location, but he didn't know how to find the next clue. When I followed you to the maze, I realized you had the answer.'

'So you've been watching us,' said Penny. 'That's a horrible thought.'

'It's what private investigators have to do sometimes. But when I saw you both running away from me, I realized it's not always the best method.'

'I wish you'd tried talking to us sooner,' said Penny. 'We wouldn't have got so worried in the maze. How did you know we were in the house on Stanford Road?'

'I've been watching the lodge for a while and this afternoon I noticed two sets of ladies' footsteps in the snow. They went in but hadn't come out again. I suspected the footprints belonged to the pair of you. So I tried the door, and it was unlocked. I expected to have a calm encounter with you. I certainly didn't expect you to hide from me then leap out like that.'

Penny laughed and Emma felt the tension finally draining from her shoulders. 'I think we've evened the score after that fright you gave us in the maze!' Penny's expression shifted quickly from amusement to intensity, leaning forward with hands clasped. 'Now, tell us what you know about the lodge and this secret society.'

'Not a great deal,' Maitland confessed, his eyes darting between them as he lowered his voice conspiratorially. 'But what I do know might be dangerous enough.' He glanced over his shoulder before continuing. 'I'll tell you everything I can.'

THIRTY-FOUR

'Lord Harpole told me he was visited by a man called Stephen Lydney a few months ago,' said Archibald Maitland. 'Mr Lydney told him he'd done some research into the Harpole family because he'd heard about a map which led to treasure hidden by Lord Henry Harpole in the sixteenth century. Lord Harpole was reluctant to believe it at first. However, he'd recently inherited Wickham House, so he ordered a search of the house. The map was discovered in a trunk in the attic where it had appeared to have been forgotten about. Stephen Lydney invited Lord Harpole to join his society which searches for hidden treasure.'

'Inveniam,' said Emma.

'Yes. Latin, is it? I don't know what it means.'

'I think it means "I will find".'

'Well, that makes sense.'

'And it also explains the book we saw on the desk in the lodge,' said Penny, her eyes widening with sudden realization as she snapped her fingers. 'The one with all those meticulous notes about treasures belonging to the Knights Templar!' She leaned forward eagerly, connecting pieces of the puzzle with animated gestures.

'Yes. As I understand it, Mr Lydney is obsessed with unearthing long-buried treasures. I've heard he found some seventh-century gold Saxon coins in a field and has gathered other treasures too. He believes there's a vast amount of old riches in this country which are yet to be discovered. Riches which were buried by invaders such as the Romans, Vikings and Danes. And people who buried their wealth during difficult times like the Black Death and the Fire of London. And then there are the adventurers like Sir Francis Drake. They apparently gave some of their plundered treasure to the Crown but kept some for themselves and hid them.'

'And I'm assuming Mr Lydney's society is secretive because treasure finds need to be reported,' said Penny. 'The coroner needs to be informed, as does the landowner. Failing to report the finding of treasure is a criminal act.'

'Indeed,' said Mr Maitland. 'And Lord Harpole told me Mr Lydney has been spoken to by the police about his activities, but nothing could be done because there was no evidence he'd actually found anything.'

'What about the Saxon coins?'

He shrugged. 'Apparently it's just rumour and there's no proof he has them. He could have sold them to a secret buyer, of course, and no one would be none the wiser.'

'So why did he create a society for this?' asked Emma.

'I suppose a society has a social and ceremonial appeal,' said Mr Maitland. 'And practical too. The members of the society either help with research or provide funds. Lydney then shares the proceeds from the finds with the members. That's how Lord Harpole explained it to me, but he didn't particularly wish to be a member. When he found the map, he felt obliged to join Lydney because he'd told him about it. But when it came to sharing the map with the society... that's when Lord Harpole changed his mind. I don't think he fully trusted Lydney. So he asked me to use the map to find the treasure. The plan was in place, but then he died and the map fell into your hands.'

'So why are you still searching for the treasure now Lord Harpole is dead?' asked Penny.

'Because it belongs to the Harpole family.'

'His brother, Richard.'

'Yes. It's only right he benefits from it.'

'And you're hoping he'll pay you well for finding it,' said Penny.

He gave a wry smile. 'That's my hope and I see nothing wrong with it. I deserve to be paid for my work. The question that puzzles me,' he said, leaning back in his chair, 'is why you ladies are pursuing this matter so diligently.'

'We didn't initially know the map led to treasure,' Penny replied, exchanging a glance with Emma. 'We were simply intrigued by the mystery and decided to follow the trail of clues.' Her voice dropped lower. 'But we've come to believe it might be connected to Lord Harpole's death.'

Maitland's posture stiffened. 'How?'

'We believe he was murdered,' Penny stated flatly.

'Murdered?' Maitland's eyebrows shot up as he recoiled slightly. 'No, that's impossible.' He shook his head emphatically. 'You were both at the inquest – the verdict was clearly suicide.'

Penny methodically outlined their theory, her hands moving with precision as she described the evidence. Emma watched Maitland's expression transform, shock giving way to doubt, then cautious consideration. His eyes widened with each new piece of information.

'Goodness,' he whispered when Penny finished, running a hand through his hair. 'You've thought this through quite thoroughly, haven't you?'

'What was Lydney's reaction when Lord Harpole withdrew the map?' Penny pressed, not allowing the momentum to fade.

Maitland's gaze dropped to the table. 'I don't know.'

'But could Lydney have been angry enough to murder him for it?' Emma interjected.

Maitland scratched his temple, a thoughtful furrow appearing between his brows. 'Now that... that's an interesting perspective I hadn't considered.' His eyes narrowed in contemplation.

'What else do you know about Lydney?' Penny asked. 'Have you encountered him personally?'

'I've shared everything I know,' Maitland said, spreading his hands. 'I've never met the man. But I do know Lord Harpole expressed a deep distrust of him.' He turned to Emma, his expression grave. 'If Lydney is indeed as dangerous as you suggest, it could certainly explain the break-in at your residence, Mrs Langley.'

Emma nodded. 'Of course. Lydney could have looking for the map.' She shivered.

Mr Maitland finished his coffee and sat back in his chair. 'So now we understand each other, what do we do? All three of us want to find the treasure hidden by Lord Harpole's ancestor before Lydney does. Shall we work together?'

Emma still didn't feel she could trust him. She tried to convey this sentiment as she looked at Penny. Penny pushed her spectacles up her nose and returned Emma's glance.

'I don't know,' said Penny. 'We need to discuss it.'

'Three heads are better than one,' said Maitland. 'Don't forget that. I'll leave you two ladies alone for a moment so you can confer. Then, when I return, you can let me know.'

He got up from his seat and left the room.

'I don't trust him at all,' said Emma in a low voice. 'He just wants to be involved so he can get a reward from the Harpole family.'

'But what's wrong with that?' replied Penny.

'I don't like his motivation.'

'But we could find out a lot from him,' said Penny. 'He knew Lord Harpole and could have some useful information which helps us find the murderer. And if we involve him, then he won't be following us anymore. I don't trust him much either, but I think it serves us better to work with him than exclude him.'

Emma gave this some thought. 'It seems risky.'

'What are the risks?'

'He could betray us. He could secretly be working for Lydney. He could even be the murderer!'

Penny nodded. 'Anything is possible.'

'So we shouldn't get involved with him!'

'I disagree. I think it's even more of a reason to work with him. If he is the murderer, it won't be long before he gives something away. We'll be ready to catch him out. On the other hand, he might be perfectly nice and decent, in which case we have some extra help.'

Emma sighed, a knot of unease tightening in her stomach. Something about Maitland's eager compliance troubled her – a performance that seemed too polished, too convenient. But Penny had that familiar determined set to her jaw that Emma had come to recognize. Once Penny Blakely made up her mind, there was little hope of changing it.

'You have more experience than me with these things,' she said. 'So if you think we can work with him, then let's do it. I just hope it's the right decision.'

'So do I,' said Penny. 'And thank you, Emma.' She rested her hand on hers. 'I won't forget your doubts about him.'

They finished their coffee and Mr Maitland returned to the room. He remained standing. 'Have you reached a decision?'

'We have,' said Emma. 'And we're happy to work with you.'

'Really? Oh, that's excellent news.' He sat down again. 'You won't regret it.'

'I hope not,' said Penny.

'So what did you find in the maze?'

'A symbol,' said Emma. She took her notebook out of her bag, reluctant to show him. She and Penny had put a lot of effort into finding it and she felt she was handing it over it to him. She opened the page and handed over her notebook. He peered closely at the drawing. 'Is that a mouse?'

'We think so,' said Emma.

'And "YOCC". What's that?'

'We don't know.'

'Do you mind if I copy this down? I'll have a good look at it and if I can work out its meaning, then I'll let you know.'

Emma hoped he would keep to his word as he took a notebook from his pocket and made a sketch from her drawing.

'Are you going to tell the new Lord Harpole about the map?' Penny asked him.

'Yes, I feel I should. But I can keep your names out of it, if you like?'

'Yes please,' said Penny evenly. 'He might demand the map from us.'

'You have every right to refuse, it doesn't belong to him. His brother left it in a case for me to collect, so it's mine.'

'He gave it to you or lent it to you?' said Penny. 'If he lent it, that means it must be returned to the family.'

'That's a good point,' he said, returning his notebook to his pocket. 'Just keep hold of it for now and I'll tell Richard Harpole that I don't know where it is.' He gave them a wink and held out his hand. 'It's going to be a pleasure working with you, ladies.'

Emma shook his hand, unsure they'd made the right decision.

THIRTY-FIVE

'The police still haven't caught the man who broke in,' said Mrs Solomon at dinner that evening. 'It's hopeless.'

'Oh, Ruth,' sighed her husband. 'There's no use in arresting a man if he didn't take anything.'

'But he still committed a crime, Ronald! He broke into our house.'

'He didn't break anything, did he? You left the window open and he climbed in. He was just trying his luck.' He broke off a piece of bread and mopped some gravy from his plate.

Mrs Solomon put down her knife and fork. 'Well, at the very least it's trespass! And he should be arrested for it.'

'The police don't bother with trespass these days,' said Mr Solomon. 'They're too busy.'

'Well, they need more officers then.' Mrs Solomon turned to Emma. 'It ruins your faith in law and order, doesn't it?'

'I'm sorry about the break-in,' said Emma. 'I feel like it's my fault.'

'He didn't take anything,' said Mr Solomon. 'So we can forget about it.'

'He was looking for the map,' said his wife. 'What's happened about it, Mrs Langley?'

Emma told them both about the Inveniam Society and how she and Penny had decided to work with Mr Maitland.

'Goodness,' said Mrs Solomon when she'd finished. 'It all sounds like a lot of work to me. Has anyone got any idea who murdered Lord Harpole?'

'Not yet.'

'There you go, the police can't sort that out either.'

'You need to stop grumbling, Ruth,' said Mr Solomon. 'Don't forget it's your birthday next week. You don't want to be grumbling on your birthday.'

She gave a coy smile. 'No, I don't. I didn't think you'd remember my birthday.'

'Why shouldn't I? I may forget most things these days, but I always remember your birthday. The sixth of February.'

Mrs Solomon's lips pursed. 'It's the seventh, Ronald.'

Later that evening, Emma updated her notebook. She crossed out the words "Mystery Man" and wrote Archibald Maitland's name next to them. At least one small part of the puzzle was solved – she knew the identity of the man who'd followed her.

Could Mr Maitland have murdered Lord Harpole? She and Penny needed to learn more about him to be sure one way or the other.

She wrote down the name Stephen Lydney. If Mr Maitland was to be believed, Lord Harpole had changed his mind about sharing the map with him. Had that angered Mr Lydney? Emma imagined it had. Had he murdered Lord Harpole so he could get hold of the map? It was a strong motive. Emma marked his name with a little star. He seemed the strongest suspect at the present time.

And it was quite a list of suspects: Lady Somersham, Mr Campbell, the new Lord Harpole, Mr Crowfield, Mr Maitland and Mr Lydney.

It was difficult to know what to do next.

THIRTY-SIX

'I have good news,' said James at dinner. 'Inspector Trotter at T Division agrees foul play could have been involved in Lord Harpole's death. So he's treating it as suspicious.'

'At last!' Penny felt relieved to hear the police were finally listening to her theory. 'So he suspects murder?'

'I wouldn't put it as strongly as that, but he agrees another person could have been in the room with Harpole when he consumed the whisky and laudanum. He's already made a start on the investigation and has been interviewing staff at the Imperial Grand Hotel today.'

'Good. And what about the second glass I found under the bed?'

'It had contained whisky, but no traces of laudanum were detected. That supports the idea that someone was drinking whisky with Lord Harpole and not putting laudanum in their own drink. However, as I've said before, it's possible Lord Harpole used that glass himself on another occasion. But treating his death as suspicious means we can question the people who knew him.'

'And the most important thing will be establishing alibis for them all,' said Penny. She then told James about her visit to the lodge on Stanford Road and the encounter with Archibald Maitland.

'I'm impressed you managed to get into the building, Penny,' said James. 'And I'm sure the Yard will be very interested in investigating Stephen Lydney's activities. If he's finding long-buried treasure and keeping it for himself, then he's committing an offence.'

'From what Mr Maitland told us, he's been rather good at hiding the evidence that he's done so. Mr Maitland mentioned Mr Lydney had found some old Saxon gold coins, but maybe he hasn't really found anything yet. Maybe that's why he's determined to find this treasure which was supposedly hidden by Lord Harpole's ancestor.'

James wiped his mouth with his napkin and sat back in his chair. 'You wonder if there's any truth in it, don't you really? It makes for a great story, of course. I think many of us would like to believe in hidden treasure. But if it's been lying somewhere for hundreds of years, you'd think it would have been found by now. Are you really sure you want to be spending your time trying to find this supposed treasure, Penny? It could lead to nothing. It could be an elaborate hoax.'

'Yes, it could be,' said Penny. 'And the idea of returning the treasure to the Harpole family doesn't seem like a particularly worthy cause when they already have a lot of wealth. However, there's clearly something in it. We've made a start and visited two locations. Perhaps it's just a puzzle or an elaborate game. But I'd like to continue with it and see where it leads to.'

'I can understand that. I just don't like the thought of this Lydney chap. It seems he may have broken into Emma Langley's home. He clearly takes it all quite seriously. If I can find a reason to interview him, then I will. I don't want you getting caught up with any nasty characters, Penny. And on that note, are you sure you can trust this Maitland fellow?'

'I probably can't, if I'm honest,' said Penny wearily. 'Emma doesn't trust him either. But I persuaded her we should, because I believe we can learn more about Lord Harpole from him.'

'I shall interview him, too. In fact, I'll do that soon because I would like to gauge what sort of gentleman he is.'

THIRTY-SEVEN

Light snowflakes fell past the window. It was a grey afternoon and Lady Amelia Somersham's eyelids felt heavy. She took a pause from her needlework and gave a loud yawn.

'Amelia!'

'I covered my mouth with my hand, Mother.'

'It's coarse behaviour. We could have had guests.'

Amelia glanced around the empty drawing room. 'But we don't have any guests at the moment.'

'No. We're waiting for them, though, and they could arrive at any moment. Perhaps you could move a little further away from the fire if it's making you feel sleepy.'

'I'm fine where I am, thank you, Mother.'

She stifled a sigh as she smoothed her black silk mourning dress. Life had been extremely boring since Charles's death. Her parents expected her to behave like an old widow. She glanced at her two sisters – both spinsters at the ages of twenty-six and twenty-eight. Neither of them had any hope of marrying soon. Now that Amelia's marriage would no longer happen, she worried she would end up like them.

She picked up her embroidery and continued with it. She

was sewing a forget-me-not flower and the work was slow and arduous. She'd always detested needlework.

'Half past two,' said her mother. 'I don't know where Lady Carrington has got to, I thought she would be here by now.'

'I'm waiting for Mr Gavan Duffy to call,' said Amelia's sister, Harriet. Her other sister, Lizzie, gave a laugh. 'You're going to have a long wait. I heard he called on Olivia Russell last week.'

Harriet dropped her sewing into her lap. 'You did not!'

'I did so.'

Harriet's brow crumpled and her lower lip wobbled. 'I don't see why he would call on Olivia. She's dull and plain.'

'It's very disappointing indeed if he has called on Olivia Russell,' said their mother. 'I'd hoped to have at least one of you married this year. But with Lord Harpole's death and Mr Gavan Duffy calling on other ladies, there isn't much hope at all, is there?'

Amelia saw her opportunity to create a scene. She dropped her sewing and got up from her chair, her chest heaving with emotion.

'What are you doing, Amelia?' asked her mother.

'I need some air,' she said.

'Why? What's the matter?'

'The way you speak about Lord Harpole's death... it's as though it's an inconvenience to you. You have no idea how enormously upsetting it is!'

'Of course it's upsetting, Amelia. And it is also an inconvenience. The man did a very foolish thing indeed. Now, there's no need to get all silly about this. Please calm yourself because we need to be ready to accept visitors.'

The butler entered the room with a card on a silver platter.

'Oh, at last. Lady Carrington is here.'

'No, she isn't, my lady. This visitor is for Lady Amelia. A Mr Archibald Maitland.' The butler crossed the room to where Amelia sat in her chair and presented her with the platter.

Her heart gave a skip. 'Thank you, Mr Kershaw.' She got to her feet. 'I wish to see him in private.'

'No, you do not!' said her mother. 'You receive him in here. And who is he, anyway?'

'He's a gentleman who was employed by Lord Harpole.'

'Employed?'

'Yes. He worked for him. He no doubt needs to speak to me regarding Lord Harpole's private affairs.'

'Private affairs? But you weren't even married!'

'No, but we were engaged to be married. And I'm mourning him as though I'm a widow, aren't I, Mother? So we may as well have been married. I don't require a chaperone for Mr Maitland's visit. Our meeting is for the purposes of business.'

Amelia's heart stirred with excitement as she stood in the morning room with Archibald. He grinned and looked even more handsome than she remembered.

'How have you been, Amelia?'

'I've been thoroughly bored. And it's been awful not being able to see you.' She stepped forward and took his hand. He gave the door a nervous glance. 'I feel like I'm trapped in my own home and I have to wear these awful black clothes.'

'You look very pretty in your black clothes.'

She giggled. 'Oh Archie, you shouldn't say such things!'

'I can't help myself.'

'How I wish I could go out and about with you and look for the treasure.'

'I have good news about that.' He guided her to a chair. 'I know where the map is.'

'You do?'

'Yes. Mrs Blakely and Mrs Langley have it.'

'Oh, those two. They're nice ladies, I'm sure they'll give it to you.'

'Yes, but the truth is I don't really want it. There are some wicked men looking for that map, Amelia. But Mrs Blakely and Mrs Langley have agreed to tell me everything they find out, and I'm confident we'll be able to find the treasure.'

'Oh Archie, that's wonderful!' She reached out and placed her hand on his cheek. His skin felt warm and a little rough. She longed to kiss him. For a moment, his eyes suggested he had the same idea. But then he slowly removed her hand from his face.

'We must be careful, Amelia. We don't want to get caught.'

'Oh, don't be such a bore, Archie.'

'I'm not a bore. I just don't want anyone to suspect us. Not yet anyway. Once we have our reward for finding the treasure, then we can do what we like.'

'Oh Archie, I can't wait until then!'

'You must be patient, Amelia. I'm going to visit Richard Harpole now and ask him to promise a reward. Then I'll find the treasure and we'll be free.'

'Hooray!'

He glanced at the door again. 'You must keep your voice down, Amelia. What if someone hears? Now, listen carefully while I explain the plan in detail.'

Amelia pretended to listen but paid little attention. She was happy enough just to watch him as he spoke. He was so handsome and clever. She'd thought she'd been in love with Charles Harpole, but then came the day when he'd introduced her to Archie – the private investigator he'd hired to find some missing family treasure. Her affection had switched immediately from Charles to Archie. She hadn't been able to take her eyes off him during that first meeting, and it had been clear he'd felt the same. Poor Charles, he'd had no idea. She felt guilty about it sometimes, but the strength of her feelings had taken hold of her. She simply couldn't help herself.

'Do you think that sounds like a good plan?' he asked her.

'Yes, Archie. Every plan you come up with is a good plan.'

'And you don't mind Mrs Blakely and Mrs Langley being involved? I'm pretty certain they'll find the treasure.'

'I don't mind at all. The more the merrier.'

'I'm not sure about merry, Amelia. This isn't a particularly merry time, is it?'

'Whoops, no, it's not. How silly of me. My fiancé has died, and I have to keep reminding myself to be sad.'

'Yes, it is a little bit silly, Amelia. But life can turn out rather strangely, can't it? A month ago, we didn't even know each other. And now we do, and all this has happened and... well... I really don't know what to think. But I do know that when I'm not with you, I miss you terribly.'

Butterflies fluttered in her stomach. 'Oh really, Archie? I miss you too. If only we could be together now!' She clasped his face with both hands.

'All in good time, Amelia.' He gently removed her hands and gave them a squeeze before returning them to her lap. 'But for the time being, I must continue with my quest.'

'You're so brave, Archie.'

'Brave?' He grinned. 'I don't know about that.'

'Good luck with it. And please visit me again soon. Promise?'

'I promise.'

THIRTY-EIGHT

'Murder?' said Joseph Campbell. 'Lord Harpole wasn't murdered.'

He'd been summoned to Kensington police station where he sat in a dingy interview room with two police inspectors. One of them was from Scotland Yard.

His stomach turned, and he tried to calm himself. Were the police suggesting he'd murdered his employer? Was he going to be arrested?

'How can you be sure Lord Harpole wasn't murdered?' asked Inspector Blakely from the Yard. He had a square face and sharp blue eyes.

'Because it's obvious it was suicide! He left a note, and he took the whisky and laudanum. I don't understand why anyone would think another person was involved.'

'His supposed suicide was a surprise to everyone who knew him,' said Inspector Trotter. He was barrel-chested and had a long chin and a light brown moustache. 'While I realize many gentlemen keep depressive thoughts to themselves, Lord Harpole's mood had always seemed to be reasonably good. He'd also made plans for dinner that evening and was engaged to be married to Lady Somersham. Does that sound like a gentleman who intentionally ended his own life?'

'It doesn't, but I don't see why anyone would wish to murder him.'

'Perhaps they didn't, but we have enough suspicion to warrant an investigation. Maybe we'll find we agree with the coroner's verdict at the inquest. But for the time being, it's been decided we shall look into his death in more detail.'

Inspector Blakely leafed through some papers in front of him. 'What time did you last see Lord Harpole on the day of his death?'

'I told the inquest everything. It was just after breakfast that morning. He told me I wasn't needed until the evening when I would help him get ready for dinner.'

'And a table had been booked for him at Verrey's restaurant on Regent Street, is that right?'

'Absolutely. I said that at the inquest, and I stand by it.'

'What were you doing at six o'clock that evening?'

The directness of the question made Joseph pause for a moment. What had he been doing? It took a moment for his mind to come up with the answer. 'I was in my room.'

'How long had you been in there?'

'An hour or two. Probably two hours, actually. I had taken a walk around London because I always enjoy visiting the city, and then I went and rested in my room. I'm not getting any younger and the walk tired me out. I planned to visit my employer's room at seven o'clock to help him get ready for dinner.'

'Can anyone confirm you were in your room between the hours of four and six?'

'No, I don't think they can.' His mouth felt dry. 'I was on my own.' Was there anyone who could vouch for him? He couldn't think of anyone at all. Perhaps a maid had seen him enter and leave his room, but he couldn't be certain. This was just what the detectives were looking for: time which wasn't properly accounted for.

He had to put up a defence. He fixed Blakely's eye, then Trotter's. 'I would never have harmed him,' he appealed. 'He was my employer. Why would I kill the man who provided me with my income? It would make no sense.'

'Absolutely,' said Inspector Blakely. 'It would make no sense whatsoever. But that doesn't mean you had no reason to kill him.'

Joseph felt a snap of anger. 'But I didn't!'

'I've made inquiries at the Imperial Grand Hotel,' said Inspector Trotter. 'And a maid states she heard raised voices coming from room thirty-seven on the morning of Lord Harpole's death.'

Joseph felt an icy chill run through him.

'Have you any idea who those voices could have belonged to?' asked Trotter.

'No.'

'Did Lord Harpole have any visitors in his room that morning?'

'He may have done. I wasn't aware of any.'

'Where were you when you saw him after breakfast that morning?'

'In his room.' There was no use lying about it, they would check.

'Did you raise your voice while you were in his room?'

'No, I didn't.'

'Did he raise his voice?'

'No. The maid must have been mistaken.'

'Are you saying she didn't hear raised voices?'

'I'm sure she heard raised voices. But they must have been coming from a different room.'

'A neighbouring room, perhaps?'

'Yes. A neighbouring room.'

'Presumably, if that were the case, then you or Lord Harpole would have heard the voices yourselves?' asked Inspector Blakely.

'I'm afraid I don't recall it.'

'Is it possible that you and Lord Harpole exchanged angry words that morning, Mr Campbell?' The inspector's voice remained casual, but his eyes narrowed perceptibly.

Campbell's posture stiffened. He felt a muscle twitch in his jaw as his hands gripped his knees beneath the table. 'Never,' he declared, too forcefully. 'He never had any reason to lose his temper with me.' A thin sheen of perspiration broke out on his brow despite the room's chill.

'I see.'

A long pause followed, and Joseph shifted in his seat. He took out his handkerchief and wiped his brow, his hands trembling.

THIRTY-NINE

'Thank you for agreeing to see me this afternoon, Lord Harpole,' said Archibald Maitland. It seemed odd addressing Richard Harpole as Lord when he'd been accustomed to addressing the previous Lord Harpole. 'Please accept my condolences on the death of your brother.'

Lord Harpole gave a solemn nod. He was stocky with thinning, dark hair. Quite different to his older brother, who'd been a slender, charming gentleman. Lady Harpole sat next to her husband and regarded him with her cool green eyes. She had delicate, attractive features and her red hair contrasted starkly with her black mourning dress.

Archibald ran his hand over his hair and continued, 'I'm a private investigator, my lord. Your brother employed me about a month ago to look into something for him. It's concerning a map. I don't know if you've heard about a map in your family's history?'

Lord Harpole shook his head and gestured for him to continue. Archibald told him about the ancestor Lord Henry Harpole and how he'd reportedly hidden some treasure gifted to him by his friend Sir Francis Drake.

'He knew Sir Francis Drake?' Lady Harpole's face broke out into a smile. 'Who'd have thought it, Richard?'

'Indeed,' said her husband gruffly. 'So, where's the map now?'

'I'm afraid I don't know,' said Archibald, pulling at his earlobe. 'However, I know the map shows St Paul's Cathedral as the first location to be visited. That's what your brother told me. So I shall continue my inquiries and track down your treasure.'

'Well, if you could find it for us, we'd be very grateful. As you can imagine, this is an extremely busy time for me. Not only has it been upsetting coping with my brother's death, but I've now inherited the Harpole estate. There's an awful lot of administration involved and I'm having difficulty finding all the relevant papers, including the will. However, I'm working with the family solicitor on all that at the moment. It's a vast estate, and it includes Wickham House, as I'm sure you're aware. Have you visited the place?'

'Yes, I visited your brother there once.' It was an impressive country seat, and Archibald felt envious. And to think Amelia could have lived there!

'So, as you can imagine, there's an awful lot to sort out,' continued Lord Harpole. Archibald listened patiently, although he found the man a bit of a bore. 'Not to mention the simple fact of moving to Berkshire. London has been my home for a long time. I shall keep this house here in Knightsbridge, of course, but I shall also have to get accustomed to living in the Berkshire countryside.' He turned to his wife. 'It's rather a lot for Constance to take on, isn't it, Constance?'

She gave a sad nod, as if it was a great burden to bear.

'But I've reassured her she'll be all right. She's just recovered from an illness, so she's not at her best. But Wickham House has a good, hardworking team of staff, and I know they'll help her enormously with the running of the place.' He patted her hand with patronizing affection. 'In a few years' time, dear, you'll be quite accustomed to it, I know it.' His chest puffed out slightly as he addressed Archibald again, with a conspiratorial male chuckle. 'Never before have I come across such a reluctant lady of the house!'

'I can imagine it's an awful lot to think about,' said Archibald, smiling politely as he glanced between husband and wife, noting how Constance's fingers twisted anxiously in her lap. 'And I hesitated about visiting you, because this hidden treasure is yet another thing for you to have to think about. However, I'm more than happy to continue this work and there is no need for you to worry yourselves about the details. I shall let you know as soon as I have any success in finding it.'

He paused and cleared his throat. Now he had to broach the difficult part of the conversation. 'It would be remiss of me not to add that your brother and I had an agreement before he died. He sought me out and retained my services to search for the treasure. In short, he agreed to pay me for my time.'

The new Lord Harpole gave a nod but said nothing.

Archibald continued. 'I've already carried out a lot of work. But I know you have a great deal to think about, so perhaps instead I could be offered a share of the treasure once it is found?'

Lord Harpole frowned. 'A share of it? But it belongs to my family.'

Archibald nodded. 'Yes, it belongs to your family, that's right. However, your brother agreed to pay me for my time.'

'My brother agreed to do that. But I did not.'

Archibald's heart sank. He'd hoped Lord Harpole would have been more gracious.

'No, you didn't agree to pay me for it. But as a gesture of goodwill—'

'I'm not obliged to make a gesture of goodwill to you, Mr Maitland.'

'No, you're not obliged. But as a polite acknowledgement of—'

'I'm not paying you anything, Mr Maitland.' His jowls wobbled with irritation. 'I'm sorry to be blunt about it, but I didn't ask you to go looking for the family treasure. I'm aware my brother did, but his decisions were his own. I conduct the family affairs in a way I see fit, and I don't wish to pay you to carry out this work.'

'You expect me to work without a wage?'

'The choice is entirely yours, Mr Maitland.'

'I'm afraid I cannot offer my services free of charge.'

'Then so be it. To be frank with you, I've got enough to be worrying about at the moment. If you were to call on me at a later date, perhaps in six months' time, Mr Maitland, then maybe I shall consider it.'

The disappointment felt heavy. Archibald got to his feet. 'Very well. Thank you for your time, my lord.'

FORTY

Mrs Tuttle was happy to mind Penny's children while Penny visited the reading room at the British Library for an hour. Since meeting Archibald Maitland the previous day, she wondered if she could find out more for herself about Sir Francis Drake, the stolen treasure and Lord Henry Harpole.

There were lots of books about Drake and Burke's Peerage gave her some information about the Harpole family. Penny sat at a desk, enjoying the peace around her. She made some notes but felt too distracted by her surroundings to get on with her research. Grey daylight streamed in through the windows of the dome above her head, illuminating the fine plasterwork and ornate galleries which circled the room. This place felt like a comfort to her after many years of reading and working here.

'Mrs Blakely?'

She turned to see a sandy-haired gentleman standing by her desk, his fringe covering his spectacles. His complexion was tanned and freckled.

For a moment, she felt transported back in time.

'Francis?' She scrambled to her feet, unable to believe it was really him. 'When did you get back? Where have you been? I had no idea you were working here again!'

He smiled. 'I returned a few weeks ago. And I took up my position here again on Monday. Fortunately, the head librarian was happy to have me back.'

'That's wonderful!'

A young man tutted and glanced at them, clearly irritated by the disturbance.

'I have a break now if you'd like to join me,' said Francis.

'Yes, of course.' She tidied away her papers and put them in her bag.

'Oh, I'm sorry. You're busy. I shouldn't distract you from your work.'

'No, it's nothing important. I don't have deadlines anymore.'

Once outside, they walked down the steps of the British Museum. Snowflakes drifted down from the grey sky and melted on the wet ground.

Penny felt her heart pound with excitement' she had always been fond of Francis Edwards. Not as fond as he'd once been of her, but she was thrilled to see him again. 'So, how are you?' she asked.

'I'm well. It feels rather odd to be back in London. And I'm certainly not used to this weather!'

'You've picked the wrong time to come back. January is always a miserable month here. You should have waited until springtime.'

Francis smiled. 'I should have done. But I was finished with my travels.'

'Where did you go?'

'I did my version of the Grand Tour. I realize it's old-fashioned these days, but it's something I've always wanted to do. Having read so much about it, I thought it would be nice to see everything for myself. So I did Paris, Venice, Rome, Athens and a few other little places. I was interested in classical architecture before I left, but now I'm completely consumed by it. In fact, I should like to study it.'

'Why don't you?'

'I need to save some money first. That's why I need to work again.' They reached the gate and stepped out onto busy Great Russell Street. 'And how are you, Penny?' asked Francis.

'I'm well. I'm a mother now.'

'How many children?'

'Two. Thomas and Florence.'

'Where are they today?'

'Oh dear, I must look like a feckless mother, don't I? I have a very helpful housekeeper who looks after them for me from time to time. So I now spend about two-thirds of my time with the children and then I get some time to work on other things. I've just written an article about motherhood for the *Morning Express*. And I've made a new friend, Emma Langley. She and I are working on a very interesting case – the murder of Lord Harpole.'

'Are you? I read about that. They thought it was suicide, but now they think it's murder.'

'Yes, that's right. James is working on the case.'

'And how is James?'

Penny felt uncomfortable talking about him, knowing that he and Francis had been rivals for her affections a few years ago. 'He's extremely well.'

'Still working hard at Scotland Yard?'

'Yes, he is. We're both being kept busy, but we're both very happy.'

'Good. I'm pleased for you, Penny. You made the right choice all along.'

She felt her face heat up. He was alluding to the time when he'd proposed marriage to her but, instead, she'd chosen James.

'I don't know if any of us can ever be sure if we've made the right choice, can we?' she said. 'Perhaps I would have found happiness if I'd made another choice. But as a bachelor, Francis, you've been able to enjoy your travels.'

'Yes, that's very true. I'm actually quite pleased you turned me down.'

They shared a laugh, and the tension was broken.

She stopped and turned to him. 'You must come to dinner,' she said. 'I would love to hear all about your travels. And James would like to see you again, too.'

'Would he?'

'Yes!'

FORTY-ONE

Lady Amelia Somersham had a second visitor that afternoon. She found his appearance rather startling. He was a tall, thin-faced man with high cheekbones. His grey hair was oiled back from his face and he wore an eye patch over his left eye. He was well-dressed in a dark woollen suit with a gold tiepin and a gold watch chain on his waistcoat.

He introduced himself as Mr Stephen Lydney. 'I was a friend of your late fiancé, Lord Harpole,' he said, 'and I thought I would call on you to offer my condolences on his passing.'

'That's very thoughtful of you,' said Amelia. She wasn't sure what to make of him; she couldn't recall Charles ever mentioning him. But she realized she had to be polite. 'Will you have some tea with us?'

'I'd be delighted to.'

Over tea, Amelia's mother asked Mr Lydney questions about the sort of business he was in. He replied with lots of dull answers about stocks, shares and banking. Amelia quickly grew bored.

Eventually, he turned to Amelia and took an interest in her. 'Have you received many visitors recently, Lady Somersham?'

'A few.'

'There was the gentleman who visited you earlier, wasn't there, Amelia?' said her mother.

'Oh yes, Mr Maitland.'

'Mr Maitland?' said Mr Lydney. 'I don't know the name.'

'He was working for Lord Harpole shortly before his death,' said Amelia.

'I see. Working in what sense?'

'Well, it's quite exciting, really. I'm not sure I'm supposed to say much about it, but I suppose it will become common knowledge before long anyway. Charles employed him to search for some ancient family treasure.'

Mr Lydney raised an eyebrow. 'Treasure? That sounds intriguing.'

'Yes. Apparently, it was taken from the Spanish and buried somewhere. Anyway, Mr Maitland is now working with two ladies to find the treasure.'

'Is that what Mr Maitland is doing?' said her mother. 'You didn't explain that to me, Amelia.'

'Didn't I, Mother? Oh, I suppose I hadn't found the chance.'

'It sounds fascinating,' said Mr Lydney. 'And he's working with two ladies, you say?'

'Yes. The ladies who found Charles when he was taken ill in his hotel room.'

'And why are they looking for the treasure?'

'They found the map.'

'Really? And where did they get hold of that?'

Amelia shrugged. 'I don't know. But anyway, the three of them are now going to look for the treasure. And when they find it, they're going to give it to the Harpole family.' Amelia also hoped Archie would be paid handsomely for his work.

'And to think you could have benefited from the find too, Amelia, if your fiancé hadn't died,' said her mother.

Amelia pulled out her handkerchief and dabbed her eyes, realizing she had to show some sorrow over Charles's death.

'Well, I really had no idea about any of that,' said Mr Lydney. 'Lord Harpole kept it all very quiet.' He drained his cup of tea and placed it back in its saucer. 'I think you're an extremely brave young lady, indeed, Lady Amelia Somersham. To endure what you have with such grace and dignity is wonderfully admirable.'

'Thank you, Mr Lydney,' she breathed, clasping her hands beneath her chin. 'Your words are very kind indeed!'

Inwardly, she shuddered at his appearance – that unsettling eye patch, the gaunt face with its hungry expression. There was something predatory in his politeness that made her skin crawl, although she maintained her performance of gentle gratitude. Strange-looking he certainly was, but she would play the grieving fiancée perfectly until he departed.

FORTY-TWO

Rupert Crowfield rested against the bar in his favourite public house. His bowler hat lay on the counter and he took a swig from his tankard as if he hadn't a care in the world. His expression soon changed when he caught sight of Lydney marching towards him.

'How did I know I'd find you in here?' Lydney hissed in his ear. 'While you've been exercising your drinking arm, I've been doing your job for you.'

He put down his tankard. 'I didn't know—'

'I told you to find the map, didn't I? But you haven't. Fortunately, I have news.'

'Well done, sir.'

'Don't patronize me! Now I have it on good authority that William Langley's widow and her friend now have the map and are working with the private detective Harpole hired shortly before his death. Archibald Maitland.'

'The three of them are working on it together?'

'Yes.'

'Have they had any success?'

'Who knows? But I don't like it at all. This was once a very well-kept secret. And now we have Langley's widow and her friend – a former news reporter married to an inspector from Scotland Yard – and Maitland. It wouldn't surprise me if Scotland Yard knows about it now, too. It's exactly what I didn't want to happen. It's become common knowledge, Crowfield.'

'How do we stop them?'

'Why are you asking me?' Anger flashed in Lydney's single eye. 'It's your job to come up with these ideas. Whatever you decide to do, we can't possibly allow them to get to the treasure before we do. And they're trouble, those two. Do you realize they've been snooping about in the lodge?'

'What?' Crowfield took in a sharp breath. How had the two nosey women got in there?

'You didn't know? Lewis called on me earlier and told me two women were looking for a cat in the lodge.'

'A cat?'

'Yes. They told him they'd lost a cat which they claimed they'd heard meowing from inside the building. He let them have a look around. The fool!'

'And did they find the cat?'

'No!' Lydney slammed his fist onto the bar, making the beer in the tankard slop. His eye blazed with fury. 'Because there wasn't one!' He leaned forward, jaw clenched and a vein pulsing visibly at his temple. 'Don't you understand what this means?' His voice dropped to a dangerous hiss. 'I questioned Lewis thoroughly about these supposed cat-seekers. His description matches Mrs Langley and Mrs Blakely perfectly.'

'So they managed to get in and look around. They wouldn't have found anything, would they?'

'No, nothing of great significance. Everything important is kept locked up, as you know. I want to know what they're planning next and I want them scared off.'

'How?'

'Use your imagination, Crowfield! But if I hear they've got anywhere near our lodge again, then you and Lewis are for it. Do you hear?'

FORTY-THREE

Two police inspectors were sitting in Lord Richard Harpole's drawing room, and he wasn't happy about it.

'Can this be quick, please, gentlemen? I have a lot to do this afternoon.'

'Of course, my lord,' said Inspector Blakely from the Yard. 'It's regarding your brother. His death was ruled as a suicide, but we believe there's a possibility he may have been murdered.'

Richard caught his breath. 'Murdered?' He turned to Constance who sat next to him. 'Do you hear this, Constance? Murder! How ridiculous.'

'I refuse to believe it!' she said.

'It appears he might have been encouraged to drink whisky with someone, and the laudanum was put in his drink without him realizing,' said Inspector Trotter. 'May we examine the note he left?'

'If you want. Although I don't see how that helps anything. I shall have to fetch it from my study.' He strode there, retrieved it from a drawer, then strode back again. There was too much to do and too much to think about. And now this!

He handed the letter to Trotter.

'Can you confirm this is your brother's handwriting?' he asked.

'It looks like it.' Richard sat down again. 'Are you saying someone forged it?'

'It's possible. It's only a short note, isn't it? And impersonal too.'

'Yes. He could have at least given an explanation for his actions.'

'Do you mind if we keep this letter for the time being?' asked Blakely.

'No, not at all. You do whatever you want with it. I can't say it's something I particularly want to reread. But why would someone murder him?'

'Did he mention a disagreement with his valet, Mr Campbell?'

'No. Was there one?'

'We think so,' said Trotter. He explained a maid at the Imperial Grand Hotel had heard raised voices in room thirty-seven on the morning of Lord Harpole's death.

'Campbell, eh?' Richard folded his arms and gave this some thought. 'And what does he say about the matter?'

'We spoke to him earlier today and he denies an argument took place,' said Blakely.

'Well, that sounds suspicious to me! What do you think, Constance?'

'Very suspicious, dear.'

'But would Campbell have murdered him?' he asked her.

'I can't imagine it. But if there was a big disagreement about something...' She fixed him with his gaze. The thought that Campbell, a man they now employed, could be a murderer was a horrible thought.

He turned back to the police inspectors. 'I'll have a word with him and see what I can shake out of him, gentlemen. He's my valet now, so this accusation and denial concerns me a great deal.'

'Of course, thank you, Lord Harpole,' said Blakely. 'May I ask what you and your wife were doing on the evening of Friday the eighteenth of January?'

Richard felt a stab of alarm. 'Why do you ask? Do you think I'm a murderer now?'

'We're establishing alibis for everyone who knew your brother.'

'Really?' Richard took in a breath. 'Very well.' He could only hope this was true, and that he wasn't about to become a suspect. 'I was here at home. I'm not usually at home on a Friday evening. Constance and I had been invited to dine with the Duke of Rutland and his wife that evening but we couldn't attend because Constance had a fever.'

'I'm sorry to hear it.'

'Yes, she was quite unwell with it. Bedridden for three or four days, weren't you, dear? I was quite worried about her, but thankfully she recovered.' He reached out to her and squeezed her hand.

'And presumably the servants will verify this?' asked Trotter.

'Of course they will!' He felt his face flush crimson and his knuckles whitened as he gripped the armrests of the chair. 'Ask any one of them!' His voice rose sharply before he caught himself, adjusting his waistcoat with trembling fingers. 'Not that my words should require verification, Inspector.' He forced a smile. 'You should trust that I'm telling the truth. A gentleman's word is his bond, after all.'

'We'd like to believe everyone is telling us the truth,' said Blakely. 'But the unfortunate fact is someone we speak to will be lying to us and we shall have to determine who that is.'

Richard nodded, keen to show he understood. 'Well, that's

the nature of a detective's job, I suppose. But I think you'll find I'm not lying. It's not in my nature.'

'I like to think we can trust you, Lord Harpole. An outsider might observe that you've benefited a great deal from your brother's death.'

Richard clenched his fists. 'Well, an outsider can go to hell! I apologise, Inspector, for my strong words, but the suggestion I murdered my brother to inherit the family estate is absolutely repugnant. Few people have any idea how much work is involved when such circumstances are thrust upon you. Ask my wife, here! She's so worried about her new duties that I'm surprised she's not fallen ill again!'

Richard was in a foul mood after the inspectors left and nothing seemed to shift it.

Constance sat by his side, pouring him tea and offering him comfort. It helped a little to know he had her support. 'I don't think Campbell could have murdered Charles,' she said. 'There has to be a mistake.'

'Perhaps there is. But what sort of valet argues with his master? There's something not right about that at all.'

'Are you going to speak to him about it?'

'Yes. But not immediately, Constance. I'm going to make some inquiries with the other servants first. They're a tight-knit crowd down there in Berkshire and I want to see if I can find out more.'

FORTY-FOUR

'It's been an interesting day,' said James that evening. Penny sipped her vegetable soup and listened as he told her about his conversations with Joseph Campbell and Richard Harpole.

'So the long and the short of it is that Campbell has no alibi for the time of Lord Harpole's death, but Harpole's brother does,' said Penny.

'Yes. It doesn't look good for Campbell, does it? Especially when you consider an argument was overheard. But I must say I like him more than Richard Harpole who seems rather obstinate and pompous to me.'

'So the one you like least has to be the murderer?' said Penny with a smile.

'I'd like it to be that way,' said James. 'Unfortunately, he has a strong alibi and he seemed to be telling me the truth. Campbell, on the other hand, is hiding something. Anyway, how did you get on in the reading room?'

'Well...' Penny's cheeks flushed, her fingers idly tracing the edge of her soup bowl as she avoided James's direct gaze. 'Francis Edwards was there.'

James's eyebrow arched sharply. 'Really?' The single word carried layers of meaning.

'Yes. He's doing his old job again.' She straightened her napkin unnecessarily.

'He just reappeared there, just like that?' James leaned forward slightly.

'Yes.' Penny tucked a strand of hair behind her ear. 'He's only been back at his job this week.'

'And what's he been doing with his time?' James's tone remained casual, but his eyes didn't leave her face.

'He went on a grand tour.' Penny's shoulders relaxed slightly, moving to safer conversational ground.

'That tour the upper classes used to do?'

'Yes. He travelled for over three years. He enjoyed it and seems happy to be back, although I don't think he's enjoying the weather here very much.' She attempted a light laugh.

'No, that doesn't surprise me.' James's lips curved into a knowing smile. 'However, I'm sure his day was brightened by seeing you, Penny.'

'There's no need to say that.' Her voice tightened slightly.

'There's truth in it though, isn't there?' James held her gaze steadily. 'He's always been fond of you, and I think it would be foolish to ignore it.'

'He asked after you and the children.' Penny took another sip of soup. 'That time in the past can be forgotten about now.'

'Yes, I know. A lot's happened since then.' James's expression softened. 'In fact, I would quite like to see him again myself. He's a good fellow.'

'Good, because I've invited him to dinner.' Penny's voice brightened with relief.

'Have you? You didn't waste any time then.' A teasing note entered his voice.

'No.' Penny smiled genuinely now. 'But I thought it was a

nice thing to do. It will be good for us to see him again. And I shall invite Emma too.'

FORTY-FIVE

Archibald Maitland chewed on the end of his pencil and reflected on his visit to Lord and Lady Harpole the previous day. They'd just inherited a vast amount of wealth, and yet they wouldn't pay him to find their family's treasure for them. The new Lord Harpole wasn't even willing to share the spoils once the treasure was found. They were remarkably discourteous.

He bit too hard on the pencil and it splintered in his mouth. Wincing with disgust, he took a handkerchief from his pocket and spat the wet fragments into it. Then he put the handkerchief back in his pocket and dropped the chewed pencil into the clutter on his desk.

He recalled how thrilled he'd been when Lord Charles Harpole had called on his services to help with the search for the treasure. It was one of the most interesting things he'd worked on in a long time, and he'd been promised some income too. His earnings as a private investigator were unreliable, and he'd assumed the Harpole family would continue paying him for his work even after Lord Harpole's death. His plan had gone awry.

Was it worth his while still looking for the map? He

reasoned that working with Mrs Blakely and Mrs Langley meant the work was shared between the three of them. And with the two ladies and Lydney all in search of the treasure, he didn't want to give up on looking for it. He viewed it now as a competition, and with a bit of luck, he would be the one who found the treasure first. Even if he wasn't paid for his time, he would benefit from the glory of finding it. It would be reported in the newspapers and would boost his reputation as a private investigator.

Fortunately, Amelia didn't seem to care that he had no money. Her family had so much of it she didn't need his income. But there was the matter of pride. He wanted to earn good money and improve his reputation. He knew the Somersham family were going to disapprove when they found out about the love affair. It was possible they would disown Amelia. That's why he had to work hard to prove his success, and maybe then he would be a little more acceptable to them.

As for Amelia, he felt overjoyed that she seemed to love him, regardless of his circumstances. At least he could rely on that.

A knock sounded at the door. He removed his feet from his desk. 'Come in!' Hopefully, it was a new customer asking for work.

But the man who entered the room didn't look like a customer, he had the officious manner of a police officer.

He introduced himself as Detective Inspector Blakely of Scotland Yard. Archibald tried not to display any concern. Was he here to discuss his wife? He couldn't be sure. He got to his feet, held out his hand, and gave a wide smile.

'Inspector Blakely, how nice it is to meet you. Your wife has told me all about you.'

'Very good.' The inspector glanced around the room, no doubt passing judgement on the mess. Archibald had been meaning to tidy up for a while.

'I understand you worked for the late Lord Harpole,' said Blakely, taking a seat. 'How long was that for?'

'About a month.'

'And what work did you do for him?'

Archibald told him about the map, ensuring his story was exactly the same as the one he'd told to Mrs Blakely. He felt sure the pair of them would discuss him and he didn't want any inconsistencies to be noticed.

'When did you last see Lord Harpole?'

'The day before his death. We had lunch together and discussed the work I was doing on the map.'

'The map he left for you in the left luggage office of Paddington Station?'

'That's right.'

'Why didn't he just give the map to you at the restaurant when you had lunch together?'

'Because he was worried we might be watched. He didn't trust the chaps at the Inveniam Society.'

'Why didn't he trust them?'

'He worried that if they found his family's treasure, they would keep it for themselves. Or at least want a large share of it. He wanted to make sure it stayed in the family.'

'And he didn't trust them because he'd gone back on an agreement he'd made with them, is that right?'

'Yes, I suppose that's right.'

'Presumably he betrayed them, and that would have made them angry.'

Archibald nodded. 'Yes, it would have done.'

'Angry enough to murder him, you think?'

'Murder? Do you think that's what happened, Inspector?'

'It's a possibility.'

'Well, I suppose they could have done. It's an awful thought, but perhaps there could be truth in it.' He'd heard

Lydney was an unpleasant man. He hoped he wasn't speaking out of turn by agreeing with the inspector.

'And what were you doing in the early evening of Friday, the eighteenth of January?'

'I shall have to think – nothing immediately comes to mind. I was obviously doing something...' He felt conscious of the detective's sharp blue eyes watching him as he started to perspire. 'You will forgive me, Inspector, when I say that it's not very easy to remember. It was two weeks ago.'

The inspector gave an understanding nod and waited.

Archibald had seen Amelia that day, but he couldn't possibly admit it. What was he going to say?

'Perhaps I can help you a little,' said Blakely. 'Where were you when you heard about Lord Harpole's death?'

'I read about it in the newspaper the following Saturday morning.'

'And where were you?'

'I was here. In this office. In fact, I was here that Friday evening, too. I work quite hard. I don't have a wife or family, you see, so I spend a lot of time in my office.'

'Was anyone else here with you that evening?'

'No.' He realized this gave him no alibi at all. 'A few people came and went, but no one was actually here with me the entire time. I work alone, you see.'

'Who came and went?'

'Just a few customers of mine.' He felt warmth in his face. He'd lied now, and he felt sure the inspector was going to notice.

'Can you give me their names?'

'They wouldn't like me to give you their names, Inspector. The work I carry out for people is confidential.'

'I'm from Scotland Yard, and I'm carrying out an investigation into a suspicious death, Mr Maitland.' Blakely leaned forward, his broad shoulders casting a shadow across the desk. His voice dropped to a dangerous calm, each word precisely measured. 'It's important that no information is withheld.' His fingers tapped once, firmly, on the desk's surface. 'If it is withheld, then I can only assume there are suspicious reasons for it being withheld.'

Archibald could see he had to be honest. 'Actually, I think I could be getting Friday evening confused with Thursday evening,' he said. 'Some people came and went on the Thursday evening, but I don't think anybody visited me on the Friday evening. It's not a busy day of the week for me.'

Blakely made some notes. 'So you were here on your own that Friday evening. What time did you leave?'

'Leave? I, er... I actually didn't leave.'

The inspector's brow furrowed. 'You worked here all night?'

'No, I didn't. I don't actually have a... This is also my home.' The admission was embarrassing. 'I sleep in the little room at the back.'

FORTY-SIX

Emma sat at a piano in the small parlour of a house in Maple Street, Fitzrovia. The clock ticked on the mantelpiece. Her pupil was five minutes late for his first lesson. She glanced out of the window at the people and carriages passing in the street. Then she looked at the keys in front of her, wishing she had time to play for herself.

Although she enjoyed teaching, she missed having a piano of her own to play. She'd spent many happy hours in her childhood home playing the grand piano in the music room. Her parents had encouraged her to play and, once she became accomplished, they enjoyed sitting and listening to her. She smiled, remembering the early days of her lessons when the household had to endure the jarring, repetitive bars of her practice.

It had been worth it. This was what she reminded her pupils when they became disheartened with their progress. Resting her fingers on the keys, she played the opening bars of Chopin's 'Nocturne in E Flat Major'. Closing her eyes, she smiled and swayed a little to the rhythm of the music. All other thoughts drifted away as the music enveloped her.

A knock sounded at the door and brought her back to the world. She stopped playing and the silence felt uncomfortable.

Her pupil's governess stepped into the room. She was a young, fair-haired woman who wore a dull grey dress. Her face was red, and she looked flustered.

'I'm still persuading Bartholomew to come downstairs.' Her voice was shrill. 'I do apologise for his behaviour, Mrs Langley.'

'It's quite all right.'

'I've already told him he'll be punished by his father when he gets home.'

'Oh no!' said Emma, horrified. 'Please don't threaten him with such things. It really doesn't matter. I expect he's just shy, isn't he?'

'Yes, he is quite a shy child. And it's about time he learned not to be. He's going away to school in September, and it won't serve him well to be a shrinking violet when he's there.'

'I really don't mind—'

'But I do mind,' she retorted sharply. 'And I'm answerable to his mother. She's paying good money for your time, Mrs Langley. There's no use in you being paid just to sit there while he sulks upstairs in the nursery.'

Emma felt sorry for Bartholomew. 'Very well. Perhaps some gentle words of encouragement might persuade him to come downstairs,' she said. 'And the time won't be wasted. I'm happy to stay a little longer to make sure we cover everything for the first lesson.'

'Well, more fool you, I say. If you're paid for half an hour, you should work for half an hour. I'll speak to him again now.'

Emma didn't like to think of the threats being administered to the small child upstairs while she waited, but there was little she could do. Clearly, the governess didn't want to let her employer down.

Emma returned to the keyboard and continued playing the nocturne, feeling soothed by its familiarity.

A few minutes later, the door opened again. The governess stood there with a small, scowling boy.

'Wasn't that beautiful, Bartholomew?' she said. 'You'll be able to do that soon. Now, all you have to do is go and sit next to Mrs Langley over there, and she'll show you how to play.'

Emma gave him a warm smile, hoping to ease his shyness. 'You don't have to play anything today,' she said. 'You can just sit beside me while I show you how to learn a tune.'

'That sounds good, doesn't it, Bartholomew?' said the governess. 'And after Mrs Langley's beautiful playing just now, I feel sure you're keen to learn, aren't you?'

'No, I'm not,' said the boy.

The governess took in a breath, and Emma could tell she was about to lose her temper again.

'It's quite all right,' said Emma. 'I'm happy to be left alone with Bartholomew for his lesson. Perhaps you can take a well-earned break?'

The governess closed her mouth, gave a nod and seemed only too happy to leave the room. She closed the door, leaving Bartholomew standing there with a sulky expression.

'Hello, Bartholomew,' said Emma. 'You can step a little closer if you like. I won't bite.'

He folded his arms and leaned against the door. Emma could see she had a challenge on her hands.

The lesson took nearly an hour, but Emma felt pleased that, for the final fifteen minutes, Bartholomew had actually sat beside her and played a few notes on the piano. She told the governess how well he'd played and requested he not be punished.

She left the house and walked along Maple Street, heading for Tottenham Court Road, where she could find an omnibus to take her home.

Tottenham Court Road was busy. Workmen in heavy boots

had dug up part of the road and now rested on their shovels as carriages and other traffic battled to pass them. A girl in a wide-brimmed hat and thick shawl offered her heather.

Emma politely declined and was glancing in the window of a furniture store when she heard a voice behind her.

'Mrs Langley!'

She turned to see a short, gaunt-faced gentleman striding towards her.

Rupert Crowfield.

Her stomach gave a turn.

'Fancy bumping into you,' he said, stepping uncomfortably close. His eyes raked over her with calculated familiarity while his mouth stretched into a smile that didn't reach his eyes. 'Where are you going?'

She didn't like the directness of his question. She wanted to tell him it was none of his business. 'I've just finished teaching,' she said.

'You're a teacher?'

'A piano teacher.'

'Is that so?' He pretended to look impressed and she felt annoyed he thought she'd fall for it.

'How can I help you?' she asked.

'Help? Oh no. I'm just making polite conversation.'

What was he doing here? Perhaps it was just a coincidence that he'd seen her. Or had he been following her? She didn't want to talk to him. She wanted to get away as quickly as possible. But she and Penny had been wanting to speak to him, and now she had the chance. She had to be brave and ask him some questions so she could gauge his response. That was what Penny would do if she were here now, so Emma had to attempt it, too.

'Have you heard that Lord Harpole's death was murder?' she asked him.

He scratched behind his ear, his eyes narrowing with

feigned casualness. 'Yes, I heard that. Quite interesting, wouldn't you say?' A smirk played at the corner of his mouth.

'Have you any idea what the motive could have been?' Emma kept her voice steady, although her heart raced.

'No idea at all.' His gaze flickered to her face, then away. 'What about you?'

'No.'

The heavy silence stretched between them. Emma felt her confidence wavering but forced herself to continue. This wasn't like her disastrous conversation with Campbell – she wouldn't let this opportunity slip away. She straightened her spine and met his eyes directly.

'Perhaps someone wanted the map,' she suggested, carefully watching for his reaction.

'The map? And what do you know about the map, Mrs Langley?'

'I think I know as much as you do, Mr Crowfield.'

'You know more than I do, don't you?' His voice dropped to a menacing whisper. 'You know where it is.'

Emma's stomach clenched. Regret washed over her – they should have rid themselves of the map when they had the chance. It had served its purpose in revealing the first location, but now it felt like a dangerous burden. Although Penny had assured her it was safely locked in her bank's vault, Emma longed to be completely free of its shadow.

'I don't know where it is,' she lied, her mouth suddenly dry. She tried to control the slight tremor in her hands by clutching her bag tighter.

His lips curled upward, eyes glittering with cruel amusement. 'I know you're lying.'

'Lord Harpole betrayed you and Mr Lydney, didn't he?' Emma pressed, desperate to shift his focus. 'Is that why you decided to take your revenge?'

His expression hardened instantly, jaw tightening.

'Revenge? What are you talking about, Mrs Langley?' The sudden venom in his voice made her take an involuntary step backwards.

'Is that why you conspired to murder him? He'd promised you the map, and yet he didn't give it to you.'

He shook his head. 'I've no idea what you're talking about, Mrs Langley.'

'I think you do,' she continued. 'You arrived at his room shortly after his death. But perhaps when you arrived, you already knew he was dead? Perhaps you poisoned him on the orders of Mr Lydney?'

He gave a laugh. 'You have quite an imagination, Mrs Langley. I can assure you Lord Harpole was a friend of mine. I told you that at the time. I was deeply saddened by his death, and it's even more upsetting to think that someone deliberately caused it. Besides, who's to say you and Mrs Blakely weren't responsible?'

'We found him when he was very unwell.' Emma insisted, her voice rising slightly.

'Did you?' Crowfield stepped closer, his breath hot on her face. 'Or did you both get to the hotel earlier that evening and ply him with whisky and laudanum?' His voice dropped to a silky insinuation. 'I know what old Harpole was like. He would have enjoyed the company of two ladies.' A lascivious smile spread across his face. 'It would have been quite easy to persuade him to share some whisky and enjoy each other's company. You claim you found him, but some say you poisoned him.'

Heat rushed to Emma's face as she clenched her fists at her sides, indignation burning through her. 'No one's saying that!' she snapped.

'Oh, they are. I would watch out, Mrs Langley. When you look at the circumstances of Harpole's death... the two ladies who claim to have found him dying have somehow got their hands on the map. If I were a police detective, the culprits would be quite obvious to me. But you've manipulated the situation. The investigating inspector at Scotland Yard is the husband of your friend, Mrs Blakely. So you've set it up rather well, haven't you?'

Emma tried to calm herself. It was obvious he was lying, and she shouldn't let him rile her. But if anyone else thought the same as he did, then she and Penny were going to have to work hard to disprove the theory.

'I refuse to let you anger me, Mr Crowfield. I need to get on my way,' she said sharply before turning and walking away.

'You were the one who brought up Lord Harpole's death,' he called after her, his voice carrying across the street. People passing by turned to stare. She made the mistake of turning to look at him and saw his face twisted with malice as he took several aggressive steps in her direction. 'And now you don't want to talk about it anymore?' He jabbed a finger towards her. 'Well, I'm afraid you've been in control of this for long enough. They're going to come for you, and they're going to come for the map, too. Just you wait and see.'

The promise in his words hung in the air like poison.

FORTY-SEVEN

The detective from Scotland Yard was quite handsome for a police officer. He had an attractive face and blue eyes. Amelia sat with her mother on the sofa, her hands fidgeting in her lap. The inspector had a serious look on his face, and she wasn't sure what he was going to say.

'I realize how upsetting Lord Harpole's death will have been for you, Lady Somersham,' he said, 'and what I'm about to tell you won't be easy for you to hear, I'm afraid. But there are some suspicious circumstances surrounding your fiancé's death, and we've decided to investigate it as a murder case.'

'Murder!' exclaimed Amelia's mother. 'Never! I refuse to believe it!'

'We might be mistaken,' continued Blakely. 'In which case, the verdict of suicide will remain. But I would like to put a few questions to you, Lady Somersham, if I may.'

'Very well,' she said, her voice sounding feeble in the large drawing room.

'When did you last see your fiancé, Lord Charles Harpole?'

'It was that afternoon. He came here, didn't he, Mother?' Her mother gave a nod. 'He called on me, and he spoke to

Mother and Father too. And we had tea and had a delightful time together. I had no idea it would be the last time I ever saw him.' She pressed her lips together and breathed heavily through her nose.

'I understand this is difficult for you, Lady Somersham. Thank you for being so helpful,' said the inspector. 'That was the last time you saw him? You didn't visit him at his hotel after that?'

'My daughter would never be permitted to visit him at his hotel,' said her mother.

'Yes, I realize that might not be appropriate. I just needed to check. Can you vouch for your daughter having been present here for the rest of that day, Lady Somersham?' He addressed his question to her mother.

'Yes, she was here for most of the time and also went on a small shopping excursion to Bond Street. Why do you ask? Do you think she went to Harpole's hotel, and murdered him?'

A bolt of horror shot through Amelia. 'No!' she exclaimed. 'I would never have done such a thing!'

'I know you wouldn't, Amelia. This is why these questions are absolutely ridiculous.' Her mother turned back to Blakely. 'Do you have any more of your silly questions? Because if not, you are free to go.'

He ignored this comment and continued. 'Do you know of anyone, Lady Somersham, who would have wished to harm your fiancé?'

'No! No one would have harmed him. Everyone liked him. He was very popular.' She pulled out a handkerchief and rubbed her eyes, hoping some tears would appear. She wished everybody would stop talking about Charles's death. She didn't know which suggestion was worse: suicide or murder. They both sounded dreadful. How she wished he wasn't dead after all. But if he wasn't dead, then how could she be in love with Archie? Everything felt very confusing.

'Very well,' said the inspector. 'I can see you're upset, Lady Somersham, and I don't wish to make things any more difficult for you. So I shall leave my questions there. I shall keep you updated, of course. As Lord Harpole was your fiancé, I'm sure you'll be very keen to know the exact circumstances of his death. I realize it's extremely distressing to talk about, but we must ensure there was no foul play involved.'

Amelia sniffed and gave a sad nod. If only Archie could be here to comfort her.

FORTY-EIGHT

That evening, James told Penny about his conversations with Archibald Maitland and Lady Amelia Somersham.

'Mr Maitland doesn't have an alibi for the time of Lord Harpole's death,' he said. 'And he could have murdered Harpole because he wanted the map for himself.'

Penny sighed and rubbed her temple. She had begun to trust Maitland, she didn't want to believe he might be deceitful – another complication in an already tangled mystery. Each new betrayal felt like another door closing on the truth.

'Think about it, Penny. If he'd successfully managed to collect the map from the left luggage office at Paddington station, then no one, other than Lord Harpole, would have known he had it. He could have murdered Harpole and planned to use the map to find the treasure and keep it.'

'That's rather risky,' said Penny. 'There's no guarantee any treasure will be found.'

'I know,' said James. 'But when people find themselves in desperate situations, they'll try just about anything. You should see where he lives and works, the place is decrepit. He's as poor as a church mouse. You need to be very wary of him.'

'Yes, James. I know how to be wary of people.' She didn't like it when he lectured her as if she didn't know what she was doing.

'And there's certainly something not quite right with Lady Somersham,' said James. 'I don't mean that personally, she seems a charming young lady. But I think she's also a good actress and I think she could be hiding something.'

'But why murder her fiancé when she would have become Lady Harpole and lived in a large stately home in Berkshire?' said Penny.

'That's a good question. Her motive for murdering her fiancé is unclear.'

'I suppose she could have been the lady in the cloak who was fleeing the Imperial Grand Hotel shortly before we got there. Does she have an alibi for the time of her fiancé's death?'

'She was shopping on Bond Street.'

'The Somershams live in Knightsbridge, is that right?'

'Yes,' said James. 'Lady Somersham may have been on a shopping trip, or she may have used that time to visit her fiancé at his hotel in Kensington. It would only have been a ten- or fifteen-minute walk from her home.'

A knock at the door interrupted them. James glanced at the clock.

'Who could that be at this hour?'

He got up to answer the door. A moment later, he returned to the sitting room with Emma. Her face was deathly pale, her eyes wide with barely contained distress.

'What is it?' asked Penny. 'Come and sit down.'

'I'm so sorry to bother you both, but I came across Rupert Crowfield on Tottenham Court Road. And I'm not sure it was by accident. I think he might have followed me.'

'Did he threaten you?' asked Penny.

'I suppose he did. Sort of. Perhaps it was my fault.'

'How could it have been your fault?'

'Well, I decided to be brave, you see.' Emma's voice quavered despite her obvious attempt to steady it. Her hands twisted the fabric of her skirt unconsciously. 'I confronted him and asked him about Lord Harpole's death. And then he turned it around—' She swallowed hard, blinking rapidly. 'He came up with this horrible accusation that you and I did it, Penny.' A single tear escaped, which she hastily brushed away with trembling fingers. 'He claims people are saying it everywhere!'

'What people?'

'He wouldn't say.'

'He's making it up,' said James.

'Tell us exactly what he said, Emma.'

Penny and James listened as Emma told them Crowfield's theory about Lord Harpole's death.

'He's just saying it to frighten you,' said James. 'And it's worked. The man is a scoundrel.'

'I want to get rid of the map,' said Emma. 'I know they're going to come looking for it. Why don't we just give it back to the Harpoles? After all, I think it belongs to them, anyway.'

'It's safe in the vault at the bank at the moment,' said Penny.

'But the vault belongs to you, doesn't it? I think this should be something for the Harpoles to deal with. In fact, I'm beginning to wish I'd never got involved in any of this. If only we hadn't encountered Lord Harpole that night and accepted his coat.'

Penny nodded. 'I agree with you, Emma. And if you feel happier returning the map to the Harpoles, then we can do that. I'll fetch the map from the vault tomorrow. After all, we don't really need it anymore, do we? And we're rather stuck on the current clue at the moment.'

'Thank you,' said Emma. She took a breath and seemed a little calmer. 'I'll return the map to the Harpoles tomorrow. I'd like to think that will stop anyone coming after us.'

'I think it's time I interviewed Mr Crowfield,' said James.

'He's on my list of suspects, and I'm annoyed I didn't get to him sooner. If I can find an excuse to detain him for a few days, then I shall make sure that happens. It's possible he's been in trouble with the police before. He sounds like someone from the criminal class.' He turned to Emma. 'We certainly don't want him pestering you on the street.'

'But what about the theory that Penny and I murdered Lord Harpole?' Emma's voice rose with barely contained panic. 'You have to admit how it appears – we discovered him dying, then somehow ended up with his precious map.' Her eyes darted between them, seeking reassurance. 'If Crowfield convinces the police to listen to him...'

Although Penny maintained a calmer exterior than Emma, she felt a stab of genuine concern. She exchanged a troubled glance with James, the possibility taking root in her mind.

'If he speaks to the police about this, then I will find out soon enough,' said James. 'It will be dealt with. Don't you worry.'

FORTY-NINE

Emma called on Lord and Lady Harpole the following day. Their smart townhouse in Brompton Square stood in stark contrast to the grey winter sky. When Emma was shown into their drawing room, the atmosphere of mourning was immediately apparent – mirrors draped with black crepe, the heavy curtains half-drawn against the weak daylight. Both Harpoles were impeccably dressed in formal mourning attire, their pale faces solemn against the dark fabric.

'It's nice to see you again, Mrs Langley,' said Lord Harpole. 'I suppose you've heard the distressing news that the police now suspect my brother was murdered?'

'Yes, I have,' said Emma. She clutched his brother's case in her hand, keen to hand it over. 'I realize this is an extremely upsetting time for you both.'

She couldn't help thinking about the large estate the younger Harpole had now inherited. Could he really have poisoned his own brother? She tried hard not to allow her thoughts to show on her face.

'I have something to give you,' she said, handing over the case which Penny had collected from the bank vault early that morning. 'This contains a map and a snuff box which belonged to your brother.'

'Ah, the mysterious map,' said Lord Harpole, taking the case from her. 'We had that odd investigator chap visiting us here, didn't we, Constance?' His wife nodded. 'He mentioned he'd been doing some work for my brother regarding a map and some treasure. It all sounded rather far-fetched to me, but it's reassuring to hear the map actually exists. Let's see it.'

He placed the case on a well-polished occasional table and opened it. Once the map was in his pudgy hand, he turned it one way and then another. 'What does it show?' he asked.

'St Paul's Cathedral,' said Emma.

'St Paul's? The treasure is buried there?'

'No. We found a symbol there which led us to another location – the maze at Hampton Court. And then we found another symbol there which we can't work out the meaning of.'

'You're working with this Maitland chap?'

'Yes, myself and Mrs Blakely.'

'And what do you plan to do when you find the treasure, Mrs Langley? You are aware it belongs to my family?'

'Yes, I am aware,' said Emma. 'And if we find anything, then we'll make sure that it's passed to you.'

'Good. Can you believe Maitland was asking me to pay him for the work? And yet here you are, willing to do it free of charge. I'm very grateful to you, Mrs Langley. You've been very helpful to my family, indeed.'

'I can't be certain we'll find any treasure,' said Emma. 'But as we've begun the work, we feel we should complete it.'

'How did you find the map?' asked Lady Harpole. 'Richard and I had never even heard of it before Charles's death.'

Emma explained how she had come across the cloakroom ticket.

'Well, thank you for returning everything to us, Mrs Langley,' said Lord Harpole.

'It's most strange, I really can't understand why anyone would want to murder him. Perhaps it was something to do with this map business. Either that or he must have made an enemy of someone, and I really can't think who.'

Emma watched him as he spoke, aware that he could be the poisoner and was trying to make conversation about his brother's death as if he had had nothing to do with it.

'The police are involved now,' she said. 'Hopefully, they'll find out who was behind it.'

'Yes, I suppose they will. We must leave it to them. Having discovered that they're treating his death as murder, I'm impatient to find the person who did it. And this has changed our lives, hasn't it, Constance?'

'Yes, dear. Enormously.'

'I'll have to divide my time between this house and the family seat in Berkshire. It's a lot for me to adjust to. We've led quite a quiet life, haven't we, Constance? And now I find myself with a title and a lot of responsibility. The estate employs many people and there's a lot for Constance to manage. She hasn't been well, and now she has all this to deal with.'

Emma found it difficult to feel sorry for the Harpoles. Perhaps she was being unreasonable. In Lord Harpole's mind, he probably felt inconvenienced.

'I'm sorry to hear you've been ill, Lady Harpole,' she said. 'I trust you're feeling a bit better now? Obviously, the death of your brother-in-law has been very distressing, but I hope your health is recovering.'

'Yes, I'm feeling much recovered in that respect, thank you, Mrs Langley.' She gave her a warm smile.

Emma thanked them for their time and went on her way, feeling relieved the map was now in the Harpoles' hands. If Lydney and Crowfield were determined to get hold of it, then Harpole would have to deal with them.

FIFTY

Rupert Crowfield drained his tankard, then pushed it across the bar to the barman.

'Another one, please, Jack.'

The barman took his tankard over to the beer pump and refilled it.

A man joined him at the bar, standing a little too close for comfort and asked for a pint of porter.

Rupert looked him up and down. He was taller than Rupert, but Rupert felt sure he could beat him in a fight. He edged back a little, then turned to face him. 'What do you want?' he asked.

'Tell me about the Inveniam Society.'

Rupert laughed. 'As if I'd tell you. Who are you, anyway?'

'Answer my question, and I'll tell you.'

'I don't think that's a fair deal.' He took his tankard back from Jack and took a large swig from it. 'Are you a copper?'

'What does the Inveniam Society want with the map which Lord Harpole was in possession of?'

'I've no idea what you're talking about.'

The gentleman turned to face him and fixed him with his sharp blue eyes.'

'You've got two choices, Crowfield. Either you answer my questions while we stand here at the bar of this pleasant old public house, or I take you down to the local station to a cold tiled room for questioning. Which would you like it to be?'

So he was a copper.

'The Inveniam Society is just a bit of fun,' said Rupert. 'We enjoy researching old treasure.'

'Do you find any?'

'No. I've told you, it's just a bit of fun. Now, are you going to tell me who you are?'

'Detective Inspector James Blakely of Scotland Yard.'

'So you're Mrs Blakely's husband.'

'That's right.'

'And you believe your wife is innocent, do you?'

'We're not here to talk about my wife, Crowfield. We're here to talk about you. How well did you know Lord Harpole?'

'Not very well.'

'But he was a member of the Inveniam Society?'

'Yes.'

'And he had a map which the Inveniam Society wanted.'

'The Inveniam Society was interested in looking at it. It supposedly led to some old treasure.'

'Lord Harpole appears to have gone to great lengths to conceal the map from you and make sure it didn't fall into the hands of the Society. If it was only a bit of fun, why would he do that?'

'I've no idea. I wanted to ask him, but then he died.' He took a swig of ale.

'And what were you doing on the evening of Friday the eighteenth of January?'

'I called at the hotel to see Lord Harpole. And then I found your wife and her friend, Mrs Langley, outside his room, and they told me he'd just died. You could argue some people might make a connection between their presence that evening and his death.'

'Spreading false rumours will get you nowhere, Crowfield. What were you doing between the hours of four o'clock and six o'clock that day?'

'I was working.'

'Where?'

Rupert wasn't sure if he should bring Lydney into it. Lydney wouldn't thank him for it, but it was likely the inspector knew he was linked to the society too.

'I was with my boss, Mr Lydney.'

'I've heard a lot about him. I'm looking forward to meeting him.'

'Do you want me to tell him you're looking for him?'

'No, there's no need. I'll find him. I trust you're keeping your nose clean these days, Crowfield?'

'What do you mean by that?'

'You know what I mean. There's no use pretending you're innocent of any wrongdoing. How many years was it you spent in prison?'

'It sounds like you know already, Inspector, so I probably don't need to tell you.'

'Good. So we understand each other, then. When it comes to a man of your reputation, it doesn't take much before we haul you in again on another charge.'

'That's very true, Inspector. I don't know what it is about the coppers, but they certainly have it in for me.'

'And with good reason, too. If I hear any word of you harassing Mrs Langley, my wife or anybody else who has found themselves caught up in this unfortunate matter, then you'll soon know about it. Do I make myself clear?'

Rupert sighed. He'd led a quiet existence for the past five years but the inspector had clearly done his research. For now, he pretended he meant no trouble.

'Absolutely clear, Inspector.'

FIFTY-ONE

'Can you think of a London location which fits the initials "YOCC"?' Emma asked Penny the following Monday. 'I've been looking at maps and I can't find anything.'

'I've been thinking about it too and I'm struggling to come up with anything,' said Penny. She picked up a small wooden horse which Florence had thrown onto the floor. 'It has to be a location, doesn't it?'

'I think so,' said Emma. 'I'm assuming it tells us the location of the next clue. Or perhaps the lost treasure?'

Penny gave Florence the wooden horse. She held it for a brief moment before hurling it onto the floor again. Her mother chose not to pick it up again this time.

'I'm still sure the symbol is a mouse,' said Emma. 'So what could a mouse have to do with the location?'

Penny gave this some thought as Florence leaned over her arm, trying to reach for the toy. 'Mouse,' she said. 'It rhymes with house. Maybe a location such as Mansion House? But I don't see what that has to do with "YOCC".'

'I think "house" is a good idea,' said Emma. 'Along with

Mansion House, there's Apsley House… and Kenwood House… Perhaps it could refer to a palace instead of a house?'

Florence cried out, frustrated at being unable to reach her toy.

'I'm not picking it up for you,' said Penny wearily. 'You'll only drop it onto the floor again.'

Florence arched her back and cried even louder.

'Oh dear.' Penny sighed, reached down and picked up the toy horse. She handed it to Florence who instantly stopped her protest and beamed.

'Mouse… house…' said Emma. 'Mice have ears and a tail and they like cheese.'

'Cheese?' said Penny. 'I can't think of anywhere in London with the word "cheese" in it.'

'I think my thoughts are getting carried away with me,' said Emma. 'Cheese is a silly idea. However… chalk and cheese. Chalk Farm? That's not far from here.'

'I've got it!' Penny's face lit up. 'How did I not think of it sooner? I used to go there regularly when I worked nearby. "YOCC". It's the public house on Fleet Street. Ye Olde Cheshire Cheese!'

Emma laughed. 'Of course!'

Florence threw her toy onto the floor again.

'We'll have to visit the place and look for a clue there,' said Penny. 'And I suppose we'll have to invite Mr Maitland along too. We agreed to work with him, didn't we?'

Emma nodded. 'We did. I just hope we can trust him.'

Archibald Maitland's office sat above a boot shop on Charing Cross Road. Leather boots were stacked high in the window with a sign saying, "Must clear entire stock. Bargains. Everything reduced." Emma deduced it was the sort of shop which always claimed its goods were reduced.

Maitland's office was a small, low-ceilinged room with a single window which overlooked the busy street. The floorboards creaked and the furniture was scruffy. Papers, empty drinking vessels and plates were piled on the desk, windowsill and a table in the corner. He invited Emma and Penny to sit on a pair of crooked wooden chairs across the desk from him. Emma took her notebook and pencil out of her bag and rested them in her lap.

'How do you know where anything is?' Penny asked, glancing at the untidy desk.

'Oh, don't worry. There's order to this chaos!' Mr Maitland grinned. 'Now, how can I help?'

'We're here to let you know we've solved the next clue,' said Penny. '"YOCC" stands for Ye Olde Cheshire Cheese.'

'Yes!' He clapped his hands together. 'Well done! I nearly got it.'

'Did you?'

'Oh yes. I knew the letters "YO" must stand for Ye Olde, but I hadn't quite solved the rest of it. What did the mouse have to do with it?'

'Cheese,' said Emma.

'Oh yes.' He gave a firm nod. 'I'd have reached that conclusion too. Well done, ladies!'

'So that's the next location,' said Penny. 'We'll need to visit.'

'And I can't say I'm unhappy about that,' said Mr Maitland. 'I'm not one to turn down a visit to a public house. When should we visit Ye Olde Cheshire Cheese?'

'How about tomorrow?'

'That's an excellent idea.'

Emma's pencil rolled off her lap and under the desk. She bent down to retrieve it then saw it had rolled further than she'd thought. Getting to her hands and knees, she reluctantly edged forward on the dusty floorboards beneath the desk.

'Is everything all right, Mrs Langley?' asked Mr Maitland.

'Yes, I've just dropped my pencil. Don't worry.' She saw it on the floor, lying next to a piece of paper.

'Have you ever met Rupert Crowfield?' Emma heard Penny ask Mr Maitland.

'I've not met him, but I've heard the name. I recall Lord Harpole telling me he worked for Stephen Lydney.'

The piece of paper next to the pencil looked like a letter. And someone had drawn hearts, flowers and kisses on it.

'Rupert Crowfield turned up outside Lord Harpole's hotel room shortly after he died,' Penny told Mr Maitland. 'He said he was a friend, but it seems he was little more than an acquaintance.'

Emma picked up her pencil and peered closer at the letter. She could read a few of the words: "...my heart misses you... can't wait to see you again...". It was clearly a love letter which had fallen from Mr Maitland's messy desk onto the floor. She wondered if she should pick it up for him then reasoned he'd be embarrassed that she'd found it.

Then she saw the name at the bottom of the letter and her heart gave a thud.

She climbed out from beneath the desk, sat back on her chair and dusted off her skirts.

'I'm sure Crowfield was little more than an acquaintance of Lord Harpole's,' said Mr Maitland. 'I'm not sure what Lord Harpole thought of him. I can only imagine he didn't trust Crowfield because he chose not to share his map with the Inveniam Society.'

Emma struggled to look at Mr Maitland now that she knew about his secret love affair. She felt impatient to leave so she could tell Penny.

'If the Inveniam Society is behind Lord Harpole's murder, then Rupert Crowfield could have had something to do with it,' said Penny. 'Mrs Langley and I have discussed this, and we thought it would be a good ruse for a murderer to turn up at the scene of the crime, pretending he'd had nothing to do with it.'

'Yes, that would be a good ruse, indeed. But not good enough if you've already seen through it, Mrs Blakely.' He gave a smile.

'We're hoping Crowfield will stay away now,' said Emma. 'I've returned the map to the Harpoles.'

'Have you indeed?' Mr Maitland's eyes twinkled. 'That's an excellent idea. We don't need it anymore and if Lydney and Crowfield want it, they can fetch it themselves.' He chuckled. 'Richard Harpole has no idea they're after it. It could be interesting!'

Emma and Penny walked along Charing Cross Road after leaving Mr Maitland's office. It was a cold but sunny day and heaps of filthy grey snow lay in the gutters and at the edges of the pavement.

'It seems Mr Maitland is willing to be helpful,' said Penny. 'Do you trust him a little more now?'

'No,' said Emma.

'Why not?'

'Because when I crawled under his desk to find my pencil, I found a letter which had fallen there. Obviously I didn't have time to read it, but I could see it was a love letter.'

'A love letter?' Penny smiled. 'To Mr Maitland?'

'Yes! And wait until you hear who it was from.'

'Who?'

'Amelia. Lady Somersham.'

Penny gasped and stopped so suddenly that a gentleman bumped into her. He muttered something then strode away.

'Are you sure?' asked Penny.

'Yes. She calls him Archie. And she'd drawn love hearts and kisses and all sorts of things on it.'

Penny stared into the middle distance, her mouth falling open in genuine shock. Her spectacles slipped down her nose, forgotten. 'Lady Somersham, with all her aristocratic privilege, and... Maitland?' She let out a short, incredulous laugh. 'I never would have imagined it. I simply cannot believe it.'

FIFTY-TWO

Joseph Campbell took out the black woollen jacket from Lord Harpole's wardrobe and walked over to the window so he could see better in the daylight. Using his trusty horsehair brush, he brushed the jacket clean, then laid it on the bed. Then he did the same with a matching pair of trousers. He took out a freshly starched shirt and found a stiff white collar to go with it. After laying the clothes out, he pulled out a drawer and selected two silk ties he thought would be suitable for the occasion. He would allow Lord Harpole to choose which one he preferred.

His employer stepped into the room moments later.

'Thank you, Campbell,' he said, avoiding eye contact as he took off his jacket and handed it to him. Joseph suspected something might be wrong.

He placed the jacket on a hanger and hung it in the wardrobe. 'Is there anything else you would like me to help you with, my lord?'

'No, that is all, Campbell. Thank you.'

Joseph turned to leave when Lord Harpole held up a pudgy finger. 'There is just one... one other thing.'

Joseph sensed he was uneasy. 'Yes?'

'I'm afraid I'm going to have to let you go, Campbell.'

It felt like a blow to the chest. Joseph fixed his face into a mask, showing no emotion. 'Let me go, my lord?'

Lord Harpole hitched up his trousers and paced the floor, avoiding Joseph's gaze.

'Yes, I'm afraid so, Campbell. This isn't easy for me to say, especially as you served my brother. However, I'm afraid I have learned about one or two unpleasant aspects of your character.'

'My lord?' Joseph resolved to stand there until he'd heard a full explanation.

'Yes. I understand you and my brother had an argument on the morning of his death.'

'We did not, my lord. As I understand it, a maid reported hearing raised voices that morning, but she was quite mistaken, I can assure you.'

'Well, the inspector from Scotland Yard seems to think there was something in it, and he mentioned it to me.'

Joseph felt his heart sink. What business did the inspector have going about saying such things? 'This is the reason for my dismissal, my lord?'

'No. Not the entire reason, Campbell. After hearing about the disagreement – which I was told you had denied – I felt there was little use in asking you directly about it myself. In fact, I made some inquiries with the staff. And while we were at Wickham House at the weekend, that's what I did. I should add that you're highly thought of, Campbell; it was quite some work to persuade anybody to say anything critical of you. But eventually, a few people could be persuaded, and I heard rumours that some personal items of Lord Harpole's had gone missing. Apparently, a young maid was blamed for it and dismissed. But after her departure, two more items went missing. A pair of silver cufflinks, I believe, and apparently a watch as well. Small items. My brother assumed he'd simply mislaid them, but after a while, he grew suspicious of you, didn't he, Campbell?'

Joseph stared at Lord Harpole and said nothing.

'I think it's fair to say that by the time you accompanied my brother on his last trip to London, relations between the pair of you were poor indeed, weren't they?'

'If the gossiping servants are to be believed, my lord.'

Lord Harpole finally fixed his gaze.

'Yes, I know servants gossip, but having looked into this, I realize there was a reason for the gossip. So I ordered that your cottage in the grounds of Wickham House be searched this morning, Campbell, while you were here with me in London.'

A cold sense of dread lurched in Joseph's stomach.

'The cufflinks and the watch were recovered from your cottage, Campbell.'

'My lord, I can provide an explanation.'

'Can you? Well, I'd be interested to hear it.'

'Both items needed to be repaired. I agreed with the previous Lord Harpole that I would see to it.'

'So why did he believe he'd mislaid them? Did you not seek to reassure him that the items were to be repaired?'

Joseph hesitated. 'I did, sir. Perhaps it slipped his mind.'

Lord Harpole shook his head. 'I'm sorry, Campbell, but I've lost trust in you. You argued with my brother on the day of his death, and you stole from him. Until you can provide evidence to the contrary, I'm afraid I'm going to have to let you go. And I dare not think of the consequences of the altercation on that fateful morning. Perhaps you returned to his room later that day and—'

'I did not poison him, my lord!' Joseph's fists clenched. 'And I shall defend myself on that most vehemently!'

'Good, because you'll need to defend yourself, Campbell. I shall inform the police about this, and they will look into it. If I am mistaken, then I apologise. If they can clear you of all wrongdoing, then I would gladly welcome you back to work for my family again. But under the current circumstances, I can only have people around me who I can trust.'

Joseph stared at him for a moment longer. The stocky, dough-faced younger brother who didn't deserve his title. He said nothing, turned and left the room.

FIFTY-THREE

'It's been a few years since I was last here,' said Penny when Emma met her in the narrow alleyway outside Ye Olde Cheshire Cheese the following day. It had narrow grimy windows and a large lamp hung on a rickety bracket above their heads.

'All the news reporters come here to exchange gossip,' continued Penny. 'And I suppose I miss that now. Although I don't miss the tight deadlines and all the rushing around that came with them.'

Archibald Maitland appeared from around the corner. Emma and Penny had agreed they wouldn't ask him about the affair with Lady Somersham for the time being. Doing so could jeopardize the arrangement they had with him. They'd decided to ask him when they thought the time was right.

'Hello, ladies! You beat me to it! Shall we have a look inside?'

Penny nodded. 'And I warn you, this place is bigger than it looks from the outside. It has lots of small rooms, so it's going to take us a while.'

'Never mind, we're in the right place if we need to quench our thirst.'

Inside, the public house was quiet. A lull before Fleet Street's workers arrived at lunchtime. The low ceiling, wood-panelled walls and small windows made the interior gloomy. Light came from a few gas lamps and a cheerful blaze in the fireplace. A handful of men sat at tables with wooden stools and benches.

'Lots and lots of wood,' said Mr Maitland. 'Perfect for carving, wouldn't you say?'

They walked around, examining the walls. It wasn't long before they caught the attention of the barman.

'Can I ask what you're doing?' he said.

'Yes, you can,' said Mr Maitland. 'We're looking for a carving which Charles Dickens made.'

Emma glanced at Penny and they couldn't help smiling at the sudden story he'd invented.

'It's true that Charles Dickens used to drink here,' said the barman. 'I'm not aware he carved anything into the timber, though.'

'It's a rumour,' said Mr Maitland. 'I read about it the other day in an interesting little magazine. It's probably not true, but we thought it would be fun to come and have a look for ourselves.' He gestured at Emma and Penny. 'These are my sisters, by the way.'

Emma stifled a laugh. His story was becoming more elaborate.

'There are a few markings on the walls which have been here for a long time,' said the barman. 'I'll ask the landlord. He'll know more.'

A short while later, a stocky man with a thick, grey moustache joined them. Penny recognized him from her many visits to the public house in the past, but he didn't seem to remember her. 'Charles Dickens carved something into the wall, did he?' he asked.

'We can't be entirely sure,' said Penny. 'It's just something my brother read about in a magazine.'

'I've worked here a long time,' said the landlord. 'Long enough to see Charles Dickens when he came here. Pleasant chap. I never saw him carve anything into the walls. If I had, then I would have asked him not to. I wouldn't have cared if he was Charles Dickens or the local ginger-cake seller. But there are a few old carvings. Some of them are very old. This public house goes back to the sixteenth century.'

They followed him as he took them around the building, showing them where markings had been made into frames, doorways, walls and tables.

'There are a lot here,' said Maitland. 'I suppose chaps like to have a few drinks and leave their mark with their pen knives.'

As they left the bar and began to climb a staircase, something caught Emma's eye on the newel post at the foot of the stairs. No one else appeared to notice it. The others climbed the stairs, while she took out her notebook and made a sketch. The carving was similar to the previous ones – it had a symbol with a cross and letters above it. The letters read: "RIOH". The symbol looked like a ball with a stick poking out of it. She felt a skip of excitement in her chest as she sketched it, she felt sure it was the carving they were looking for.

Once Penny reached the top of the stairs, she turned to see where Emma was. They caught each other's eye and Emma grinned. Penny returned it, realizing what she'd found.

Once the tour of the public house was finished, Maitland seemed subdued. He clearly thought they'd missed the clue.

'I don't know where you got the idea that Charles Dickens carved something here,' said the landlord. 'He may have done, he may not have. But I can tell you he used to come here. Just about every public house in London claims he was a regular. Although, in this place, he actually was.'

'That's fascinating,' said Penny. 'Thank you for your time.'

They stepped out into the alleyway and out onto Fleet Street.

Emma pulled out her notebook and showed Penny and Mr Maitland the carving she'd sketched.

'So you did find something!' he said. 'How did I miss it? You kept it very quiet. "RIOH" and a ball on a stick. What does that mean?'

'I don't know,' said Penny, adjusting her spectacles with a frown. 'We'll need to spend some time trying to work out what it leads to.'

'Yes, that's the tricky bit.' Maitland rubbed his chin thoughtfully. 'And I don't understand the cross.'

'Me neither,' said Penny.

'It will be nice to see where this ends, won't it?' Maitland's eyes gleamed with barely contained excitement.

'And I hope it will end quite soon,' said Penny with a weary sigh. She massaged her temples. 'I'm growing a little tired of chasing one obscure carving to the next. I'm beginning to wonder if there's actually anything worthwhile at the end of this trail.'

'Oh, I'm sure there is,' said Mr Maitland. 'Stephen Lydney seems quite convinced about it. For as long as he's interested, then I'm interested too. I'm going to go back to my office and have a proper think about this.'

They said goodbye, and he went on his way.

'I can't work out if Mr Maitland is helping us or not,' said Penny. 'He hasn't really contributed anything yet, has he?'

'Not yet,' said Emma. 'But I think it's useful having regular contact with him. It means we can keep our eye on him just in case.'

'Just in case he's not who he says he is?'

Emma nodded. 'I still don't trust him.' She spotted a young man bounding enthusiastically towards them. His eye was fixed on Penny.

'Mrs Blakely! You're here again on Fleet Street. Does this mean it won't be long before you're returning here as a news reporter?'

He was about twenty-five and had handsome, boyish looks with dark hair and hazel eyes.

'Hello, Mr Wright,' said Penny. She introduced him to Emma. 'This is Harry Wright, the new reporter on the *Morning Express*. I met him recently.'

'It's a pleasure to meet you, Mrs Langley.' He held out his hand to her and grinned. She met his gaze and felt her eyes held there. And although she wore gloves, she felt a tingle in her hand as he shook it.

'I had a good chat with Inspector Trotter yesterday,' he said. 'We've got a whole page devoted to the murder of Lord Harpole. It will be printed in the morning.'

'An entire page?' said Penny. 'Goodness.'

'Perhaps I could interview you for it as well?'

'No, there's no need. I'm not officially working on the case. I'll leave it to the police to comment.'

'As you wish, Mrs Blakely. So, who do you think the murderer is?'

'There are quite a few suspects, Mr Wright. I really wouldn't want to speculate. I'm not speaking in any professional capacity.'

'I'm not going to publish what you say, Mrs Blakely. I'm just interested to hear.'

'Well, there are the people who were close to Lord Harpole – his valet, his brother and his fiancée. And then he was a member of the Inveniam Society, and it's possible someone from the society could have been behind it.'

'Ah yes, Inspector Trotter told me about the Inveniam Society. I'm doing a lot of research into them at the moment. That Stephen Lydney is quite a character. I'm going to try to interview him.'

'You are?' said Penny. 'I've heard he's not a particularly nice person, so do be careful.'

'Oh, I shall, Mrs Blakely. Anyway, I should get on, I've got a deadline.' He turned to Emma. 'It was lovely to meet you, Mrs Langley.' He tipped his hat and went on his way.

'I don't think he was lying just then,' said Penny. 'I think he was genuinely pleased to meet you, Emma.'

Emma blushed. 'He was just being polite.'

'If you say so. He's extremely enthusiastic, isn't he? I don't suppose he's been a reporter long enough to suffer the disappointments and rejections which chip away at you and wear you down. He'll probably be a different person in two years' time.' She stopped and chuckled. 'Oh dear, I sound a bit old and bitter, don't I?'

FIFTY-FOUR

Archie was sitting on a bench overlooking the lake in St James's Park. Amelia's heart gave a skip as soon as she saw him. She dashed over to him as quickly as her heavy skirts and delicate shoes would allow.

'Archie, how are you? I've got so much to tell you!'

He got up from the bench and grinned broadly. 'Darling Amelia. Did you manage to get away all right?'

'Yes, I told Mother I wanted to visit the shops. She made a fuss about it and said that one of the maids could go for me instead. But I told her I absolutely insisted on it, and so I've managed to get out on my own. Isn't it wonderful?'

She glanced up at the sky, which was overcast and grey. 'Do you think it will snow? I really want more snow. Proper snow.'

The air was chilly, and she was worried it would make her nose red. But she didn't mind because she was with Archie.

'What do you need to tell me?' he asked as she took his arm. They began to walk along the path around the lake.

'A detective from Scotland Yard visited, and he told me they think Charles was murdered!' She stared up at his face, her eyes wide, keen to see what he made of this.

He gave a small nod. 'I think the same detective visited me, too. And he said much the same.'

'Did he ask you lots of questions, Archie? He asked me so many questions that my head hurt. And it was awful because I couldn't really understand why someone would murder Charles.'

'Me neither. It must be something to do with the map.'

'But why murder him for a map? It seems such an awful waste of life. And then I couldn't believe it when the detective asked me where I was at the time he was murdered. As if he suspected me of doing it!'

'You mustn't worry about that, Amelia,' he said, patting her hand. 'The detectives always ask questions like that. He asked me the same too.'

'So he thinks you did it as well?'

'He'll be speaking to lots of people about it, and he will ask them all the same question. He's trying to establish alibis for us all.'

'But the problem is, we were together, weren't we, Archie? And we can't tell anyone that – it's supposed to be a secret.'

'That's right. That's the dilemma I was faced with as well. We could come clean and tell him we were together at the time, but then he might tell other people, and we certainly don't want anyone else finding out. And he might even think that we carried out the murder together.'

'Which is so awful! I don't want anyone thinking that! There must be something we can do.'

'I don't see what we can do, Amelia. Once a police detective gets an idea into his head, then he's going to keep following it until he finds evidence one way or another.'

'But there isn't even evidence that we did anything!'

'No, there isn't. It's possible he'll find something and convince himself that it's evidence. We'll just have to wait and see.'

Amelia shivered. 'I don't like it at all, Archie. I don't like the fact we have to keep our love affair secret. And I don't like the fact that the police are asking lots of questions now. And it was awful when they said Charles committed suicide, but now it turns out that he didn't. And all of it is just simply horrible. I wish I could go back to a few weeks ago before any of this happened. Sometimes I close my eyes and wish it so much that I almost believe I could. Sometimes I want to go to sleep for a long, long time and then wake up and discover all this has gone away. It just feels awful.'

'Yes, it does, Amelia. But we should be all right, I feel sure of it. I'll find this treasure, and I'll make the Harpole family pay me a good sum of money for it.'

'Will you, Archie?' She peered up at him, earnestly. 'I do hope you get it. My family has lots of money, but when they find out about us, they're probably not going to let me have any of their money anymore.'

'Yes, that is a concern, because we really could do with it. But don't worry about it for now. I have a plan, and I feel quite sure we'll be all right. And whatever happens, we have each other, don't we, Amelia?'

'Oh yes, we do, Archie.' She stood up on her tiptoes and gave him a light kiss on his cheek. 'It's so romantic of you to say such things. I can't wait for all this to be over. Oh, I almost forgot to tell you. I had a visitor who told me he was a friend of Charles's. He was an odd-looking fellow and he wore an eye patch.'

'What was his name?'

'Mr Lydney.'

Archie stopped and the colour drained from his face. He turned to her. 'Lydney? What did he want?'

'He didn't want anything. He just visited to pass on his condolences.'

'He wouldn't have visited for that.' He placed his hands on

her shoulders. 'What did he ask you, Amelia? Think very carefully.'

She didn't like the way Archie was behaving so seriously now. She felt her chin begin to wobble. 'I can't really remember what he asked. He didn't stay for long. I remember we talked about you and the map...'

'The map? Did he ask where it was?'

'I told him one of the ladies had it. Mrs Langley or Mrs Blakely.'

'Oh, good grief!' He clasped his forehead.

Amelia felt panic rising within her. 'What is it, Archie? What have I done wrong? Oh please don't be cross with me!' Tears stung her eyes.

'No, I'm not cross with you, Amelia. Please don't cry. You've done nothing wrong. You weren't to know.'

'No, I wasn't to know. I don't know everything that's going on. I've never even met him before!' She pulled out her handkerchief and sobbed into it.

FIFTY-FIVE

Emma arrived at Penny and James's home at seven o'clock that evening. She'd been invited to dinner with Francis Edwards. Penny had told her he was an old friend who had found her missing plant-hunter father in South America.

Emma thought he sounded fascinating.

When she was introduced to him, he seemed an ordinary, humble gentleman with sandy hair and spectacles. His tanned face was the only thing which suggested he'd spent time in exotic, far-off places.

'It's a pleasure to meet you, Mrs Langley.' He shook her hand. 'Please, call me Francis.'

They gathered in the sitting room with a drink before dinner. Mrs Tuttle brought the children downstairs to say goodnight.

'It's lovely to meet you at last, young Thomas,' said Francis, crouching down to his height. 'When you're older, I'll tell you all sorts of stories about your parents.'

'Oh Francis, don't!' said Penny, blushing.

'They're lovely children,' said Francis, standing up again. 'You must be very proud parents.'

'We are,' said James with a proud smile. 'And it's good to see you again, Francis, after all these years.' He gave him a friendly slap on the shoulder. 'You must tell us all about your travels.'

'I really don't want to bore you,' said Francis.

'No, you won't bore us. We're interested to hear. Penny and I haven't had an opportunity to travel in recent years, have we, Penny?'

Penny shook her head. 'No, we've been rather busy here with the children.'

They said goodnight to the children, and Mrs Tuttle took them back upstairs.

'They're quite delightful,' said Francis. 'It's lovely to see you all so settled.'

He smiled broadly, but there was a hint of sadness in his eyes. Emma sensed he was a little envious of the happy family.

'What are your plans now that you've settled back in London, Francis?' asked James.

'I'm not entirely sure yet. I'm renting some rooms in Camden and I shall get settled back into work.'

'And remain a bachelor?'

His face reddened. 'That all depends on whether I meet the right sort of lady.'

'I'm sure there are many ladies who would like to be Mrs Francis Edwards,' said James with a playful glint in his eye, watching his wife's face carefully for her reaction.

'Oh, I don't know about that.'

'There's no need to tease him, James,' said Penny. 'I'm sure the very last thing Francis is thinking about is marriage. I'd say enjoy your freedom while you can, Francis.'

'Thank you, Penny. I think I've done quite a good job of enjoying my freedom over the past few years. But I shall see what happens. I don't like to plan too far ahead.'

Mrs Tuttle had prepared a delicious meal of chicken in

white wine sauce. As they ate, Penny told Francis about the map and the Harpole family treasure.

'What an interesting story!' he said. 'Although I can't help thinking Sir Francis Drake's loot should be returned to the people he stole it from.'

'Wasn't it the sort of thing everyone did in those days?' said James. 'I can't say the Spanish were particularly well-behaved back then, either.'

'I suppose not. And looking back on those days from a time where we're all a little more civilized can cause us to make critical judgements. Sir Francis Drake is a rather complicated fellow. He did some useful things, but let's not forget he was also a pirate.'

'He saw off the Spanish Armada,' said James. 'I'd say that was more than merely useful.'

'He played a part,' said Francis. 'But there were other factors, too. Not least, the wind direction.'

The debate continued and the mood grew uncomfortable as it descended into bickering. Emma ate her chicken and kept quiet. She noticed Penny's jaw was tense.

'Shall we change the subject?' said Penny eventually. 'I don't think we're going to solve the question of how good, or bad, Sir Francis Drake was. It was all quite a long time ago.'

'Very well,' said James sulkily.

Emma could tell Francis wished to say more, but was biting his lip.

Penny looked as though she was regretting getting the two men together.

FIFTY-SIX

Stephen Lydney removed the monocle from his eye and took a sip of port from his chalice.

What was he going to do about Crowfield? The man was hopeless. Nearly three weeks had passed since Lord Harpole's murder and they'd made no progress with finding the treasure. He'd put so much work into his research and there was a risk of it all coming to nothing.

A knock sounded at the door.

'Enter!' Perhaps that was Crowfield now.

But a gentleman in an overcoat and bowler hat stepped in through the door. A gentleman who was unmistakeably a Scotland Yard inspector – Lydney knew one when he saw one. It had to be the same gentleman who'd called on Crowfield a few days ago.

'Inspector Blakely!' He gave him a wide smile and got to his feet. 'I'm delighted to meet you at last. I've heard so much about you.' The inspector took a seat opposite him at his round table. 'You're a detective at the Yard who's highly thought of.'

'Am I indeed? That's very kind of you, Mr Lydney. I wasn't expecting to be so warmly welcomed.'

'I afford respect to those who earn it, Inspector.'

Blakely looked at the maps and books on the table. 'This all looks very interesting,' he said. 'What's it all about, then?'

'How nice of you to ask. Few people are interested in my little hobby.'

'Which is what, exactly?'

'Surely you've heard by now? I'm extremely interested in tracing old treasure. Take this map, for example – it shows a location in Essex, one of the first sites occupied by the Knights Templar in the thirteenth century. It's a farm these days, but from the research I've done, I have reason to believe the Knights Templar buried some of their treasures there for safekeeping. Now I need to speak to the landowner about it, of course. I like to keep everything legitimate.'

'Do you really?'

'You sound sceptical, Inspector. But I'd like to assure you I'm very professional about my work.'

'Did you report your find of the Saxon gold coins?'

He chuckled. 'I must be frank with you. Despite my determined efforts, I haven't actually uncovered any treasure yet. That was a little rumour I started myself, just to get people interested.'

'Interested in what?'

'My society, of course. The Inveniam Society. I've heard it described as secretive, but I can assure you there's absolutely nothing secretive about it whatsoever. We just keep things to ourselves to keep out the lower classes. You're most welcome to attend our meetings whenever, Inspector.'

Blakely raised an eyebrow, suggesting he was surprised to hear this.

'Now then, allow me to tell you a little more about this site in Essex.' He spent some time describing it to Blakely, showing him the details on the map, and then pointing out references in books he had found.

'That's impressive indeed,' said Blakely. 'I hear you're also interested in finding Sir Francis Drake's hidden treasures.'

'Oh, absolutely. I can only assume you're referring to the map owned by the Harpole family. It was drawn up by Lord Charles Harpole's great-grandfather, Theobald Harpole. Talk of where the lost treasure may be hidden has been passed down through generations of the Harpole family. I learned about the map from an interesting book about ancient Spanish treasures. I presented my research to Lord Charles Harpole. He was obviously very interested, and rather dismayed that his own father, who died early last year, hadn't passed the knowledge on to him. Perhaps it had been forgotten about. Anyway, we made a deal. He would retrieve the map, I would find the treasure for him and we would share the proceeds. Unfortunately, he changed his mind.'

'That must have been disappointing.'

'Yes, it was. He then hired a private detective called Maitland to do the work for him.' He shook his head. 'I don't think he had any hope of finding the treasure. From what I've heard, the map shows a symbol that is supposed to be in St Paul's Cathedral. There's a clue there which leads to the next clue and so on. It really is a good old-fashioned treasure hunt. As I haven't got the map, I hope to bypass a step or two in the treasure hunt and find the treasure using my own research.'

'It sounds like Lord Theobald Harpole drew up the map for a bit of fun,' said Blakely.

'Oh yes, he did. By all accounts, he enjoyed puzzles and games, and he created the map for his family. His son, however, doesn't appear to have shown much interest in the game, and neither did his son after that. By the time Lord Charles Harpole became a grown man, practically all knowledge of the map and the game had been lost. A great shame. And the Harpoles only have themselves to blame. If they'd put in the effort to find the treasure, it would be in their family now.'

'If you find the treasure, would you share it with them?'

Lydney gave a laugh. 'Now that's an interesting thought, Inspector. We have a new Lord Harpole now, of course, and I don't know him at all.'

'How did you feel when you discovered Charles Harpole went back on his word to give you the map?'

'I can't deny I was angry. I had some words with my assistant, Rupert Crowfield, about it. He was disappointed, too. But there was nothing we could do about it, was there? Lord Harpole had gone back on his word, and that tells you all you need to know about a man's character.'

'Perhaps you asked Crowfield to visit Lord Harpole at his hotel on Friday the eighteenth of January?' The inspector's tone was deceptively casual.

Lydney chose to keep his expression impassive, but he tapped his fingers on the arm of his chair. 'No, not at all.' He leaned back with calculated ease. 'I've since learned that Crowfield did call on Lord Harpole that evening, but he was too late.' A thin, cold smile touched his lips. 'Lord Harpole was already dead. I suspect Crowfield went there to have a word with him and try to persuade him to change his mind about the map.'

'And Lord Harpole refused, therefore Crowfield poisoned him.'

'Oh no.' Lydney shook his head. 'That's not a nice accusation at all, Inspector. As I've told you, Crowfield arrived after Lord Harpole had died. Now, I'm sure that some decent investigation by your men will reveal who was in that room with him. The hotel staff must have seen people coming and going from Lord Harpole's room. They must have an idea who he was with. I'm quite surprised the police haven't worked it out yet.'

'We haven't worked it out yet because we've only just decided that Lord Harpole's death was murder. The murderer made a good attempt to stage his death as a suicide. It was so convincing, in fact, that the coroner was fooled.'

'Yes, what a shame. It wasted time, didn't it? If it had been treated as a murder immediately, I'm sure you'd have caught the culprit by now. However, it's not for me to tell you how to do your job, Inspector, is it? I've been honest and open with you about my work and my dealings with Lord Harpole, and I trust now that you have all the information you need from me.'

'Where were you on the evening of Friday the eighteenth of January, Mr Lydney?'

'So you'd like an alibi, would you? Well, that's quite easy. I was here. I don't socialize much. We hold our monthly meetings of the Inveniam Society and I occasionally meet with friends, but that's all I do. You're going to ask me if someone was with me, and I shall tell you they weren't. However, a nosy lady lives above the shop across the road. She sees everyone coming and going on this street. I'm sure if you have a word with her, she'll be able to tell you what my movements were that day. She doesn't miss a thing.'

He smiled at Blakely, confident he'd presented himself with a strong defence. He sensed Blakely's mind working, trying to find something he could take issue with. Thankfully, the inspector got to his feet. 'Thank you for talking to me, Mr Lydney. I may need to call on you again soon.'

'Very well, Inspector, as you please. If you'd like to know anything further, just let me know.'

As soon as the door closed behind Blakely, Lydney got to his feet.

What did Blakely know? And what had his wife found out?

He paced the room as he ruminated. He'd asked Crowfield to work on this and he'd achieved nothing.

It made his blood boil.

FIFTY-SEVEN

After a piano lesson in Kensington the following day, Emma visited the nearby Harrods store to buy a pair of French kid leather gloves. Mrs Solomon enjoyed shopping at Harrods and Emma paid a little extra to make sure the gloves were expertly wrapped for her birthday.

As she stepped out onto Brompton Road, a familiar lean figure strode past – Lord Harpole's valet, Joseph Campbell. He wore a long, dark overcoat and had a determined expression on his face.

What was he up to? Emma decided to follow him.

From what she'd heard, there'd been a disagreement between the valet and Charles Harpole on the morning of his death. However, Campbell was denying it had happened.

The traffic in the road was moving slowly. As a horse-drawn omnibus drew alongside Campbell, he jumped onto the platform at the back and climbed up the stairs to take a seat on the top.

If she didn't get on board too, she would lose him. Emma caught up with the omnibus and saw there was space on the lower deck to sit inside. She skipped onto the platform and went in.

The omnibus slowly made its way east along Brompton Road, through Knightsbridge and past Hyde Park. Emma kept a keen eye on the platform at the back, waiting to see when Campbell would disembark.

They reached Piccadilly and Emma began to worry she'd missed him getting off. If he had, then she consoled herself with the thought she was heading in the right direction towards home.

After passing through Piccadilly Circus, the omnibus moved on to Leicester Square. When it stopped outside the Empire Theatre, Campbell hopped off. The omnibus moved on again before Emma could follow.

She departed at the next stop, hoping she could find Campbell again. The pavements thronged with people and she realized she'd lost him in the crowds.

Then she caught sight of the lean figure crossing the road and her heart gave a skip.

He was walking towards Charing Cross Road. Emma followed. He turned right and she paused on the corner. They were very near the boot shop which Archibald Maitland's office was situated above.

Emma held her breath as she watched Campbell cross Charing Cross Road and call at the door by the boot shop.

He was calling on Archibald Maitland.

FIFTY-EIGHT

Mr Campbell had a lot to say about his former employer. Archibald Maitland listened patiently as the valet grumbled and vented his anger about being dismissed. Campbell was bitter but he also had some useful information which Archibald assured him they could use to their advantage.

The conversation was thirsty work. Archibald invited the valet to join him in The King's Arms but he declined. After Campbell had left, Archibald put on his overcoat and headed out alone.

It was getting dark and a light drizzle fell as he crossed Charing Cross Road. He'd almost reached the public house when someone knocked into him. He was about to protest when he was shoved into an alleyway and up against the wall.

It happened so quickly, he'd had no time to react.

The man was shorter than him but he was stronger and his forearm was pressed up painfully against Archibald's throat. In the gloom, he could see his face had a strong jawline and deep-set blue eyes.

His mouth felt dry. 'What do you want?' It was an effort to speak with the pressure on his neck.

'Don't you want to know who I am?'

'All right then. Who are you?'

'Rupert Crowfield.'

'I've heard of you.'

'Good. That's what I was hoping.'

'Could you release your grip a little? I'm struggling to breathe.'

'I won't fall for that.'

'I mean it! I shan't run away. I've been wanting to talk to you, in fact.'

'Oh, have you?' The pressure eased a little. 'About what?'

'The map.'

'Where is it?'

'I don't know.'

'You're lying.'

'I don't!'

'Shame,' said Crowfield. 'I need you to help me.'

'Help with what?'

'You're working with Mrs Langley and Mrs Blakely, aren't you? How much progress have they made with finding the treasure?'

'Not much. But if you really want to know, why don't you ask them yourself?'

'No, it's easier if you find out for me.'

'I refuse to.'

The arm pushed against his neck again. 'Now that's not what I want to hear, Maitland.' His voice was low and quiet now. 'Especially when there's Lady Somersham to think about.'

Maitland's blood ran cold. 'What of her?'

'You've been having a love affair with her. And while she was engaged to Lord Harpole!'

'There's no affair.'

'What will Lady Somersham's parents think when they find out about you and their daughter?'

Maitland's fists balled. How did this man know so much about him? 'Keep Lady Somersham out of this.'

'It's impossible, I'm afraid. She's already caught up in it, isn't she? Perhaps the pair of you murdered Lord Harpole.'

'Ridiculous!' Maitland gritted his teeth and tried to push Crowfield away. But he wasn't strong enough.

Crowfield increased the pressure on his neck. Pain shot through his throat and he gasped for breath.

'From now on, Maitland, I want regular updates from you about those ladies. I want to know how close they are to finding that treasure. Do I make myself clear?'

FIFTY-NINE

'Jones tells me he's had a good response to the advertisement for a new valet,' Richard told Constance at breakfast the following morning. 'Hopefully we shall have a new man in place next week.'

'That's excellent news, dear.' Constance pushed her kedgeree around her plate with her fork.

'I've asked Jones to ensure the chap has a good working knowledge of Berkshire. We're going to be spending quite a bit of time there, so I'd like to have a valet who is used to the area and will know the locals. You know you're going to have to get to know everybody down there, Constance.'

She sighed. It was another thing she was going to have to do. She didn't really like meeting new people; she preferred her own company. But she had to accept her new status meant acquainting herself with all the important people in Berkshire.

'Well, I suppose that makes sense, then,' she replied. 'The valet should be able to give you some advice on that matter.'

The butler came into the dining room with the morning post on a silver tray. He handed them each a pile of letters.

'Goodness, look at all this correspondence,' said Richard.

'Are you feeling important now, Constance?' He gave her a smile.

Although the pile of post looked daunting, she quietly admitted to herself she was enjoying feeling a little more important. She picked up her letter opener, opened the first letter and gave another sigh. 'Oh dear, the fabric I ordered for the drawing-room curtains isn't available in the quantity we need. They say they have a similar design but in a slightly different colour. Oh, that is annoying. I shall have to go into the store again.'

Richard was silent. She glanced up at him. He was holding a letter in his hand and his face was pale.

'Is everything all right, Richard? Have you received bad news?'

'No,' he said. He folded up the letter. 'Not bad news.'

She didn't want him keeping anything from her. 'You're not fooling me, dear. I know you too well. Something awful has been written in that letter. What is it?'

'You don't need to worry yourself about it, Constance.' Richard turned away dismissively, his shoulders tense. 'You have enough to think about.'

'But I shall worry about it.' She leaned forward, heat rising in her face. 'And I shall worry about it even more if you don't tell me what it is.' Her voice was sharp.

'It's nothing I can't sort out with the solicitor.' He ran a hand over his brow, refusing to meet her gaze.

'Richard!' Her grip tightened on the letter opener. 'I demand to know what you're looking at!'

His head snapped up, jaw tightening. 'Do you really, Constance? Well, if it upsets you, then you've only got yourself to blame. I'm trying to protect you, you know.' His tone shifted to condescending. 'I know how fragile your nerves are at the moment.'

He tossed the letter across the table to her. The wording was short:

I know your secret and will keep it confidential if you send £100 to the General Post Office in St Martin's Le Grand for the attention of Frank Duncan.

Constance felt the blood drain from her face. 'What secret, Richard?'

'I don't know.'

'And who's Frank Duncan?'

'I've no idea, Constance.'

'Have you ever known anyone with that name?'

'No. But it could be a false name.'

'But this is awful, Richard. This is blackmail! What does this person know? What secret are they talking about?'

SIXTY

'I wonder why Joseph Campbell was visiting Archibald Maitland,' said Penny. 'We have a few things to ask him now. There's his apparent affair with Lady Somersham and now a meeting with Lord Harpole's valet. And he's never mentioned either of them to us!'

'It's a puzzle,' said Emma. They sat in Penny's sitting room. Tiger the cat dozed on a chair while watching Thomas with one eye. He was arranging a fort of building blocks around his toy train. Baby Florence sat on Penny's lap, chewing on a rubber teething ring.

'I don't know what to think about Mr Maitland,' continued Emma. 'He's supposed to be helping us and yet there are things he's not sharing.'

'I can understand why he'd keep an affair with Amelia Somersham secret,' said Penny. 'It would be a scandal for her if her family found out.'

'And perhaps he's keeping it secret for another reason,' said Emma. 'Perhaps the pair of them conspired to murder Charles Harpole?'

They heard the front door open then close.

'That must be James,' said Penny. She glanced at the clock on the mantelpiece. 'Very odd. It's only half past two.'

He entered the room, his hat in his hand and his face downcast.

'Is everything all right?' Penny asked him.

'No. I've been taken off the case.'

'Oh no. Why?'

'Because you were involved.'

Penny frowned. 'That doesn't make sense.'

'It does when you think about it.' James explained, his expression grim. 'Now that it's a murder case, both you and Emma need to be formally interviewed by the Yard. And I can't interview you, Penny, because you're my wife.'

Penny sighed, shoulders slumping as realization dawned. 'Of course. It makes sense now.' She turned to Emma, worry etching lines around her eyes. 'We were the ones who found Charles Harpole, so the Yard will want to speak to us.'

Emma's heart sank, and heat drained from her face. 'And consider us suspects?' Her voice dropped to barely above a whisper.

'But we're innocent and they have no evidence.' Penny's voice carried a forced confidence that did little to reassure Emma.

'But we gave evidence at the inquest,' said Emma, clutching the edge of her chair. 'Surely that's enough?'

'I'm afraid not,' said James. He ruffled his son's hair and slumped into a chair. 'You gave evidence to the coroner at an inquest. This is an investigation by Scotland Yard now.'

'So it's different.' Emma looked down at her hands. Her stomach knotted as she thought about being interviewed by the police. Would they treat her like a criminal?

'Detective Inspector Fenton is in charge now,' said James.

Penny gave a groan which made Emma feel even worse.

'The detective inspector from Holborn?' she said. 'He's at the Yard now?'

'I'm afraid so.'

'Who is he?' asked Emma.

'I encountered him while I was reporting on the murders in St Giles,' said Penny.

'And what's he like?'

'Officious and stubborn.'

'It's nothing to worry about,' said James. 'It's just procedure. And it's quite obvious neither of you poisoned Lord Harpole.'

'But what if Rupert Crowfield tells him we did?' said Emma. 'He could tell him we poisoned Harpole to get hold of the map. It's quite believable.'

James shook his head. 'Fenton is a better detective inspector than that. He won't believe some nonsense a criminal tells him.' He shrugged his shoulders. 'It's frustrating, but maybe it's for the best. The case has been giving me an uneasy feeling.'

'What do you mean?' asked Penny.

He rubbed the back of his neck. 'It sounds foolish to say it, but I've had the sensation of being watched recently.'

Emma shuddered. 'Has someone been following you?' she asked.

'I don't think so. I've not noticed anyone. But it's just a sensation. I've felt it ever since I interviewed Mr Lydney. He's an unpleasant type. Perhaps he... Oh, don't listen to me. I'm probably just imagining it.' He rubbed his neck again. 'How about I make a pot of tea? It will help us feel better, I'm sure.'

SIXTY-ONE

The following morning, Emma sat in a sombre wood-panelled room in Scotland Yard. A fire burned in the grate but the heat seemed to be escaping up the chimney while a draught from the window chilled the room.

Detective Inspector Fenton had greying mutton-chop whiskers and a sharp nose.

'I've solved many murder cases in my time,' he told Emma. 'And you'd be surprised how often the person who found the body turned out to be the murderer.'

'I didn't find a body,' she said. 'We found Lord Harpole seriously unwell in his hotel room.'

He shuffled his papers and nodded disinterestedly.

For the next twenty minutes, Emma responded to his detailed questions about that evening. She took her time, answering carefully and consistently. She was determined not to let him fluster or panic her.

'There's something else I'd like to say,' she said at the end of the interview. 'If Mrs Blakely and I had intended to murder Lord Harpole that evening, we wouldn't have summoned a doctor, would we? We would have simply left him to his fate.'

Fenton gave a nod. 'That's a fair point, Mrs Langley.'

SIXTY-TWO

'How did it go?' Penny asked Emma once her interview with Detective Inspector Fenton was finished. She looked weary.

'As well it could, I think. Good luck.' She gave Penny a smile.

'No conferring please, ladies,' said Fenton, appearing in the waiting room. 'Come along, Mrs Blakely. Your turn.'

Penny rolled her eyes and followed him.

They sat at the wooden table in the draughty interview room and Fenton looked through his papers. 'Mrs Blakely, formerly known as the ace reporter, Miss Penny Green.' He sat back in his chair and smiled. 'So old Detective Inspector Blakely made an honest woman of you.'

'Yes,' said Penny, impatiently. 'What would you like to ask me, Inspector?'

'Just a few questions about the circumstances of Lord Charles Harpole's death. We're treating it as murder.'

'I know,' said Penny. 'I was the first person to suggest there could have been foul play involved.'

'Really?' He sat forward and looked through his papers. 'There isn't a record of that here.'

'No. I don't suppose there is.'

'So you suggested it, eh? Still up to your old tricks, then. Even though you're a mother.'

Penny's teeth clenched. 'Are mothers not allowed opinions, Inspector?'

'Oh, they're allowed opinions, all right. But all this gallivanting about on dark foggy nights and calling on peers in their hotel rooms... If you were my wife, then I'd have a word or two to say about that.'

Anger balled in Penny's chest but she managed to remain calm. 'It sounds like you have a word or two to say about it even though I'm not your wife, Inspector.'

He gave a dry laugh. 'So you know my thoughts on the matter then. Once a news reporter, always a news reporter, I suppose. And one could argue Blakely knew what he was getting himself into when he married you.'

Penny couldn't keep in her anger any longer. 'A proper detective conducts himself without prejudice or judgement!'

Fenton seemed taken aback.

'Can we just get on with the interview now?' she added.

'Of course.'

When Penny returned home that evening, there was a telegram waiting for her from Archibald Maitland:

```
Solved it! Royal Italian Opera House tomorrow
midday.
```

Penny smiled to herself. The Royal Italian Opera House. That's what RIOH stood for. She hadn't fathomed what the symbol meant, but she presumed Mr Maitland had worked it out.

He'd solved a clue and was proving himself useful. But still her doubts about him lingered. Did he want to help her and Emma, or did his loyalty lie elsewhere? With Lady Somersham perhaps? Or Mr Campbell? Or perhaps his only motivation was serving himself.

Mrs Tuttle left after preparing dinner and Penny was expecting James home at seven o'clock. When it was eight o'clock, she decided to eat without him and kept his food warm on the sideboard.

After dinner, she tidied and sorted the children's laundry. Then she read for a while and tried not to worry about James. The nature of his work meant his hours could be unpredictable. But he usually sent her a message if he was going to be very late. She told herself not to worry until ten o'clock.

Ten o'clock came and went. Why hadn't she heard anything from him? Penny paced the floor, tidied some more and tried to ignore the unease which gnawed in her stomach. By half past ten, she wondered if she should do something. It was completely out of character for James not to contact her. She went into the hallway, put on a hat and coat, and dashed out to Mrs Tuttle, who lived about fifty yards away.

She didn't like leaving her children sleeping alone in the house, but she would only be a few minutes, and there was little else she could do.

'Goodness, Mrs Blakely. Are you all right?'

'No. It's probably nothing, but I don't know where James has got to.'

Mrs Tuttle patiently listened while Penny explained.

'I'll come over and sit in the house and mind the children while you do what you have to do, Mrs Blakely. I'm sure there's nothing to worry about.'

Back at the house, Mrs Tuttle made herself comfortable in the sitting room.

'I'll go to the local police station nearby,' said Penny quickly. 'They'll be able to get a message to Scotland Yard and find out what's detained him. I know I'm worrying unnecessarily, but I can't help it.'

'Hopefully you'll be reassured soon, Mrs Blakely.'

SIXTY-THREE

Outside, a heavy fog dimmed the streetlamps. Penny wrapped her coat tightly around her and hurried as fast as she could the police station. Inside, the desk sergeant listened patiently to her flustered explanation and request for help.

She waited by the desk as the sergeant went to make inquiries. The station's harsh gaslight cast everything in an unflattering yellow glow, making the dingy walls look even more grim.

An elderly man with a dishevelled appearance shuffled through the door, his rheumy eyes lighting upon Penny immediately. 'Are you selling eggs, miss?' he asked, his voice tremulous.

'Not this evening,' she replied tersely, her nerves too frayed for pleasantries.

'Well, that's a shame.' He moved closer, his moth-eaten coat giving off a strong smell of tobacco. 'Have your hens not been laying recently?'

'I don't have any hens,' said Penny, turning away pointedly. 'Please leave me alone.'

A young constable appeared from a side room, sighing with

familiar resignation. 'Not this evening, Mr Watkins,' he said, gently taking the old man's elbow.

'Her hens have stopped laying,' the old man announced loudly, gesturing at Penny.

'Can you leave, please, Mr Watkins?' The constable's voice firmed as he guided him towards the door.

Penny drummed her fingers on the counter, her anxiety growing with each tick of the clock on the wall. Ten minutes past eleven – where was James?

The desk sergeant returned. 'I sent a wire to the Yard and received a prompt reply. Your husband's not there, I'm afraid.'

'Maybe he's been called out on an investigation?'

'I feel sure they would have said so if that was the case, Mrs Blakely.'

Nausea swirled in her stomach. She sensed something bad had happened.

'I'm sorry we can't help any more than that, Mrs Blakely. It's possible he got caught up in something and hasn't been able to tell anyone about it yet.'

'I hope so,' said Penny. Her voice quavered with worry. 'I hope there's a suitable explanation for it.'

'I'll send a wire to the Yard again and ask them to let me know as soon as they've heard of his whereabouts. Just leave me your address, Mrs Blakely, and I'll make sure someone gets back to you.'

He was doing the best he could. Penny thanked him, wrote down her address and went on her way.

Where had James got to? How could he just disappear? She had to look for him.

She walked through the quiet, foggy streets, making her way towards the underground railway station. From there, she would follow the route he would have taken back home. Perhaps something had happened to him on the way. She shuddered at the thought. She didn't want to entertain the idea that he could have come to harm.

The station was closed for the night. She stood outside it, glancing around at the shuttered shops and quiet roads. A hansom cab passed by, but the street felt cold, lonely and quiet.

There were a couple of routes James could have taken through the streets to get back home. Penny chose the route she thought he was most likely to have used. It was difficult to see in the fog. She checked every doorway and narrow alleyway she passed.

Occasionally, a figure would loom out of the fog. Often, it was someone on their way home from a public house. She came across a constable and asked if he'd seen James.

'I'm afraid not, madam. Have you reported it at the police station?'

'Yes,' she answered irritably. 'I've already done that.'

It wasn't long before she reached her street again, and there was still no sign of him.

She retraced her steps, this time walking on the opposite side of the road and checking every doorway and passageway.

The bell of St. John's Wood church struck midnight, each sombre tone vibrating through Penny's chest like a physical blow. The dread that had been building all evening crystallized into something cold and terrible.

What had happened to James? She ransacked her memory – had he mentioned plans? A late meeting? A duty she'd forgotten in the chaos of children and household? No, there was nothing. James was meticulous about such things, always sending word if delayed.

Her thoughts raced in darkening spirals. An accident? A sudden illness? Or something worse – someone with a grudge, someone they'd crossed in their investigations? The possibilities multiplied with each passing moment, each more terrifying than the last.

She reached the church and headed for the path which ran down the side. She could just about see her way in the faint glow of a streetlamp. Outlines of tombstones rose out of the gloom and the back of her neck prickled. There was nothing to be scared of and she repeated the thought in her mind as she slowly made her way along the path. But no matter how much she tried to be rational, the graveyard stirred her most primitive fears.

A sack lay at the foot of the church wall. Penny was about to pass it when something made her look again. A sack? What could it be doing there?

She stopped abruptly, her breath catching in her throat. What she had taken for a discarded sack in the shadows was unmistakably the outline of a man's overcoat.

'Hello?' Her voice emerged as a frightened whisper, barely carrying in the night air. No response came.

She inched closer, her heart hammering painfully against her ribs. Perhaps it was just a drunk who'd stumbled in from a nearby tavern? Or a vagrant seeking shelter from the bitter night?

But as she drew nearer, recognition struck her like a punch to the chest. That dark wool coat with the distinctive collar – James's coat.

'James?' Her voice broke on his name as she rushed forward, falling to her knees beside the motionless figure.

He lay face down on the frozen ground, utterly still. With trembling hands, she gently turned him over, a strangled cry escaping her lips as his beloved face came into view. Even in the dim light, she could see the violent discolouration, the crusted blood.

She tore off her glove with her teeth and pressed her bare hand to his ice-cold cheek, desperately searching for signs of life. 'James,' she whispered, her voice raw with terror. 'James, please...'

Her fingers found his neck, searching for a pulse with frantic determination. There – faint but present. He was alive.

SIXTY-FOUR

Emma ran up the steps of St Mary's Hospital in Paddington the following morning. After making several inquiries, she finally found her way to the ward where James was being treated. She strode past a line of iron beds and recumbent patients to where Penny sat by a bed at the far end.

She was holding her husband's hand and looked exhausted.

'Oh, Penny, I'm so sorry. How is he?'

'I don't know.' Penny's voice cracked. 'I don't think he knows I'm here. But I'm talking to him all the same.'

Emma couldn't form words; her body felt paralysed with shock. The man in the hospital bed barely resembled the strong, confident inspector she knew. His face was a grotesque mask of purple and yellow bruising, one eye swollen completely shut. She focused on the slight rise and fall of his chest beneath the thin hospital blanket, clinging to that rhythmic movement as proof that James still existed somewhere beneath the damage.

'What happened to him?'

'I don't know. He hasn't been able to tell me. But the doctors think he was attacked by someone. A group, even. I found him shortly after midnight, he must have been there for hours.' She got up from her chair and rubbed a hand over her face.

'Oh, Penny.' Emma rested a hand on her arm. 'I really believe he's going to be all right. He won't let them get the better of him.'

'I don't know who did it,' said Penny, her voice cracking. She paced beside the bed, unable to stay still, her fingers constantly reaching to smooth James's blanket or adjust his bandages. 'And his watch and wallet are missing so perhaps it was robbery.' She halted suddenly, her eyes flashing with sudden ferocity. 'But I don't understand why they had to hurt him so much.'

She turned to Emma, her face transformed in anger. 'Perhaps it was Lydney and Crowfield trying to put a stop his investigation. Maybe they took his belongings to disguise their true motive.' Her hands clenched into fists at her sides. 'It's too horrible to even contemplate.' Her voice dropped to a whisper. 'And if it's them, that means we're responsible for this, Emma. We brought this danger into our lives – into James's life.'

'The only people responsible are the savage people who attacked James,' said Emma. 'And we'll find out who they are. He'll wake up soon, and he'll be able to tell us. I just know it.'

As she spoke, Emma prayed she would be right. All they could do was be hopeful. They had to keep praying James would recover.

'He told us he felt uneasy about the case, didn't he?' said Penny. 'He told us he felt he was being watched. He was right!'

Emma nodded. 'He could have been followed for a few days as the culprit waited for the right moment to attack him.' She shivered. 'Such a horrible thought.'

'If only he'd seen who was following him,' said Penny. 'He could have done something about it instead of it coming to this. The more I think about it, the more I'm convinced that Lydney is responsible. We just need James to wake up and tell us.' She took a handkerchief from her pocket and wiped her eyes. Emma squeezed her shoulder, trying to offer some comfort. 'I had a message from Mr Maitland last night,' Penny continued. 'He wants to meet at midday today outside the Royal Italian Opera House. I shan't be able to go, obviously. But if you feel you would like to go...'

'I'll go,' said Emma. 'The Royal Italian Opera House. Why didn't we think of that before?'

Penny managed a smile. 'I know. I thought the same. But somehow it doesn't even matter anymore. I just want James back.'

Emma nodded. But she couldn't say anything because she knew she would cry.

SIXTY-FIVE

A raised voice woke Lady Constance Harpole. Her husband was shouting somewhere in the house. It was morning, but she couldn't be sure what time. Daylight streamed in through the curtains. She rang the bell to summon her maid.

'What's happening, Minnie?' she asked, propping herself up in bed.

'Unfortunately, there's been a burglary, my lady.'

'A burglary?' Her heart gave a thud. 'What's been taken?'

'Lord Harpole believes it's a map, my lady.'

She felt her shoulders relax. 'Just the map? Anything else? Silverware? Ornaments? Jewellery?'

'We haven't noticed anything else that's gone missing yet, my lady. But we're checking every room in the house just to make sure. You were undisturbed in here last night, I take it?'

'Yes, I think so. Open the curtains a little so I can see the room more clearly.'

The maid did so, and Constance could see the room was just as it had been when she went to sleep the previous evening.

'Thank goodness they didn't come in here. They must have been after that map. Well, they can have it as far as I'm concerned. I've grown tired of hearing about it. Why is Richard shouting about it?'

'He's angry someone got into the house so easily.'

'How did they get in?'

'They climbed onto the roof at the back, my lady, and forced open a window on the landing.'

'Oh, that is dreadful. It shouldn't have been so easy for them to get in. And while we were asleep, too! It's very worrying. We shall have to make sure that window has a lock put on it.'

'That's what Lord Harpole has also said, my lady. How are you feeling this morning?'

Constance felt her head. 'A little warm still. But I must get up.'

'He was quite anxious that you shouldn't be disturbed.'

'Well, if there's been a burglary, then I want to know about it. Can you prepare a bath for me, please?'

'What about breakfast, my lady?'

'I won't have any just yet. I would like to speak to Richard first.'

Half an hour later, Constance joined her husband in his study.

'What are you doing up and about, Constance? You felt unwell again yesterday and I told the maid not to disturb you.'

'Your voice woke me up this morning, Richard. I heard you shouting about the burglary. I understand the map's been taken.'

'Yes. They got in through the window on the first floor, came down the stairs, entered my study and took it. They must have known it was here. They knew exactly what they were looking for. Once they had it, they must have gone on their way again. We should be grateful that was all they were after. But I wish now I'd hidden it. I didn't expect anybody to come into the house and find it. Now I suppose we shall have to speak to

Maitland again and ask him to help us find the treasure. But I don't know how we're going to do that without the map.'

'Surely Maitland won't need the map anymore, dear. He's already put quite a bit of work into it.'

'Hopefully.' He reached out to her and took her hand. 'I was worried about you yesterday when you said you felt unwell again. I can't bear the thought of you coming down with another fever.'

'I'm all right, thank you, dear.' She eased herself into a chair. 'I got up because I was worried, and I still don't like the thought that someone's been in the house. But if all they've taken is the map, then thank goodness we're all right. Just think what they could have done. They could have harmed us.'

'I really don't want to think about that, Constance. Now then, you're up and about. Does that mean you're well enough to have lunch with Mr and Mrs Graves? He's the High Sheriff of Berkshire. They're going to be neighbours of ours and they wrote to say they will be in London for a few days and would like to meet.'

'Yes, I remember, dear. You wrote them a letter, didn't you? I think I'll be well enough for that. It's important we get to know our new neighbours.'

'Good. And then I shall think about speaking to Maitland again. He's going to want payment, isn't he? I suppose I have to make a decision. Do I pay him to help us find the treasure, or do I forget about the nonsense altogether? There really is too much to think about at the moment.'

Constance sighed. 'Yes,' she said. 'I'm afraid there is.'

SIXTY-SIX

Archibald Maitland's grin seemed out of place when Emma met him outside the Royal Italian Opera House on Bow Street. She couldn't bring herself to smile while Penny and James were detained at the hospital.

The opera house was an imposing building fronted by a row of tall, classical columns. To Emma, it looked a little too large and grand for the narrow street.

A shabby ginger-cake seller approached them, rattling a pot of coins. He carried a tray which was supported by a leather strap around his neck. 'Ginger cake for your lady?'

'No, thank you,' said Maitland. 'And she's not my lady.'

The ginger-cake seller gave Emma a toothless leer and went on his way.

'You can't walk about the West End without someone accosting you, can you?' said Maitland. 'Anyway. Here we are.' He glanced up at the grand edifice and rubbed his palms together with glee. 'Where's Mrs Blakely?'

Emma told him what had happened, carefully observing his reaction.

Mr Maitland's face fell. 'Goodness. Is Inspector Blakely badly injured?'

'Yes, he is. He hasn't gained consciousness since he was found. Mrs Blakely is extremely worried about him. As am I.'

'Awful. Simply awful. I hope he makes a full recovery. Have they caught the person responsible?'

'No. They have no idea who carried out the attack at the moment. But I have my suspicions it could have been Lydney and Crowfield. Inspector Blakely questioned them both recently and perhaps they took objection to it.'

Maitland nodded. 'That wouldn't surprise me. It sounds like a cowardly act. Exactly the sort of thing you'd expect Crowfield to do. And perhaps Lydney too.' He paused and glanced around. 'I sometimes wonder what we've got ourselves into.' He lowered his voice. 'I feel sure someone was watching me from the street last night.'

A knot tightened in Emma's stomach. 'Really? Could you see who it was?'

'No. Just a figure. I could barely see them, but I could... feel them there.'

Emma recalled the sensation of being watched as she'd stood outside the house on Stanford Road. 'I know that feeling,' she said. 'It makes my skin crawl.'

'Yes! My skin crawled.' He shrugged his shoulders, as if trying to shake off the sensation.

'I suppose we've got ourselves caught up in something, haven't we?' said Emma. 'The map fascinated me to begin with, but I've realized now it's caused nothing but trouble. And what will we find here in the opera house? Another symbol which will take a few days to work out, and then that leads us to another one, and another one, and so on. There may not be any treasure at the end of it, after all. It could be someone just playing a prank.'

'I'd like to think there's some treasure at the end of it. Mr

Lydney did a great amount of research into this and, when he told Lord Harpole about the map, he was quite convinced some treasure would be found.'

'But do you trust Mr Lydney?'

'No, I don't. But... Well, we're here now. Let's have a look around the opera house and see if we can find the next symbol. You're more than welcome to join me, Mrs Langley, obviously. We're working on this together. But if you'd rather be with Mrs Blakely and her husband, then I understand.'

'No, I'll accompany you,' said Emma quickly. She glanced up at the building. 'Look at the size of this place, it's enormous. Where are we supposed to look? In the foyer? In the auditorium? Perhaps the symbol has been carved in one of the dressing rooms. How could we possibly get access to those?'

'I can see you're quite disheartened today, Mrs Langley. And that's understandable too. But I'm good at talking my way into things. That little story about Charles Dickens in Ye Old Cheshire Cheese was good fun, wasn't it?'

He smiled, and Emma could tell he was trying to cheer her up. It wasn't working.

'All right then, Mr Maitland. Let's go inside and have a look, and I'll let you do the talking.'

They walked up to a set of doors. Mr Maitland tried the handle but the doors were locked. They walked to another set of doors which were also locked.

'Well, this is a good start,' he said. He rattled the doors to get someone's attention. 'Hello!' he shouted. He rattled the doors again.

'I don't think we can get in,' said Emma.

'Of course we can get in. Hello! Let us in!'

His shouts attracted some glances from passers-by and Emma felt a little embarrassed. 'Perhaps we can come back another—'

'Absolutely not. Hello!'

A man in red livery appeared in the foyer on the other side of the door. He gestured dismissively through the glass.

'What?' shouted Mr Maitland through the door.

The man approached the window, pointing emphatically to a sign. 'Closed,' he mouthed.

'I know that. Let us in!' Maitland pounded on the glass.

The man's face contorted with obvious frustration. Then he reluctantly undid the locks at the top and bottom of the door and opened it an inch. 'We're closed,' he said through the narrow gap, his voice tight with irritation.

'I know you're closed,' said Maitland. 'But I dropped my wallet here last night. Can I come in and look for it?'

'No. But it may have been handed in to our cloakroom. What does it look like?'

'It's leather. Brown. I think I dropped it in the auditorium and it's probably tucked away beneath a folded seat or even in a folded seat somewhere. It won't be obvious so I think it's best I come in and find it myself.'

'Where were you seated?'

'Er, the dress circle.'

'Row and seat number?'

'I actually can't remember. E or F. Twenty something. I could be mistaken. But if I actually could get in there…'

'I'm afraid not. I shall look for your wallet and if I find it then I shall let you know. Perhaps you could let me have your name and address?'

Mr Maitland took a step back. 'No. Forget it! I'm not going to all that trouble. This is the last time I attend a performance here, do you hear me? The very last time. My wallet is somewhere inside this building and yet you refuse to let me in and look for it!'

'Simply leave your name and—'

'No!' Mr Maitland dismissed him with a wave of his arm

and strode off. Emma felt surprised by his sudden loss of temper. She bit her lip as she watched him march away.

The liveried man closed and locked the door and she followed Mr Maitland. 'There's something I've been meaning to ask you,' she called after him. 'Did Mr Campbell call on you the other day?'

'Campbell?' he said over his shoulder. 'Oh yes, he did.'

'Why?'

'He was just passing. He wanted to tell me the new Lord Harpole has dismissed him. He accused him of stealing from his brother.'

'And did he?'

'I don't know. Campbell denies it, but who knows what to believe?' He stopped by a public house called the Bow Street Tavern. 'I'm going to drown my sorrows in here, fancy joining me?'

'No thank you, Mr Maitland.'

He glanced up and down the street.

'Is everything all right?' asked Emma.

'Sort of. You never know who's watching, do you?'

Emma felt a shiver. She looked around her. The passers-by seemed disinterested and there was no one loitering and looking suspicious. 'Hopefully no one's watching,' she said.

'Good. Looks like I'm safe for now. Goodbye, Mrs Langley.' He pushed open the bar door and she caught a whiff of beer from within. He disappeared inside and she continued on down Bow Street. As she walked, she recalled their conversation in her mind.

Maitland hadn't been entirely truthful with her. He'd told her Campbell had called on him because he'd been passing his office. But she knew Campbell had deliberately gone there by omnibus.

Had Campbell lied to Maitland? Or was Maitland lying to her?

SIXTY-SEVEN

Emma returned to St Mary's Hospital, hopeful James might have woken. But her hopes were dashed when she found Penny at his bedside, just as Emma had left her that morning.

Her face was drawn and pale and Emma suspected she'd had little to eat or drink.

'There's a chop house nearby,' said Emma. 'Shall we go there for a short while and get something to eat?'

'I can't leave him.' Penny gripped James's hand a little tighter.

'I know you don't want to,' said Emma. 'And that's understandable. But you need something to eat. You'll need your strength for when he wakes.'

Penny nodded, her eyes remaining on James.

'We can be very quick,' said Emma. 'And the nurses will watch him while we're gone. Don't forget you need to keep your strength up for the children too. They'll be keen to see when you get home later. The chop house does a ten-ounce steak for five pence with an extra pence for fried onion. It says so on the sign in the window.'

Penny turned to her. 'I don't feel hungry,' she said. 'But

you're right. I should eat. For the children's sake and James's sake too.' She cautiously let go of his hand. 'We have to be quick, though. Very quick. I don't want him to wake and wonder where he is.'

'I know. Let's tell the nurses where we're going. Perhaps one of them will be happy to fetch you if James wakes.'

Penny got to her feet. 'All right then. You've persuaded me.'

Emma took her arm. Penny seemed diminished and it was saddening to see. Emma was so accustomed to Penny being the older, experienced one. Just like a big sister. And now their roles were reversed. Penny was too filled with concern for James to care for herself, so Emma had to look after her.

'My mouth's already watering at the thought of that ten-ounce chop,' said Emma as they walked along the ward.

'You can have mine too,' said Penny. 'I don't feel hungry.'

'We're not leaving the chop house until you've eaten some of it,' said Emma. 'And if you don't finish it, that's all right. I'll have the rest.' They shared a smile. 'And if you're in the mood to hear it, I'll tell you how I got on with Archibald Maitland at the Royal Italian Opera House.'

SIXTY-EIGHT

Emma returned home that afternoon, feeling despondent. She was worried about Penny and James and she and Maitland had failed to find the next symbol.

She was also anxious that Detective Inspector Fenton suspected her and Penny of poisoning Lord Harpole. Had they done enough to defend themselves?

Laurence the shaggy cat strolled past her. She smoothed her hand along his furry back as he passed.

A knock sounded at the door. It was probably the Scotland Yard inspector. Emma tried to calm her pounding heart.

'There's a young gentleman here to see you, Mrs Langley,' called Mrs Solomon from the hallway.

Young? Who was Mrs Solomon referring to?

She gasped and got to her feet as the *Morning Express* reporter, Harry Wright, stepped into the room. His familiar boyish grin caught her off guard, sending an unexpected flutter through her chest that she hastily attributed to surprise.

'It's a pleasure to meet you again, Mrs Langley.' He held his hat in one hand and shook her hand with the other. 'I'm sorry for calling on you unannounced like this.'

'How did you know I live here?'

'I looked you up in the directory. I hope you don't mind.'

'You're a news reporter?' asked Mrs Solomon. She'd followed him into the room.

'Yes, that's right. For the *Morning Express*. The same newspaper that Mrs Blakely used to write for. If I can do a job half as good as she did, then I'll be extremely happy.'

'Indeed,' said Mrs Solomon. 'Would you like some tea?'

He nodded. 'Yes, please.'

Emma gestured for him to take a seat.

'I've heard about the terrible attack on Inspector Blakely,' he said, taking out his notebook and pencil. 'What can you tell me about it?'

'Now just a moment,' said Emma. 'Are you writing an article about it?'

'Yes, of course. A detective from Scotland Yard has been attacked. That's important news indeed.'

'Yes, I suppose it is.' Emma thought of poor Penny sitting by her husband's bedside. Then again, Penny had been a news reporter herself and would have written many similar stories in the past. 'Please don't print anything I tell you because I can't be certain if it's true or not,' she said. 'I know nothing about the attack, and I don't want to be named in your story either.'

'That's fine, I won't put your name down. What do you know about the attack?' He fixed her with his keen hazel eyes. There was a hint of playfulness in his expression, as if he enjoyed his work. Or perhaps he just enjoyed talking to her. The thought made Emma's face flush a little.

She looked down at her skirts and smoothed them. 'I've just told you, Mr Wright. I know very little. Mrs Blakely found her husband lying beside the church in St John's Wood, and he'd probably been there for a few hours. It's likely he was attacked on his way home. He must have left St John's Wood railway station, crossed the road and been attacked as he passed the church. I can only imagine he was dragged into the churchyard.' She gave a shudder and met Mr Wright's gaze again. 'It was a foggy night, so few people would have seen exactly what happened.'

The reporter made some quick notes.

'But I don't know if those are the actual facts,' she added. 'I'm only telling you what Mrs Blakely told me while she was at her husband's bedside. If you want the facts, then the police can tell you.'

'They're not talking to me,' he said with a grimace. 'They don't like reporters very much.'

'Well, I think that's a shame because you do an important job.'

'Thank you, Mrs Langley. I like to think so.' A pause followed while they held each other's gaze. Emma looked away, her face flushing some more. She could only hope he hadn't noticed. Why did the annoying, pushy news reporter make her feel this way? Her mouth lifted at the corners and she corrected her expression, keen to appear serious. To distract herself, she leaned forward and peered at the writing in his notebook. 'Is that shorthand?'

'Yes. It speeds everything up.'

'And you understand those squiggles?'

'Absolutely. I had to be trained in it, of course. But anyone can learn it. Here, you can have a closer look.' He handed her his notebook. As he did so, her fingers brushed against his. A tingle rushed up her arm and down her back. Embarrassed, she avoided his gaze and leafed through the notebook.

'Obviously I can't read any of this,' she said. 'But it's all very clever.'

'No, there's nothing clever about it. It's a bit like learning a foreign language. Or reading music, for example.'

Emma couldn't resist mentioning her love of music. 'I'm a piano teacher. I can't write in shorthand, but I can read music.'

'There you are, you see.' He grinned. 'That's even cleverer than knowing shorthand.'

'It's not clever, it's just a skill, as you've explained yourself, Mr Wright.' She handed the notebook back to him.

'So let's have a look at the facts,' he said. 'Inspector Blakely was found by the side of the church, is that right?'

'Yes, that's what Mrs Blakely told me.'

'And he was on his way home from work?'

Emma nodded.

'And he was found shortly after midnight, is that right?'

'Yes, those are all facts which I suppose you can use.'

'You do realize that the more information we can put into this article, the more helpful it will be for the police? People will read it and recall they were in the area at the time. Then they'll pass on information to the police. And all because they read about it in the newspaper! I don't want to sensationalize the story, I just want to make people aware this has happened. And if witnesses come forward, then that helps us!'

'I hope so. Although I suspect I know who's behind this.'

His eyes widened, and she realized she'd given away too much.

'Who do you think it is?' he asked.

'I can't say. But I think it might be someone who Inspector Blakely interviewed recently. He didn't like being asked questions. Don't write that down!'

She was too late; he was making notes again.

Emma put her head in her hands. 'Oh dear, Mr Wright, speaking to you is exhausting.'

He laughed. 'Really? I'm sorry if I'm annoying you, Mrs Langley.'

'Yes, that's it. You're annoying me. Everything I say, you write it down. Can't we have a conversation without you recording it?'

'It's important it's recorded, Mrs Langley. A reporter's notebook is an official record. It must be kept so it can be referred to at any time.'

'Well, in that case, I wish I'd never even allowed you in this house, Mr Wright. If every single word I've said is going to be in your notebook for eternity, then I shall close my mouth and not speak anymore.'

She stared at him with her lips pursed. He returned her gaze and a smile played on his lips. Emma found it difficult to sustain her anger. There was something amusing and likeable about him.

'All right then.' He closed his notebook and put it in his jacket pocket with his pencil. 'Why don't we have a conversation about something else? And I promise not to write anything down.'

Emma returned his smile and tried to think of something else to talk about.

'What's it like to be widowed so young?' he asked.

The directness of his question made her struggle for words. 'It's... probably the same as any other age, really. I've never been widowed before and I don't know what it's like to be older and...' She trailed off, then laughed at her hopeless reply. 'I'm sorry,' she said. 'No one's asked me that question before and I don't suppose I've given it much thought.' The last time a gentleman had showed this much interest in her had been during her early days of courtship with William. And he'd soon lost interest once he'd married her and got his hands on the money she'd inherited.

Harry Wright was remarkably different to William. His enthusiasm seemed earnest and she couldn't help liking him. She also felt wary; she couldn't allow herself to be betrayed again.

'I suppose it was a rather foolish question,' he said, scratching his neck. 'I should have known better considering I ask questions for a living! Let me think of another. Oh!' He appeared to suddenly remember something. 'Did you hear about the burglary at Lord and Lady Harpole's house?'

'No. When was that?'

'This morning.'

'This morning? You hear about these things quickly, Mr Wright. What was taken?'

'Nothing.'

'Nothing?'

'Officially they took nothing,' said Mr Wright. 'But they actually stole the map.'

Emma gasped. 'Lydney and Crowfield must have taken it! The Harpoles should have done a better job of keeping it safe.'

'They should. Apparently it was easy to get into the house. The burglar climbed onto a roof at the back and got in through a window.'

'You'd think someone as rich as Lord and Lady Harpole would make more effort to keep their doors and windows locked.'

Mrs Solomon walked into the room with tea.

'Here we are,' she said. 'And some biscuits too.'

'Thank you, Mrs Solomon,' said Mr Wright. He glanced around the room as she poured the tea. 'Where do you keep your piano, then?'

'We don't have one here,' said Emma.

'So how do you practise?'

'I don't at the moment. In fact, I don't really have many opportunities to play.'

'Goodness. You teach piano to people and yet you're unable to practise yourself. How can you possibly ever get any better at it?'

'Mrs Langley is already quite accomplished,' said Mrs Solomon, smiling proudly as she handed him a cup of tea. 'But you're right, Mr Wright. Emma could do with a piano here.'

'Please don't get a piano just on my account, Mrs Solomon,'

said Emma. 'After all, I'm only staying in a room here temporarily. Before long, I'll find a place of my own. And perhaps I shall get a piano then.'

'I don't mind getting a piano at all,' said Mrs Solomon. She made herself comfortable in an armchair. 'In fact, I once played myself many years ago. As a girl, actually. I've forgotten all of it.'

'Sometimes you don't, though,' said Emma. 'Some people sit at a piano years, even decades, after they last played. And once they begin to recall a song, they sometimes find their fingers can remember some of it, if not all of it. It's quite incredible what the mind can retain.'

'I'd like to hear you play, Mrs Langley,' said Mr Wright.

'You'd be better off going to a proper recital where you can listen to a professional musician.'

'No, I want to hear *you* play.'

'Really?' Embarrassed, she sipped her tea and burned her lip on it.

Mr Wright glanced at his watch. 'Oh, I've just noticed the time. I must get on.' He put down his cup.

Emma felt disappointed he had to leave so suddenly. 'Good luck with the article, Mr Wright.'

'Thank you. Hopefully it will help the police effort. Goodbye!'

He dashed off before anyone could see him to the door.

'What a pleasant young man,' said Mrs Solomon. 'And he's taken a shine to you, Mrs Langley, hasn't he?'

SIXTY-NINE

Maitland was woken by a knock at the door. His room was in darkness; he had no idea what the time was. His head felt thick and heavy and his mouth was dry. He'd fallen asleep in his chair with his feet on his desk. He winced as he moved his legs. They felt stiff and achy.

The knock came again.

'Just a moment,' he said, rubbing his face.

Slowly, he remembered that he'd visited the Bow Street Tavern after his failed attempt to get into the opera house. He couldn't remember how much he'd drunk in there, but he'd consumed it quite quickly.

What was the time now? He fumbled with the gas lamp on his desk and turned it on. Then he checked his watch – it was half past five. Was it evening or morning? He lifted himself out of his chair and staggered over to the window.

Outside, the street was busy with traffic and people. Definitely evening. He'd probably only been asleep for an hour.

The knock sounded a third time. He shook his head to wake himself up. 'Come in.'

The door opened, and his visitor stepped into the room.

'Good evening,' he said with a smile of recognition. 'This is a surprise. How can I help?'

His smile wasn't returned. Something didn't feel right.

SEVENTY

Emma couldn't believe what she was reading at breakfast the following morning. She read it again, trying to ensure she hadn't been mistaken.

Had she got the name right? Was it possible more than one person was called Archibald Maitland? But the address was on Charing Cross Road. It had to be him.

She recalled him rattling the doors of the opera house the previous day and losing his temper because they couldn't get inside. And then he'd gone into the Bow Street Tavern and that had been the last time she'd seen him.

She sat motionless, waiting for her mind to fully realize what had happened.

'Mrs Langley?' said Mrs Solomon.

'Oh goodness, I'm sorry. I've just read some terrible news.'

'What is it?'

'Archibald Maitland. The private detective who was working with Penny and me. He was found dead at his office on Charing Cross Road last night. They think it's murder.'

Mrs Solomon rested down her knife and fork. 'Goodness. That is shocking. Do they know who did it?'

'No.'

'How awful. First, that intruder in this very house. And then Inspector Blakely was attacked just two nights ago and now the murder of Mr Maitland. Mrs Langley, this all began when you decided to find out about that mysterious appointment your husband put in his diary. Just look at what it's led to. That man was nothing but trouble. I don't mean to speak ill of the dead, but I can't help it in his case. He's dragged you into this even after his death!' She shook her head in dismay.

Her words offered little comfort. Emma lost her appetite for any more breakfast and put her napkin next to her plate.

'I'm going to go there and see if I can find out more.'

'Find out more? Mrs Langley, I think you should stay away from there!'

'I can't sit here not knowing what happened. I need to see it for myself.'

A small crowd had gathered outside the boot shop on Charing Cross Road. Emma's tears blurred the scene as she approached. She wished now she'd trusted Archibald Maitland a little more. She felt guilty that she'd been suspicious of him.

People stood in the street, discussing what had happened.

'Blood everywhere... He was a private detective...'

Her heart gave a skip when she caught sight of a friendly face. Harry Wright.

'Mrs Langley.' He gave her a faint smile; the sombre situation didn't allow for much more.

'I read about it in the *Morning Express* this morning,' she said. 'Was it your article, by any chance?'

'Yes, it was. I've been here most of the night, actually. I heard something was up late yesterday evening, so I came here straight away.'

'What do the police know so far?'

'According to the chap who runs the boot shop, he heard some noise in the room above at about half past five. He thought it was unusual, apparently Mr Maitland was normally a quiet tenant. And then... well, I don't really want to say. I left out the details in the news report.'

'What details?' asked Emma.

'You don't want to hear.'

'I do want to hear.'

'Are you sure?'

'Absolutely. I'm fully capable of hearing whatever it is you don't want to tell me.'

'All right, then. If you're sure.' He swallowed. 'The proprietor of the boot shop, Mr Smith, heard the disturbance. However, he didn't report it to the police. He says it was unusual, but he didn't think it was anything serious. He thought perhaps someone had fallen over or knocked something over. But then... about twenty minutes later, he noticed something dripping through the ceiling.'

Emma shuddered. 'Blood?'

Mr Wright gave a nod, his lips pressed tight.

'How very unpleasant. I suppose it's what happens with a knife injury.'

'Yes, it does,' said Mr Wright. 'Mr Smith says he ran out into the street calling for the police and that's when they found him up there. Dead.'

'Did Mr Smith see the culprit coming or going?'

'No. They have very little to go on at the moment. I expect Scotland Yard will get involved with this, and we shall find out more as they investigate. In the meantime, I'll keep asking around to find out if we know who could have been behind it.' He turned to Emma. 'I don't suppose you know, do you?'

'I have no idea,' she said. 'The person behind it could be the same person who attacked Inspector Blakely. That makes me think of Mr Lydney or Mr Crowfield. Perhaps both of them. My thoughts keep coming back to them every time.'

She thought of Lady Somersham, imagining the young woman's face when she learned of Maitland's brutal end. Would there now be genuine grief behind the mourning rituals for Charles Harpole, private tears shed for a forbidden love? Or had she too been playing a part all along?

SEVENTY-ONE

Penny arrived at the ward and asked a nurse how James was faring.

'He stirred a little yesterday evening,' she said, 'but then he lapsed back into sleep. The doctor is hopeful he's making a good recovery.'

'It doesn't seem hopeful to me,' said Penny. 'He must have had a very serious injury to his head.'

'It's possible,' said the nurse, 'but it may not be as bad as you fear, Mrs Blakely. Sometimes a period of prolonged rest like this is the body's way of healing itself. I have nursed many people in a similar condition before, and I'm happy to tell you that most of them make a full recovery.'

Penny noticed she said 'most'. She didn't say 'all'. Penny couldn't bear the thought of losing James. It had been extremely difficult telling the children their father was in hospital. They wanted to see him, but she didn't want them to see him in his current state. And she couldn't bear the thought of him never recovering. She immediately pushed the thought from her mind as tears sprang into her eyes.

'Please have hope, Mrs Blakely,' said the nurse, her weathered hand resting briefly on Penny's shoulder. Her eyes carried the gentle authority of someone who had witnessed countless bedsides, both tragic and triumphant. 'I've seen men recover from worse. I have great hope for your husband.'

Penny managed a thin smile, drawing unexpected strength from the woman's quiet confidence. 'Thank you,' she whispered, turning back to James's still form with renewed determination.

'Good morning, James.' She took his hand and squeezed it. Perhaps the nurse was right. Perhaps he would recover. He had a little more colour in his face this morning, and now that the swelling was going down, he was looking more like himself. But his head was still heavily wrapped in bandages, and she worried about the wound beneath them.

'I got a copy of the *Morning Express* on my way here,' she said. 'I like to read it regularly now. In fact, I must finish editing my article for Edgar. He'll be wondering where it is.'

Did she see his mouth twitch? She couldn't be certain. It was the sort of thing she wanted to happen, so perhaps she was just imagining it. She rested the newspaper over the bedcovers and slowly flicked through it.

It wasn't long before she found an article about the attack on James. It was short and factual and hadn't been sensationalized, but she didn't enjoy seeing it there in print. The attack had been so personal. The effect on her and her family had been enormous, and yet here it was – just a few words in a column that people would read before moving on to the next story.

But it was newsworthy; she realized that. As a news reporter, she'd written many similar stories over the years. She'd always written with consideration for the family's feelings, but she believed it was an important service. People needed to know what was going on. Reading an article about her husband's attack gave her complicated feelings. 'You're in the newspaper, James. You're famous,' she said. 'It's a shame you're not in the newspaper for some successful police work, but here you are mentioned all the same. I can only hope it will help them catch the culprit.'

James gave a grunt.

She looked up at him. 'What was that?'

Nothing. She was imagining it again. She looked back at the newspaper, then startled when she read about the murder of Archibald Maitland. She sat back in her small metal chair for a moment, trying to comprehend it. Emma hadn't sent her a message about it, but then she wouldn't have done – she wouldn't have wanted to bother her. She wondered if Emma had been able to find out anything more.

'Archibald Maitland murdered,' she said. 'Who could have done such a thing? Why? At least you're still with us, James. At least they couldn't take you away from me.'

'What?'

Penny jumped to her feet. The sound was unmistakable. James had spoken.

She gripped his hand. 'James? James? Can you hear me?'

He grunted again. His eyes twitched, and then they opened.

'James.' She leaned over him, eager for him to see her face. 'James? Can you hear me? Are you all right?'

He tried to speak but had to clear his throat before trying again. 'Of course I can hear you, Penny. I've heard everything you've been saying.'

Tears sprung into her eyes as her concern turned to joy. She fell onto him, embracing him. He was too weak to respond. The nurse came running down the ward.

'Is he awake, Mrs Blakely?'

'Yes, he is.'

Tears ran down her face, soaking James's cheek as she held him. She felt the nurse's hand on her shoulder, gently pulling her back, presumably so James could have some air.

'What did I tell you, Mrs Blakely? Just be hopeful. And

here he is – he's back with us.' She turned to James. 'Good morning, Mr Blakely. How are you doing this morning?'

'Where am I?' he mumbled.

'St Mary's Hospital. You've been in the wars, but you'll be all right. Would you like a bit of breakfast?'

SEVENTY-TWO

Emma called at the smart Somersham home in Knightsbridge. She was shown into the drawing room where Lady Amelia Somersham sat with her mother and two sisters. As soon as Emma's eyes met Lady Amelia's, she detected anguish behind them. The poor young woman had clearly been unable to express any grief for Mr Maitland.

'It's Mrs Langley, isn't it?' said the senior Lady Somersham. 'I hear you were in the unfortunate position of discovering Lord Harpole when he was gravely ill.'

'That's right, my lady. I wonder if I may speak to your daughter, Lady Amelia, please? There's something about Lord Harpole I'd like to discuss with her.'

The elder Lady Somersham pressed her lips together; she clearly wanted to know what was going to be discussed. 'Very well.' She turned to her youngest daughter. 'You may want to speak to your visitor in the morning room, Amelia.'

Lady Amelia Somersham gave a nod. Her face was stiff and impassive, and Emma sensed she was desperately trying to keep control of her emotions. She followed her through the house to a comfortably furnished room that overlooked the garden.

As soon as the door closed behind them, Lady Somersham burst into tears.

Emma didn't know what to say. She stepped forward and embraced her until the tears began to subside.

As Lady Somersham recovered herself, she was apologetic. 'Oh, I'm so sorry. I don't know why I did that. I suppose I just felt overcome with emotion. So much has happened.'

'It's Archibald Maitland, isn't it?' asked Emma.

Lady Somersham gave a nod and pressed her lips together, desperately trying to hold her tears in.

'I shan't say anything for the time being,' said Emma, 'unless your love affair had anything to do with the murders of Lord Harpole and Mr Maitland.'

'No.' She shook her head vehemently, tears spilling down her face again. 'No, it has nothing to do with that.'

'You clearly loved Mr Maitland a great deal.'

'I did. Very much. It was our secret. We were going to start a life together. He was going to become a successful and wealthy investigator and impress my parents so they would agree to our marriage. But now this has happened, and I can't talk to anyone about it. I can't even go to his funeral.'

She fell back into a chair and sobbed some more. Emma glanced at the door, wondering if anybody would hear on the other side of it.

'Please try to compose yourself, Lady Somersham.

'I can't! And I have to keep my feelings hidden. Even though Archie's dead, my parents will disown me if they find out about what happened between us. My reputation will be ruined! How could I ever find myself a husband?'

'It must be very difficult for you,' she said. Lady Somersham's tears seemed genuine, but was it possible she and Maitland had conspired together to murder Charles Harpole?

She sat in the chair next to her and allowed a moment to

pass before she asked her next question. 'So you loved Mr Maitland. But you didn't love Lord Harpole?'

'I thought I loved Charles. I felt sure of it. He was such a pleasant gentleman. And then he employed Mr Maitland to work for him. The moment we met, I couldn't think of anyone else but Archie. I'm a dreadful person. I betrayed my fiancé. And I've betrayed my family too. But I couldn't help how I felt. Once I felt those feelings, I couldn't put them away again!' She turned to face Emma. 'Do I look like I've been crying?' Her eyes were red and puffy and her face tear-stained.

'Yes,' she replied gently.

'Oh dear. Will you sit with me until my face returns to normal?'

'Of course.'

She couldn't upset her further by asking more questions. Her distress was too real.

But had Lady Somersham been the cloaked lady fleeing the Imperial Grand Hotel that night?

SEVENTY-THREE

The following afternoon, Emma arrived at the reading room of the British Museum. She pulled open the heavy door and peered inside. The electric lights were switched on and people worked quietly at the long wooden desks which radiated from the centre of the room. Emma cautiously stepped inside, not wishing to disturb anyone at work. She glanced around, looking for Francis Edwards.

Sitting at the desk on the dais in the centre of the room was a stern-faced man, who she guessed was the head librarian. He stared at her, clearly wondering who she was.

'Mrs Langley?' she heard a whisper at her shoulder.

She turned to see Francis Edwards. He smiled and pushed his spectacles up his nose. 'Are you here to see me?'

'Yes, I am,' said Emma. 'Is there any chance I can meet with you when you finish work here today?'

'Yes, of course. I finish at half past five. That's only an hour away. If you wait for me outside, we can talk then. How's Inspector Blakely? I read about the attack in the newspaper. It's terrible.'

'He's still in hospital,' said Emma. 'But Penny sent me a telegram yesterday to tell me he's woken up.'

'Well, at least that's something. Thank goodness.'

Emma looked in some bookshops nearby to pass the time before returning to meet Francis Edwards. He was already waiting for her when she arrived.

'I hope you don't mind me asking,' she said, 'but I could do with some help. Poor Penny has a lot of other things to think about at the moment and I really want to solve the puzzle which supposedly leads to the treasure. The map has fallen into the wrong hands now and Mr Maitland is no longer around to help. I feel a bit lost but I want to finish what I've started.'

'What sort of help do you need?'

'Well, I think it will take a lot of research. I've heard that Mr Lydney, the founder of the Inveniam Society, uses a lot of books in his research. And you have access to such a vast, impressive library here, surely we're capable of finding something out? If he can do it, then so can we.'

'You're quite right, Mrs Langley. I believe that too. Why don't we go into the library now? I know you don't have a reading ticket, but I'll tell the head librarian you're a friend of mine and I'm helping you with some research.'

'Will he be all right about that?'

'He will if I tell him I'll close the library tonight,' Francis confided with a conspiratorial wink, adjusting his spectacles. His fingers tapped a silent rhythm on the book in his hands, betraying his excitement at their shared adventure. 'Which means he can leave for home a little earlier than usual.'

A short while later, Emma and Francis sat at a desk in the empty reading room, surrounded by piles of books. Several were about Sir Francis Drake, while others were about naval sea battles, Spanish galleons and the British aristocracy.

Francis was flicking through the books, leaving some open at certain pages and writing down notes with a pencil, which he kept tucking behind his ear for safekeeping.

'The Harpole family is actually quite fascinating,' he said. 'I can't say they've ever been an important family in the history of Britain and her empire, but they've done an excellent job of befriending those in power. If you go back through the generations, you can find many informal links to royalty and politicians of the day. And this ancestor, Lord Henry Harpole, he was a friend of Sir Francis Drake's. He appears in a few contemporary accounts of the time.'

'You've found out all this just now?' Emma asked, eyebrows raised.

'No. In fact, I took the liberty of looking into it after the Blakelys' dinner last week. I found the topic quite fascinating, so I thought I'd see what I could find out. Lord Henry Harpole left his wife to live with his Irish mistress.'

'Goodness. How scandalous.'

'Yes, it caused quite a stir at the time. And the two ladies argued long after his death. It's said his mistress exhumed his remains and took the coffin with her to Ireland where she lived out the rest of her days with him reburied in her local churchyard.'

'Is that really true?'

'I don't see why it shouldn't be. The great-grandfather of Lord Harpole, Lord Theobald Harpole, was an interesting gentleman who enjoyed carriage racing and had a large collection of smoking pipes.'

'Smoking pipes? I wonder if the new Lord and Lady Harpole have been lucky enough to inherit those,' remarked Emma.

Francis laughed. 'Lord Theobald Harpole also made his

own velocipede, had a morbid fascination with burial grounds and enjoyed practical jokes and puzzles. He had several puzzles printed in *The Gentleman's Magazine*.'

'Really?' said Emma. 'So that explains why he drew the map and created the symbols. It was a puzzle. He created the trail for people to follow around London to find the treasure.'

'That's right. Apparently he was often asked about the treasure which Sir Francis Drake had supposedly given to his ancestor Henry Harpole. It has been quite an obsession of treasure hunters over the centuries and I get the impression Theobald Harpole got quite annoyed when people asked him about it.'

'Presumably because it was his family's business and no one else's,' said Emma.

'I agree. But there's always been a fascination with Sir Francis Drake's hidden treasures and many people are keen to find them. If Theobald Harpole had been forthcoming about what the treasure was, then it would have lost some of its mysterious appeal.'

'Perhaps he should have explained what the treasure was and the treasure hunters would have left him alone. Is it possible the treasure never existed?'

Francis chuckled. 'What an interesting thought! I've tried to find out exactly what Sir Francis gifted to Henry and what it was worth, but I've been unsuccessful. That doesn't mean it never existed though. There must have been something because Theobald Harpole declared that someone could find it if they solved his treasure trail.'

'It sounds as though he created it for his own enjoyment,' said Emma. 'And for the frustration of the treasure hunters. I wonder how long the trail is.'

'It could stretch to twenty or thirty locations, couldn't it?' replied Francis. 'In which case, it could take someone a year, perhaps even more, to find the location of the supposed hidden treasure. What we need to do is learn what we can about Lord Theobald Harpole and work out where he would have buried it.'

A couple of hours later, Emma and Francis left the reading room and Francis locked up.

Emma thanked him for his help. 'I've made lots of notes,' she said. 'And I'm going to go home and look at them all now and try to make sense of them.'

'It's been a pleasure,' he said. 'I enjoy looking into things like this. I can only hope that something comes of it. Perhaps when James has recovered, you'll be able to discuss it with Penny. She has a sharp mind for these things. I always thought she would make a good detective, although I don't think she ever wanted to be one.'

It was a cold, clear night and a nearby gas lamp illuminated their clouds of breath in the air. Some stars were visible in the night sky.

'Look at that,' said Francis. 'Stars. Usually, the sky is so full of cloud or smoke or fog that it's rare to see them, isn't it? I saw them a lot on my travels, of course. They're quite something when you're in the desert.'

'They must look magical,' said Emma, craning her neck to look up at the sky. 'It must have been difficult coming home again.'

'No, I was ready for it.' A wistful smile played across his features. 'There's nowhere quite like home, is there? It's nice to come back and see everyone.'

His eyes grew distant, remembering. 'While I was away, I often wondered how everyone was getting on. Penny was expecting a child when I left so I knew that when I returned life would be quite different for her. It's been lovely to meet young Thomas and baby Florence.' His smile tightened almost imperceptibly. 'They seem a very happy family indeed.'

'They are,' said Emma. 'Penny misses the work she did before but she enjoys being a mother too. And she's been writing some articles about motherhood for the *Morning Express*.'

'Has she? That doesn't surprise me at all. She's found the perfect way to combine her two passions. Family and writing.' He looked up at the night sky again. 'If we look closely enough at the stars, I wonder if we can see our fate?'

'What do you mean?' asked Emma, puzzled.

He gave a soft laugh. 'The Elizabethans believed their fates were written in the stars, that's why Shakespeare refers to them so often in his plays.'

'Do you believe that?'

'Oh no. The Elizabethans were a superstitious lot and our scientific understanding has improved an awful lot since those days. It's just a thought I like to muse on from time to time. The idea of fate. What if our lives had taken different paths?'

Emma thought of her marriage to William Langley, her fingers unconsciously twisting her wedding ring. 'I often wish I'd taken a different path,' she admitted quietly.

'But maybe you couldn't?' Francis's voice softened. 'Maybe fate decided for you?' His cheeks coloured slightly. 'Actually, there's no need to respond. I think I'm just in an introspective mood.'

'I think you're making an interesting point,' said Emma, meeting his gaze. 'Perhaps I couldn't avoid marrying William, perhaps fate decided that for me.' She paused, her voice barely audible. 'Perhaps fate made me fall in love with him.'

'Ah yes. Love. Is that decided by fate? It can certainly feel like it. It's funny, when I... Oh, forget about it. It's late. How will you get home?'

'I'll walk. It's just over a mile away.'

'No, you can't walk alone in the dark, I'll help you find a cab.'

He began to walk down the steps.

'What were you going to say?'

'Say?' His shadowy silhouette turned to face her. 'Nothing.'

'Yes you were. You said "it's funny" and then you said "forget about it".'

'Oh that. It was nothing.'

'No it wasn't. It was something. And I was enjoying our conversation so I want to hear it.'

He sighed. 'All right. But it's not important. It's that idea of love being decided by fate or not. It's funny because there was a time when I proposed marriage to Penny.'

Emma smiled with genuine surprise. 'Did you?' she asked softly, 'I didn't know that.'

'It's quite obvious she declined,' he said. 'She was in love with James Blakely, you see. She was in love with him and I was in love with her. And that's fate I suppose. She and I were never meant to get married, despite my feelings for her.'

Emma felt sympathy for him. She'd heard unrequited love was painful. 'It's possible to love more than one person,' she said. 'I'm sure you'll meet someone one day who—'

'Yes that's what I've been telling myself for some years now. I'm not sure it's true though.' He turned and continued down the steps.

SEVENTY-FOUR

The hansom cab stopped in Northampton Square, and Emma paid the driver and disembarked. Francis had offered to give her money for the fare because he'd insisted on her travelling home in a cab, but she had assured him there was no need for him to do so. She smiled as she recalled his kindness.

She was just approaching the Solomons' house when she heard a voice.

'Mrs Langley.'

She spun around, her heart thudding in her chest. A tall, lean man stepped into the light beneath a gas lamp. His appearance startled her. His face was thin, and the overhead light cast dark shadows in the hollows of his cheeks. An eye patch covered one eye.

She backed cautiously towards her home; she was only yards from safety.

'There's no need to be alarmed, Mrs Langley. I don't mean you any harm. It's nice to meet you at last. My name is Stephen Lydney.'

She climbed up the steps backwards so that she was standing right by the front door.

'If you come any closer to me, I shall shout and scream and make such a noise that the police will be called.'

He held out a palm and remained where he was. 'Please don't be anxious. As I've already said, Mrs Langley, I don't mean you any harm. I thought it would be nice to meet and discuss all this silly nonsense. After all, it began with your husband, didn't it?'

'Yes. He gave you money didn't he? Why?'

Mr Lydney nodded. 'He was very generous. My society is funded by investors. They pay me to carry out my research and when I recover lost treasure, they share in the spoils. They get a generous return on their money.'

'Did William receive anything?'

'Sadly... his untimely death meant that—'

'He didn't receive anything, did he?' Her hands tightened at her sides. 'And do you know where he got the money from? He stole it. From me. I inherited it after my parents died and he stole it all. Perhaps you could return the money to me?'

He rubbed his brow and gave an awkward laugh. 'It's not quite as simple as that, Mrs Langley. The money has been—'

'No, I don't suppose it is simple to return it. It never is with people like you, is it?' Her jaw ached with anger and she worried now she might antagonize him. She backed against the door, one hand on the handle.

'I'm very sorry to hear your husband stole that money from you,' said Mr Lydney. 'I thought he was a decent gentleman and I liked him very much. I'd assumed he'd come by it by legitimate means. It's a shame when you hear something disappointing about someone.'

Emma wanted him to leave. 'I don't have the map anymore,' she said. 'I don't know where it is. It was stolen from Lord and Lady Harpole.'

'Ah, but who does it really belong to? The previous Lord Harpole agreed to share the map with me. We had an agreement. I don't believe the Harpoles have a right to it anymore. But what does it matter? You probably don't need it now, do you?'

Emma said nothing.

'I know you and Mrs Blakely won't rest until you have answers,' continued Mr Lydney. 'But it's a very dangerous business, you know. If you didn't realize that before poor Maitland was murdered, then surely you've realized it now.'

Emma's stomach gave a turn. 'You murdered him?'

'Do I look like the sort of man who would do such a thing?'

'Did you attack Inspector Blakely?'

He laughed and shook his head. 'Goodness, you appear to have a terribly low opinion of me, Mrs Langley.' He took a step towards her and her hand tightened on the door handle.

'It's cold out here,' he said. 'You'd better get inside. And once you're in there, I advise you stay there. Ladies like you and Mrs Blakely have no business getting involved in these matters. If you continue on this fool's errand, you will have to pay a price.'

Emma said nothing, but her heart thudded heavily in her chest. His eye stared unblinkingly at her.

Then he turned and vanished into the darkness.

SEVENTY-FIVE

Emma slept badly that night. Whenever she closed her eyes, she saw Lydney's gaunt features, shadowy beneath the gas lamp. How long had he been waiting there for her?

Although he'd kept his distance she'd felt threatened. His appearance had been a warning. She shivered. She couldn't bear the thought of him returning.

Deciding she couldn't possibly return to sleep with her mind so active, Emma rose and lit the gas lamp. The warm glow cast long shadows across her small room as she retrieved the notes she'd made during her research with Francis. She climbed back into bed, spreading the papers across her eiderdown.

His handwriting mingled with hers on the pages – neat, precise annotations beside her more hurried script. She hadn't found time yet to properly review all he'd shared. Now, in the quiet solitude of night, she carefully read through each page, reorganizing and refining the information, determined to extract every useful thread from the tangled skein of history.

Francis had told her they needed to learn what they could about Lord Theobald Harpole and work out where he would have buried the treasure. She recalled his carriage racing, pipe collection and interest in old graveyards. Then she read her notes about Lord Henry Harpole and how his body had reportedly been moved to Ireland by his mistress. She couldn't imagine how his mistress had managed that. Had she employed gravediggers to help her? Why did no one try to stop her? It was probably just a silly story, but Emma had noted that Henry Harpole had first been buried in the churchyard of St Bartholomew the Great in Smithfield. It was an old and well-known church next to St Bartholomew's Hospital.

She turned to her notes on the eccentric Lord Theobald Harpole and how he'd enjoyed practical jokes and puzzles. An idea came to her. She considered it for a while, then put it out of her mind. It seemed too obvious. But was it?

She sighed and made some notes in her notebook. She decided she'd discuss them tomorrow with Penny. She closed her notebook, gathered her papers together and put them to one side. Then she turned out her light, lay down in the dark and tried to get back to sleep again.

The following day, she called on Penny.

Penny looked weary, but was pleased to see her. 'James is getting better every day, and he'll be out of hospital soon.'

'That's wonderful news.'

'I read about Maitland's death in the newspaper,' said Penny. 'So much has happened in just a few days.'

Emma told her what she knew about Maitland's death and then about Stephen Lydney's visit.

Penny shuddered. 'Something needs to be done about him. He shouldn't be allowed to wait for you in the dark like that. I would have been terrified. I'm very impressed you didn't scream for the police.'

'I was close to it,' said Emma. 'But I wanted to see if he had anything useful to say for himself.'

'Did he?'

'No, not really. I think he just wanted to intimidate me. And to be honest with you, it worked. I hardly slept last night.'

Penny reached out and held her hand. 'I'm sorry to hear it, Emma. This sorry business needs to come to an end, doesn't it?'

'I think Lydney stole the map from the Harpoles, though.'

'Oh dear, really? So he's going to get his hands on the treasure after all.'

'I hope not. I decided I needed some more help, so I called on Francis Edwards.'

'Excellent.' Penny smiled. 'I'm sure he would have appreciated that. He enjoys being involved with working out puzzles. Was he helpful?'

'Yes, very. He gave me lots of information.'

'That sounds like Francis.'

'And while I was awake last night worrying about Stephen Lydney, I had a thought about the puzzle.' Emma explained to her what Francis had told her about Lord Harpole's ancestors. 'I think I know where the hidden treasure could be buried.'

'Really?' said Penny. 'You've worked it out?'

'I think it lies in Lord Henry Harpole's grave in the churchyard of St Bartholomew the Great.'

Penny's jaw dropped. 'How did you work that out?'

'I can't say I'm completely certain. But apparently his body was moved to Ireland by his mistress, and that means that Henry's grave could be empty – unless they've since buried other family members there. But if it's empty, then it would be the perfect burial place for treasure, wouldn't it? Apparently, Lord Harpole's great-grandfather, Lord Theobald Harpole, had lots of eccentric interests, and one of them was exploring old graveyards. Perhaps Theobald buried the treasure in Henry's empty grave. That's where I think the trail ultimately leads to. And I think that explains the cross marked in each of the clues. Perhaps his grave is marked with a cross?'

'Yes, that's what it could mean! Well, I suppose we'll have to find out. Although we can't go digging in the grave, can we? We'll have to speak to the vicar at the church there and see what he makes of the theory. And if there is a possibility it's there, then I suppose we'll have to involve the new Lord Harpole and his wife, Lady Harpole. It's their business after all, isn't it? But at least we'll have hopefully helped the Harpole family be reunited with the lost riches.'

A pause followed. Emma wondered if Penny was thinking the same as her – that the Harpole family didn't exactly need to be reunited with their lost riches. But if they were correct, then it drew the puzzle to a close, and they could feel relieved that Stephen Lydney hadn't got his hands on the treasure.

'So that settles it,' said Penny. 'Let's go and have a look.'

SEVENTY-SIX

Snow clouds had gathered after the clear night and snowflakes fell as Emma and Penny approached the beamed Tudor gatehouse leading to the church.

Once they'd passed through the gateway, they saw the church ahead of them. To their left was a small graveyard.

'This must be where Lord Henry Harpole was buried,' said Emma, feeling her heart pound with excitement.

The graves were old, and many of the headstones were crooked and worn. Ivy, lichen and dirt covered the inscriptions, and they had to wipe the stones clean with their gloved hands to read the lettering.

Snow gently settled on the tombstones and graves. A lone blackbird sung a tune from a nearby yew tree.

Emma and Penny moved silently between the tombstones, searching for the grave belonging to Lord Henry Harpole. Before long, they'd covered the small graveyard.

'He's not here?' said Penny. 'I struggle to believe it.'

Emma's shoulders sank. 'Perhaps I was foolish for thinking I'd solved it.'

'Just a minute,' said Penny, stepping over to a corner of the graveyard. 'Did we check this section?'

Emma realized they'd overlooked it. Three old sunken tombstones occupied the corner. They had probably once stood taller and prouder but they'd slumped and sunk over the centuries.

One of the headstones was shaped like a cross. In front of it was a small patch of freshly dug earth. Emma's heart dropped like a stone. 'No, this can't be true.'

'Someone's already been here?' Penny asked.

'We don't know yet whether this is Lord Henry Harpole's headstone,' said Emma. She stepped over to it, stooped down, and peered at the gravestone. The letters were just about visible. She traced them with her gloved finger. Sure enough, she could make out the word "Lord" and then "Henry", followed by "Harpole". Beneath the lettering were the dates: 1770 to 1835.

'It's him, all right.' She got to her feet. 'And someone has had the audacity to dig into his grave!'

'Lydney,' hissed Penny.

Snowflakes were already covering the disturbed earth. Before long the grave would rest under a blanket of snow and no one would ever know Lydney had been here.

'I remember James saying he was very diligent with his research,' said Penny. 'We had Francis Edwards to help us, but it seems that Stephen Lydney is just as clever.'

'I don't know why I feel disappointed,' Emma said. 'If you think about it, that treasure was stolen in the first place. Sir Francis Drake then gave it to a friend, but it wasn't his to give away, was it? And then it's been the property of a wealthy family for centuries. Until recently, the family had forgotten it even existed. It wasn't exactly a noble endeavour, was it?'

Penny smiled and took Emma's arm, her steps lighter despite their disappointment. 'You're absolutely right, Emma. No one truly deserved that treasure in the end.'

She squeezed Emma's arm affectionately. 'I suppose what really disappoints me is that we wanted to solve the puzzle ourselves. The challenge was the real treasure, wasn't it?' Her expression brightened. 'And we did solve it – just not quite quickly enough to beat Lydney to the punch.'

Her practical nature reasserted itself as she gestured towards the disturbed grave. 'However, someone has desecrated this resting place, which is both disrespectful and illegal. I think we should find the church authorities and report it immediately.'

SEVENTY-SEVEN

Emma and Penny warmed themselves in a restaurant advertising four-pence dinners near Smithfield meat market.

The vicar of St Bartholomew the Great had been perturbed to hear the grave of Lord Henry Harpole had been tampered with and told them he'd tell the sexton to look into it.

'Let's forget about the treasure for now,' said Penny. 'It was a bit of fun to begin with, wasn't it? But the resolution was disappointing. And as you rightly pointed out, Emma, do the Harpole family really deserve their treasure anyway?'

'They particularly don't deserve it if they're murderers,' said Emma.

'You think Richard Harpole could have murdered his brother?'

'I think he's the most obvious person. He's inherited a large estate. And he chose the perfect time to do it. His brother was due to be married, and if the marriage had produced an heir, then Richard Harpole had no chance of inheriting Wickham House. However, if he could somehow stage his brother's murder as a suicide, then not only would he inherit the estate, but he would also be free of suspicion because everyone would believe his brother had committed suicide.'

'It makes sense,' said Penny. 'But I don't think it can be Richard Harpole. James established he had an alibi, didn't he? In fact, he had several alibis. The servants in the Harpole household said he was at home that evening.'

Emma sighed. 'This is so difficult. Whenever you think you've cracked it, a complication arises. Do you think it's possible Richard Harpole persuaded his entire staff of servants to lie for him?'

Penny shook her head. 'I think it's unlikely. If he had then I think at least one of them would have examined their conscience and come forward by now. I just don't think it's possible.'

'So who's left? Lady Somersham and Joseph Campbell,' said Emma. 'Lady Somersham could have murdered her fiancé so she could have a love affair with Archibald Maitland. But it seems she knew her family would never have approved of a relationship with him, anyway. So would she really have risked so much to murder him? I think we have to speak to Joseph Campbell again. He denies arguing with Lord Harpole on the morning of his death, and yet many people are certain the argument took place. And furthermore, he's been dismissed by the new Lord Harpole for apparently stealing from his brother. So perhaps Richard Harpole suspected Campbell murdered his brother and got rid of Campbell before he could do the same to him?'

'So Joseph Campbell could have murdered him for the map?' said Penny.

'Yes, that's the only motive I can think of at the moment. I would like to speak to him again after my last disastrous attempt. I don't know where to find him, but if I call on Lord and Lady Harpole, perhaps they might tell me.'

SEVENTY-EIGHT

Stephen Lydney gave the tin chest a gentle shake, just to reassure himself it had something inside. In fact, it felt quite full. He grinned and proudly placed it in the centre of his round table.

The story about Henry Harpole's grave had been true! He hadn't enjoyed digging in a graveyard in the middle of the night, but he'd been rewarded for his efforts.

The chest had a small, rusty padlock on it, which he would be able to prise off with his pliers. His hands trembled with excitement as he took the pliers out of a drawer. He'd always told the members of the Inveniam Society that any finds would be opened in front of everyone. But now that he finally had some treasure, he couldn't wait until they were all together. Instead, he would look at it now and then pretend to open it for the first time at their next gathering.

He pushed his monocle into his eye and set to work with the pliers on the padlock. It took a lot of strength to break it, but eventually the metal thread of the padlock bent and gave way.

How ancient was this box? He wondered if it was an original chest dating back to the sixteenth century. Was it possible that Sir Francis Drake had handled it himself? He pictured the moment Sir Francis Drake had handed it over to his dear friend, Lord Henry Harpole – a gift he had brought back from his travels around the globe. Gold coins and jewellery from a Spanish port or galleon. The Harpole family had lost their rights to this treasure through their own foolhardiness. The secret had lain in their own family for all these years, forgotten. But now, the treasure was his.

He took in a breath, then slowly and carefully lifted the lid. He could feel the grit scraping in the hinges as he opened it.

His immediate thought was that the contents of the chest looked dull. The treasure had presumably tarnished over time.

He peered in to take a closer look. All he could see were some old smoking pipes. He pushed his hand in, assuming the treasure lay beneath them. But he found more pipes.

Frustrated, he picked up the chest and emptied it out onto the table. Old pipes scattered across it; some fell off the edge and bounced onto the floor.

There was no sign of any treasure. Had he made a mistake? He could only assume there'd been another chest buried in the grave which he'd missed. He had to get back there.

Then a slip of paper caught his eye and he picked it up. Turning it over, he saw it was a short, handwritten note:

Congratulations. You have found the treasure! It may not be what you had hoped for, but you solved the clues to find it and I commend you for that.

I hope you enjoy my precious pipe collection, it gave me many years of joy.

Lord T Harpole

Lydney clenched his fists and let out a violent roar of anger.

SEVENTY-NINE

Emma called at the Harpoles' home in Brompton Square in Knightsbridge. Even the snow was cleaner and prettier in this wealthy part of London.

'I'm afraid Lord Harpole is out at the moment,' said the maid who answered the door, 'and Lady Harpole has been taken unwell.'

'Oh dear,' said Emma. 'I'm sorry to hear it. Actually, you may be able to help me yourself. Do you mind if I ask your name?'

'Minnie.'

'Thank you, Minnie. I'm looking for Lord Harpole's former valet, Mr Campbell. Do you know where I can find him?'

'I don't know myself, but I can ask for you,' Minnie offered, her eyes darting nervously to check if anyone might overhear.

'Thank you. Do you know why he was dismissed by Lord Harpole?' Emma kept her voice casual.

Minnie leaned closer, her voice dropping to a conspiratorial whisper. 'He'd been stealing from Lord Harpole's brother,' she confided, her eyes wide. 'Valuable items, they say. When Lord Harpole found out, he dismissed him on the spot.' She straightened, smoothing her apron anxiously. 'Never seen the master so angry before.'

'That's interesting to hear. Thank you, Minnie.'

'I'll ask Mrs Simmons, the housekeeper, where you can find Mr Campbell,' added the maid.

A short while later, she returned with an address written on a piece of paper.

'Thank you, Minnie,' said Emma. 'You've been very helpful.'

EIGHTY

Joseph Campbell had taken rooms in a rundown lodging house near Victoria railway station. It stood on a mean-looking, narrow street – a stark contrast to the comfortable, wealthy homes he'd worked in before.

The wiry-haired landlady of the lodging house told Emma she could talk with Campbell in her parlour. The pair sat at a dainty table covered with a lace tablecloth. Small, framed pictures of animals adorned the walls, and a row of china cats was neatly arranged along the mantelpiece.

'What do you want from me, Mrs Langley?' asked Campbell glumly. His appearance was more dishevelled since they'd last met. He wore a brown woollen suit, old-fashioned and worn, and his shoulders slumped.

'Have you heard about Mr Maitland's murder?' Emma asked.

'Of course I have. I was very saddened to hear about it. He was a good man.'

'Do you know who did it?'

'Of course not! It's been a complete shock.'

'He told me he met with you shortly before his death.'

'Yes. It's a shame I didn't get better acquainted with him sooner. I remember Lord Harpole – the proper Lord Harpole – employing him. We didn't speak much initially, but I discovered, sadly too late, that he was a decent chap.'

'Can you think of anyone who would have wanted to murder him?'

'I don't know what my opinion is worth, Mrs Langley. You can see what's happened to me, haven't you? I'm renting a small room in this house having been dismissed from my employment. Eventually my savings will run out. There are no prospects of another position at this time. I'm old and my reputation is in tatters.'

'And this is because you stole from Lord Charles Harpole?'

He shrugged. 'Call it that if you like.'

'Did you argue with Lord Harpole about the theft on the morning of his death?'

He sneered. 'That maid was mistaken.'

'But she wasn't, was she? She was certain she heard you and Lord Harpole arguing. You don't want to admit it because you're worried you'll be accused of murdering him.'

Mr Campbell rubbed a hand over his unshaven chin. 'I was defending myself.' He pointed a finger at her and lowered his voice. 'I didn't murder him, though. And I don't know who did. It probably had something to do with this map nonsense.'

'What did you and Mr Maitland discuss when you met?' asked Emma.

'That's our business, I'm afraid, Mrs Langley.'

'Even though Mr Maitland is now dead?'

He gave her a stern look. 'I was sworn to secrecy, and I stand by that.'

Emma decided to change the subject. 'Do you think Richard Harpole murdered his brother?' she asked.

He sat back in his chair. 'That's a very direct question, Mrs Langley. My answer is no. He couldn't have done.'

'Why are you so sure? He's benefited a great deal from his brother's death.'

'He has, for the time being. There's been a delay with the paperwork since his brother's death and the will appears to have been mislaid. If you ask me, someone hid it. But the truth will come out before long.'

'What do you mean?' asked Emma.

'I can't say.' He folded his arms.

'But you must! If he can easily be ruled out as his brother's murderer, then please tell me why.'

He scratched his chin and looked up at the corner of the room as he thought. 'Very well,' he said. 'Richard Harpole is illegitimate.'

Emma gasped. 'So he's not actually Charles Harpole's brother?'

'They shared the same mother, but not the same father.'

'And does Richard Harpole know that?'

'Oh yes. He's known for a few years, ever since their mother died. She confessed it to Charles Harpole on her deathbed. But it was kept a family secret, as these things always are.'

'Tell me more.'

'Very well. When the elder Lord Harpole died early last year, his estate passed to his eldest son, Charles. The fact his younger son, Richard, was illegitimate didn't matter to anyone. The elder Lord Harpole never knew that Richard wasn't his son. Charles and Richard decided not to tell him because he adored his wife. I can vouch for that. The shock of the news would have killed him. Despite his illegitimacy, Richard Harpole very much remained part of the Harpole family.'

'But it mattered when Lord Charles Harpole was murdered,' said Emma.

'Oh yes. It matters very much now. Richard has inherited

an estate that doesn't belong to him. It's not officially his yet because of the administrative delays, but he's enjoying living as though it is.'

'Who else knows?' asked Emma.

'Until a few days ago, only Charles and Richard knew. And I knew because Charles confided in me. It was a secret I kept... until I needed to use it.'

'What do you mean by that?' Emma pressed, noting how Campbell's demeanour had changed.

'I used the information for revenge.' A cold gleam appeared in his eyes as he leaned forward. 'When Richard Harpole dismissed me, I sought out Mr Maitland. I knew he was also displeased by a recent encounter he'd had with him.' His voice dropped to a whisper. 'So the two of us hatched a plan.'

'And what was the plan?' Emma's heartbeat quickened.

Campbell's face transformed with an unexpected smile – the first Emma had ever seen from him. It wasn't pleasant; it crawled across his face like something predatory. 'Blackmail,' he announced with obvious satisfaction.

Emma nearly gasped. 'You blackmailed Richard Harpole? What happened? Did he pay you?'

Campbell rubbed his palms together with barely contained excitement. 'We sent a note demanding a hundred pounds be sent to the General Post Office in St Martin's Le Grand for a man called Frank Duncan.'

'Who's he?'

'An alias we used. But nothing came of it because Archibald Maitland was murdered.'

'He was murdered because he was blackmailing Richard Harpole?'

'I've already told you, I don't know who murdered him. I don't know how Richard Harpole could have known the identity of his blackmailers. And I'm still here, aren't I?'

'So there would have been no point in Richard Harpole

murdering his brother,' said Emma. 'Because he knew he wouldn't be able to inherit the Harpole family fortune. Even though he's tried to do so, he'll be found out eventually.'

'That's exactly right,' said Mr Campbell. 'And I'm very much looking forward to the day that happens.'

EIGHTY-ONE

Emma left Joseph Campbell's lodging house wondering if he'd been honest with her. He'd seemed earnest enough, but was he the murderer?

She had more questions for the Harpoles' maid, Minnie. With Lord Harpole out and Lady Harpole indisposed, she reasoned now was a good time to return.

As she approached the house, she noticed the narrow passageway at the side which presumably led to the rear. It must have been the route the intruder had taken to steal the map.

Feeling nosy, Emma opened the gate and went down the passageway. At the back of the house, a long snow-covered garden stretched ahead of her to the mews at the far end.

The house was four storeys high and had a single-storey section built onto the back. It looked more recent than the rest of the house and its paned doors and tall windows suggested to Emma it was a summer room or something similar. It had a good view of the garden.

She looked up at the roof of the summer room, which gently sloped to meet the main part of the house. Just above the roof was a large sash window, which she guessed the burglar had slid open to get into the house.

But how had the burglar got onto the summer house roof? She glanced around but could see no way he'd climbed up there. Had it been Rupert Crowfield? Or Stephen Lydney? Whoever it had been, they were clearly good at climbing.

'Mrs Langley?'

The voice startled her. She turned to see Minnie addressing her from a ground-floor window.

Her mind worked quickly as she tried to come up with an explanation. She couldn't think of anything.

'Oh, I'm sorry, Minnie,' she smiled. 'You've caught me being very nosy, I'm afraid. I heard about the burglary at this house, and I was wondering how someone had found it so easy to get in. I should have asked your permission before I came here, and it really is none of my business. I'm sorry.'

Minnie smiled nervously, her fingers twisting in her apron. 'They got in frightfully easily,' she admitted, glancing over her shoulder as though her employer might materialize at any moment. 'They climbed up onto that roof and got in through the window there.' She pointed with a trembling finger.

'But how did they reach the roof?' Emma asked, studying the considerable height.

'There was a water butt there, just below.' Minnie's voice quickened with the thrill of sharing forbidden information. 'Lord Harpole ordered it to be moved after the break-in. And there's a lock on the window now too, so no one can get in again.' She shivered visibly. 'It terrifies me to think someone was walking around the house like that while we were all asleep.'

'Yes, it must have been dreadful,' said Emma sympathetically. Encouraged by Minnie's openness, she leaned closer. 'I've been wondering about something else, Minnie. Do you mind if I ask you a few more questions?'

EIGHTY-TWO

Emma called on Penny the following day and was delighted to find James at home. He sat in an armchair, his face still badly bruised.

'You're looking well, James,' said Emma.

'No I don't,' he replied. 'I look awful.'

'But hopefully you're feeling better?'

'Yes, a lot better, thank you, Emma. I'm just impatient to get back to work again.'

'Well, you shouldn't be,' said Penny firmly. 'You need to take all the time you can to rest.'

'Daddy's poorly,' said Thomas.

'He's getting better now,' replied Emma.

'I've got a train.' He held it out for her to see.

'It's a very nice train. You like trains, don't you?'

Thomas nodded and resumed his game on the hearthrug.

'Have you any idea who attacked you?' Emma asked James.

'I suspect it was either Rupert Crowfield or Stephen Lydney, but neither of them can be found at the moment.'

'Stephen Lydney has probably escaped abroad with his treasure,' said Penny.

'If he has, he won't get far. We'll find him,' said James confidently. 'I feel sure of it.'

Penny turned to Emma. 'How did you get on with Mr Campbell yesterday?'

'Quite well, actually. He was friendlier this time, even though he's down on his luck.' Emma recounted her conversation with Joseph Campbell.

'So Richard Harpole is illegitimate?' said Penny. 'And yet he's parading around pretending to be Lord Harpole when it isn't his title at all!'

'That's very interesting,' said James. 'It seems unlikely that he murdered Charles Harpole. He had nothing to gain from it, did he?'

'But he gains if everyone believes he's entitled to the estate,' said Penny. 'I wonder what's happened to the will?'

'Campbell thinks someone could have hidden it,' said Emma. 'Richard Harpole, probably.'

'He'll get caught out,' said James. 'If Campbell knows then he's not going to sit back and allow him to assume the title of Lord Harpole.'

'Campbell had better be careful he's not murdered for knowing it,' said Penny, her expression grim. 'I think Richard Harpole could be ruthless when cornered.'

'His wife certainly is,' said Emma suddenly, her voice taking on a certainty that made both James and Penny turn to her in surprise.

'Richard Harpole didn't murder his brother – I'm convinced of that now. However,' she leaned forward, her eyes intense, 'I believe Constance Harpole did.'

'Constance?' James's eyebrows shot up in disbelief. 'But she's spent much of the past few weeks laid up in bed with illness.'

'Exactly,' said Emma. 'It's been the perfect way to escape

detection, hasn't it? The ailing wife who never leaves her room – what better alibi?'

'No,' said James, shaking his head firmly. 'When I spoke to Richard Harpole about the evening of his brother's death, he told me Constance had a fever. The servants confirmed it.'

'She pretended she had a fever,' said Emma. 'She pretended because she was planning Charles Harpole's murder.'

'But why?' asked Penny. 'Why would she do that when she knew her husband was illegitimate and couldn't rightfully inherit the estate?'

'Because when she murdered Lord Charles Harpole, she didn't know her husband was illegitimate. He must have kept it from her. I suspect she's now discovered the truth.'

A pause followed as Penny and James considered this.

'Interesting,' said James. 'She must have been devastated when she found out the truth. Although I still don't understand how she could have murdered her brother-in-law when she was bedridden with a fever.'

'Emma has already said she didn't have a fever – it was all an act,' said Penny. 'Constance probably did what I once did when I faked a fever to avoid lessons with my governess. I sat by the fire in the nursery until I overheated, then convinced my mother I was ill. It worked remarkably well.'

James smiled. 'I can imagine you causing your mother a lot of trouble, Penny. But back to Constance Harpole. She was bedridden. What did she do? Sneak out when no one was looking?'

'That's exactly what she did,' said Emma. 'It was easy for an intruder to get into their house, and it was just as easy for her to get out too.'

EIGHTY-THREE

'I visited the Harpole house twice yesterday,' explained Emma. 'And I spoke with a maid called Minnie on both occasions. She told me Constance Harpole fell unwell two days before Charles Harpole's death. She retired to her bedchamber and Minnie and another maid called Jane looked after her. Apparently Constance occasionally asked to be left undisturbed for a few hours.'

'So she could sneak out of the window?' said James.

'I think so,' said Emma. 'Constance must have known her brother-in-law planned to spend a few days in London. This allowed her to begin feigning illness a few days before his arrival. She clearly prepared well. She would have obtained the whisky and laudanum from somewhere. Maybe she had such items in the house already or maybe she went out to purchase them. She must have written her brother-in-law's suicide note in advance so she could leave it on the table with the empty bottles.'

'How chilling!' commented Penny.

'Minnie says at half past four on the evening of Charles Harpole's death, Constance requested to be left alone for three hours so she could sleep undisturbed. During that time, Constance must have dressed and put on her cloak. She presumably chose a cloak because it had a hood and she could conceal her identity. Then she escaped from the house with the whisky and laudanum. It was dark and foggy so few people would have seen her leaving. The Imperial Grand Hotel is a mile from the Harpoles' home and I think she could have covered the distance in about twenty minutes. I think she may have got there around five o'clock. Maybe someone in the hotel noticed her arrive.'

'I'll tell Fenton to speak to the hotel staff again,' said James. 'Someone must have noticed a cloaked lady arriving at around five o'clock that day.'

'They must have done,' said Penny.

'Charles Harpole could have been surprised when his sister-in-law arrived at his hotel room, I don't know for sure,' continued Emma. 'But he was clearly happy to have a drink or two with her. My guess is she poured the whisky out of his sight so she could add the laudanum without him noticing. As soon as he showed signs of illness and incapacity, Constance left.'

'Shortly before six,' said Penny. 'Because that's when we met, wasn't it?'

'That's right,' said Emma. 'She'd just rushed out of the hotel, losing her cloak pin on the way. Perhaps she'd fastened it hastily in the hotel room in her hurry to leave and it wasn't properly closed.'

'We encountered the doorman picking up her cloak pin from the floor, didn't we?' said Penny. She turned to her husband. 'The police should speak to him too.'

James nodded.

'I'm sure the cloak pin is hers,' said Emma. 'Because Minnie told me that a few days later, Constance asked her to go to the hotel and collect the cloak pin.'

'Was Minnie not suspicious about that request?' asked James.

'I don't think she questioned it,' said Emma. 'It is suspicious when you consider it now. But Minnie's is only fifteen or sixteen years old and she was following her employer's orders. I asked her about the cloak pin because the hotel told us it had been collected by a maid.'

'So Constance rushed back home and climbed into the house and went back to bed?' said James.

'Yes, she must have,' said Emma. 'She could have got home again by twenty past six.'

'And Richard Harpole was none the wiser,' said Penny. 'This all makes sense.'

'And there's something else I remembered last night,' said Emma. 'Something which struck me as odd at the time but I didn't dwell on it. I wish now that I had. Do you remember when we spoke with Richard and Constance Harpole after the inquest, Penny?'

'Yes, I do.'

'And Constance said something which gave her away. When her husband commented that everyone at the scene of his brother's death had a tough job, Constance agreed. She then remarked how dark the room must have been and how awful it would be to see a dying man in the chair in front of you. Her words put a picture in my mind. And it was the same picture of the scene. She'd described it as if she'd been there.'

'Which she had!' said Penny. 'How else would she have known the room was dark and that Charles Harpole was in a chair facing the door?'

'And when we saw her at the inquest, she appeared to have made a remarkable recovery from her fever hadn't she?' said Emma. 'I thought she looked very well indeed.'

'Good point,' said James.

'And what about the notepad the suicide note was written

on?' said Penny. 'And the pen? They're probably in her bedchamber.'

'The police need to search the room,' said James.

'But what about Archibald Maitland?' said Penny. 'Constance Harpole couldn't have murdered him, could she?'

'I think she could,' said Emma. 'Joseph Campbell told me he and Maitland tried to blackmail Richard Harpole and threatened to reveal his secret. I suspect Constance found out about the blackmail attempt and the truth about her husband's illegitimacy. I think she decided to silence Maitland.'

'But how would she have known he was one of the people behind the blackmail?' asked Penny.

'Mr Campbell told me they sent Richard Harpole a note asking for one hundred pounds be sent to the General Post Office in St Martin's Le Grand for a man called Frank Duncan.'

Penny nodded. 'And now I understand. All Constance Harpole had to do was visit the post office and ask them to look out for a Frank Duncan collecting the money and to give her a description of him.'

James nodded. 'She would have soon worked out who it was.'

'We need to tell Inspector Fenton,' said Penny. 'And Inspector Trotter, too.'

'Good idea,' said James. 'It sounds like you need to explain everything to them. I just wish I could come with you, but I'm not up to it. This needs to be put to the Harpoles, and then we'll see what Constance has to say for herself.'

EIGHTY-FOUR

'I refuse to let all of you into my house!' said Lord Harpole. 'There are too many of you!' Emma and Penny stood at the doorway of his home with Inspector Fenton, Inspector Trotter and two police constables.

'And who's he?' Lord Harpole pointed past them. Emma turned to see Harry Wright behind them on the steps. She couldn't resist a smile.

'Harry Wright, from the *Morning Express* newspaper, my lord,' he said.

'Not now, Mr Wright,' said Inspector Trotter. 'Leave, please, and I'll update you once we're done here.'

Mr Wright flashed Emma a conspiratorial wink before tipping his hat and striding purposefully down the steps, his notebook already in hand.

'We would like to speak with your wife, Lord Harpole,' said Inspector Fenton.

'I'm afraid you can't,' replied Lord Harpole. 'She's currently unwell in bed. Now, perhaps you can tell me what this is all about?'

'Perhaps we can go into a room where you can sit down, my

lord. What you're about to hear may come as quite a shock to you.'

They were admitted into the house and followed Lord Harpole into the drawing room. He stood by the fire with his hands behind his back.

'Do you not wish to sit down, my lord?' asked Fenton, gesturing to a nearby chair.

'No, I'm quite fine standing, thank you.' Lord Harpole planted his feet firmly, arms crossed defensively. 'Now, what is this intrusion about?'

'I'm afraid this won't be easy for you to hear,' Fenton began, his voice carefully measured, 'but we are here to arrest your wife on suspicion of murder.'

Lord Harpole's jaw dropped, and he staggered sideways as though physically struck, his hand grasping blindly for support. Inspector Trotter stepped forward quickly, catching his him and guiding him into a nearby chair.

'Constance?' he gasped, his voice barely audible. Murder? Murder who?' His hands trembled visibly as they gripped the armrests.

'Lord Charles Harpole and Mr Archibald Maitland.'

'Never!' Lord Harpole surged halfway out of his seat, face flushing crimson. 'Constance would never do such a thing! You've got this completely wrong!' Spittle flew from his lips as he shouted.

'I think it's best we speak with her now, my lord,' said Inspector Fenton, moving towards the drawing room door.

'Just wait! I shall fetch her and ask her about this ridiculous nonsense. You'll see that she had nothing to do with any of it.'

They waited as Lord Harpole went upstairs. Minutes passed. Then a few more.

'Oh, damn it,' muttered Inspector Fenton. 'I'm going up there myself.' He'd just left the room when he returned, accompanied by a bewildered-looking Lord Harpole.

'I can't find my wife,' said Lord Harpole, his face ashen with confusion. He stood in the doorway, swaying slightly. 'She's not in her bedchamber.' The implication of her absence slowly dawned in his eyes, horror replacing bewilderment. 'Oh God... What has she done?'

EIGHTY-FIVE

'Search the house,' ordered Detective Inspector Fenton. The constables left the drawing room. Lord Harpole scratched his head, his brow furrowed with concern.

'She could have got out through the window again,' said Emma.

'Got out through the window?' said Lord Harpole. 'What on earth are you talking about?'

'We think she's done it before,' said Penny, hurriedly. 'We'll check outside.'

On the front steps, they encountered Harry Wright.

'A lady just ran out from the back of the house,' he said. 'In her nightdress!'

'Why didn't you stop her?' asked Emma.

'She took me by surprise! I didn't know what she was doing.'

'It's Lady Harpole,' said Penny, glancing up and down the street.

'Lady Harpole?' gasped Mr Wright. 'What's she doing running off in her nightdress? She went that way, towards Hyde Park.'

'Let's go,' said Penny.

Emma's feet slipped in the snow as they attempted to run to the end of the street. They had only gone a few yards when she spotted something on the ground. A crumpled, wet slipper. She stopped and picked it up. Penny noticed another one lying close by.

'These must belong to her,' said Emma. 'She must be running barefoot!'

Penny shook her head incredulously. 'She's lost her mind.'

They continued on and caught up with Mr Wright by the main road. The snow had soaked into Emma's shoes and her toes felt cold and wet.

Small, icy flakes fell as they looked left and right on Knightsbridge Road.

'There!' cried Penny, pointing.

Between the passing traffic, Emma caught a glimpse of a woman running alongside the high wall of Hyde Park Barracks on the other side of the road. She was barefoot. Her fox-red hair flowed loose and her white nightdress billowed as she ran. It was an ethereal sight on a cold, busy London street.

Emma felt concerned for Constance Harpole. She clearly wasn't thinking straight and she was going to catch a dangerous chill in her state of undress.

They waited for a pause in the traffic then followed her. The flakes of snow stung Emma's eyes and her legs ached as she braced herself against slipping on the icy pavement.

Passers-by stopped and stared as Constance passed them. To Emma's frustration, no one attempted to stop and challenge her. She reached the end of the barracks wall and turned right into Hyde Park.

'She's moving fast!' said Mr Wright. 'It's a struggle to catch her!'

The park was a white expanse of snow with grey, bare-branched trees. Constance was easily distinguishable with her flash of long red hair. She moved with ease in the colourless landscape, possessed by a desperation to escape.

Emma's throat was dry from the cold air and her chest ached with exertion. She wasn't sure how much longer she could run for. Mr Wright sprinted ahead of her and Penny, clearly determined to bring the chase to an end.

He gained ground on Constance and called out for her stop. His words appeared to make her move faster. Then suddenly he tumbled and hit the ground heavily.

Emma winced, concerned he'd hurt himself. She and Penny ran up to him as he staggered to his feet and brushed the snow from his clothes.

'Are you all right?' asked Emma.

'Yes, I'm fine,' he grunted, although he was clutching his lower back. 'Don't worry about me.' He limped a few steps, clearly unable to run anymore. 'Just go after her!' he said.

Emma and Penny continued the chase. Ahead of them, Lady Harpole had reached Rotten Row – a horse track which crossed her path. A line of horses and riders trotted towards her. Emma guessed it was the Household Cavalry exercising their mounts. Lady Harpole darted across the track before the horses could reach her, but there wasn't enough time for Emma and Penny to follow. They sighed as they had to stop and wait for horses to pass.

The thud of hoofbeats and jangle of harnesses filled the air. Breath and perspiration rose in small clouds. Emma's frustration grew as the troop steadily made its way past them. She knew this time would allow Constance to make her getaway. Concerned for Harry Wright, she turned around to see him walking towards them. Unfortunately, his limp looked bad. She raised her hand to acknowledge him and he raised his in return.

Once the Household Cavalry had passed, Emma and

Penny hurried on, crossing the churned-up track of snow and mud.

Constance was still in sight. 'I think she's slowing,' puffed Emma.

'Thank goodness,' said Penny, panting. 'We need to get her somewhere warm. There's a police station on the other side of The Serpentine.'

The Serpentine was the long, curved lake in the centre of the park.

Lady Harpole was now running towards a road which crossed the park. Emma and Penny were much closer to her now. She moved wearily, her limbs floundering.

'She's exhausted,' puffed Penny. 'Hopefully she'll have to stop soon.'

A carriage slowed on the road, its occupants staring at the woman with loose hair in a nightdress. Emma thought she heard the driver call out to Constance, but she ignored him. Eventually, the carriage continued on, heading for the bridge over The Serpentine.

Constance slowed to a walk.

'We've nearly got her,' said Penny continuing her jog. Emma tried to keep up with her, ignoring the stiff pains in her legs.

'Lady Harpole!' called out Penny, her voice carrying across the snow-covered park. 'We want to talk to you!'

Constance continued forward without acknowledging them, her bare feet leaving bloody footprints in the snow. Her movements were mechanical, purposeful.

Finally catching up, Emma and Penny positioned themselves on either side of her, trying to slow her determined pace. When Constance finally turned to them, Emma barely suppressed a gasp. The woman's face was flushed with fever or madness, her green eyes unnaturally wide and glittering with an intensity that seemed beyond sanity. Her hair, wild and untamed, whipped around her face in the bitter wind. Emma recognized the dangerous detachment in her gaze – the look of someone who had stepped outside the boundaries of ordinary human constraints.

EIGHTY-SIX

'Do you remember us?' Penny asked Constance Harpole. 'Mrs Blakely and Mrs Langley.'

'I remember,' she said, breathless.

Emma glanced down at her feet, they were white with cold and smeared with blood. She felt pity for her. 'Please put on my coat,' she said, unbuttoning her overcoat. As she did so, she recalled Lord Charles Harpole making the same gesture.

Constance held up a palm. 'No. I'm not cold.'

'But you must be!' said Penny.

Constance shook her head.

'Why did you run away?'

'Because I will hang for what I did.' She quickened her step, heading for the bridge ahead of them.

'What did you do?' asked Penny.

'I killed my brother-in-law,' she said. 'I poisoned him so I could become Lady Harpole.' She gave an odd laugh then stopped and stared at the ground. 'But it was all in vain.'

'What do you mean?' asked Emma.

Constance lifted her face and fixed her gaze. 'Richard was illegitimate. I only found out last week. He never told me. If only he'd told me! He should have told me years ago. I'd lived in hope of being a lady one day. If I'd known, then...' Her gaze returned to the bridge ahead of them.

'Then what?' asked Penny.

'No one would be dead,' she replied. 'It's all Richard's fault.'

'You can't blame your husband for the awful murders you've committed,' said Emma.

Constance turned on her. 'You have no idea what it's like! My husband kept a secret from me. He lied to me! He pretended to be someone he wasn't!'

The similarity to Emma's experience struck her like a physical blow – a husband's betrayal, the foundation of one's life revealed as a lie. For a moment, sympathy threatened to overwhelm her judgement. But she thought of Lord Harpole, dying alone in that hotel room, and of Maitland, bleeding to death in his office.

'Nothing justifies murder,' said Penny firmly, taking Constance's arm gently. 'We're going to take you somewhere warm now.'

Constance shrugged her off. 'No you're not. You're not taking me to the police. I refuse to go!'

'They'll be here soon, anyway,' said Penny, giving a hopeful glance around. Emma looked too. There was no sign of anyone other than poor Mr Wright limping in the distance.

Where had the police got to? Emma felt sure they would have realized by now that Constance wasn't at home. It felt eerily quiet and lonely in the park. The only sound was the distant thud of hoofbeats.

Constance jogged towards the bridge, the cold wind tugging at her nightdress and hair.

Emma and Penny followed. 'Please come with us,' pleaded Penny. 'It will be easier for you if you talk calmly with us now. If you keep running, you'll only make things worse for yourself.'

'It can't get worse,' said Constance.

'There may not be a death sentence,' said Penny. 'Sometimes leniency is shown! Especially for women. Please come with us now. This can all be dealt with decently and respectfully.'

Constance didn't reply. They followed her onto the bridge. Mist curled over the cold, grey Serpentine. A pigeon sat on the low balustrade wall. It took off as they approached, swooping over the water to the bare trees on the far side.

Constance stopped and looked out over the lake. 'I used to come here as a child,' she said. 'I raced my sisters around the lake. Nanny told us off. She said we had to behave like proper little girls. But I ignored her.' She smiled. 'I thought I was better than her. And I was. I always wanted to be someone special. A lady or even a princess. We often passed Kensington Palace on our walks and I dreamed I would one day live there.' She sighed. 'The best I could manage was to marry the second son of a lord. Only the second son.'

A pause followed. Penny broke the silence. 'So you reasoned that if something happened to the first son, then you could become Lady Harpole.'

'Yes. And it was surprisingly easy.' Constance turned to them. 'Charles was surprised to see me that evening, but it wasn't difficult to charm him. I brought him a bottle of his favourite whisky. With that and a lady for company, he was very amenable. He always had a fondness for me, but don't tell Richard that.'

'And the laudanum?' asked Emma.

'I brought that with me too. I keep it at home because I need a drop of it now and again for my nerves. I poured his whisky that night and I added the laudanum to his third drink. He commented it tasted a little different but I told him he was imagining it. Her believed me! Then I added it to his fourth and so on... Before long he didn't really know what he was drinking.

I know it was the wrong thing to do, but I had so much to gain from it.'

Emma recalled the awful state they'd found Lord Harpole in that evening. 'You didn't feel any remorse?' she asked, incredulous.

'I don't really know what that feels like.' Constance's gaze drifted out over the lake again.

Harry Wright had now caught up with them and stood about twenty yards away. He caught Emma's eye and seemed to understand it was best he remained where he was.

'And Mr Maitland?' asked Penny. 'Why did you murder him?'

'He knew Richard was illegitimate! And then he tried to blackmail us. It had to stop. These men...' She shook her head and smiled bitterly. 'They're just so stupid!'

'Why do you say that?' asked Emma.

'Maitland put a false name and the General Post Office address on the ransom demand. All I had to do was visit the post office and ask a clerk there to alert me as soon as the man with that name came in to collect the money. I told the clerk I wanted a description of the man and he obliged with a telegram the following day. It was easy to work out who the blackmailer was from the description. Maitland called on us once to ask for payment to search for family treasure. The nerve of the man! He was clearly desperate for money and would stop at nothing to get it.'

'So you called on him?' asked Penny.

'Yes. He had to be dealt with. He knew Richard's secret and he thought he could use it to get money from us. There was a risk he would tell others, too. I hid a knife in my muff and called at his office on Charing Cross Road. That was another easy one. I told him I wanted to discuss the search for the family treasure. And I pretended to be upset about having just damaged the heel of my shoe in the street. I asked if he could have a look at it and see if it could be repaired. A gentleman can never resist trying to help a lady, can he? It was while he was holding the shoe next to the lamp that I struck. He was too distracted to stop me. He never expected his genteel lady caller to attack him with a knife!' She laughed and Emma and Penny exchanged a glance. It was hard to comprehend how Constance could talk about her callous crimes so calmly.

The smile faded from Constance's face. 'But it was all for nothing... I worked so hard to become Lady Harpole. I even pretended I was reluctantly inheriting the title! I fooled Richard and I thought I'd fooled everyone, but...' She turned and gave Emma and Penny a grim look. 'I failed.' A tear rolled down her cheek. 'What am I now? What have I become?' She looked down at her nightgown and bare feet. 'I'm stripped of everything. No status. No dignity. For a brief time, I was a lady. Just as I'd dreamed. But not now. I'm worthless now.'

She clambered onto the balustrade wall, knocking off clumps of snow. She knelt at first, then carefully rose to a standing position.

Emma's heart leapt into her mouth. 'Please come down,' she said. 'We need to get you out of the cold.'

Constance stared down at them with a strange, serene smile. The wind blew flakes of snow around her. Her long red hair played over her shoulders and her nightdress whipped around her bare legs.

'Tell Richard he should never have kept his secret from me,' she said. 'Tell him this is all his fault.'

'No,' said Penny. 'You must tell him yourself. Come down from there. Come with us.' She held out a hand.

'Never.'

Constance raised her arms and stepped back off the wall, her gaze still fixed on them.

Then she fell from sight. Emma felt sickened as she heard the splash. Could anyone survive the freezing water?

She and Penny rushed to the wall and peered over. They caught a glimpse of white nightdress beneath the surface and then it was gone.

'Oh, goodness,' gasped Penny. 'How can we get her out?'

'Help!' Emma shouted. 'Someone's in the water!'

Her voice echoed across the lake.

Harry Wright ran onto the bridge. 'Don't go in after her!' he urged. 'You'll die in there.' He glanced around. 'There should be a life buoy at the side of the lake somewhere. I'll go and find it. But we can only rescue her if she wants to be saved.'

EIGHTY-SEVEN

A warm fire burned in the grate of the waiting room at Hyde Park police station, but Emma struggled to warm up. She and Penny sipped at cups of sweetened tea, trying to come to terms with what had happened.

Harry Wright paced the floor. 'Perhaps we shouldn't have chased her?' he said. 'Do you think that's why she did it?'

Penny shook her head sadly. 'I suspect she made up her mind to do it as soon as she heard us arrive this morning.'

Emma's heart felt heavy. 'I feel responsible,' she said, wringing her hands together. 'I accused Constance Harpole and now look what's happened!'

Mr Wright stepped over to her and tentatively rested a hand on her shoulder. 'You didn't accuse her unfairly. You were right about her.'

Penny nodded. 'You were, Emma. And you did the right thing. You told me and James first and then we involved the police. Don't forget how much we tried to persuade her to come with us, but we couldn't force her. She knew her fate would be a death sentence, so she chose another way out.'

Inspector Trotter and Inspector Fenton entered the room.

Mr Wright lifted his hand from Emma's shoulder which she felt a little disappointed about.

'They've pulled Lady Harpole's body from the water,' said Fenton. 'On a day like today I suspect the shock of the cold killed her rather than drowning. I need to take statements from all three of you so we can establish exactly what happened. Who wants to go first?'

Emma exchanged glances with Penny then Harry Wright. None of them seemed keen to talk about the tragic event. It felt too recent.

'All right then,' said Mr Wright. 'I'll go first.'

EIGHTY-EIGHT

'A box of smoking pipes?' said James shaking his head. 'That's what Stephen Lydney found in Lord Henry Harpole's grave?'

'That's what the article in this morning's *Morning Express* says,' said Emma. As soon as she'd read it that morning, she'd called on Penny and James to share the news.

'And he's been charged with unlawfully disturbing a grave,' said Penny.

'Good,' said James. 'So that's Lydney and Crowfield both arrested now.'

'Crowfield?' said Emma.

'Yes, I haven't found the chance to tell you yet,' said Penny. 'We got a telegram last night from the Yard to say Crowfield has been charged with attacking James.'

'Thank goodness they've got him!'

'And the frustrating thing is, I can't remember anything about the attack,' said James. 'I remember leaving the railway station that evening and crossing the road, and then... Nothing. The next I knew, Penny was smothering me while I lay in a hospital bed.'

'I was overjoyed you'd woken up, James! I can't tell you how awful it is sitting at your loved one's bedside like that and worrying they're never going to be the same again.' She reached over to him and squeezed his hand.

'So how does the Yard know Rupert Crowfield attacked you, James?' asked Emma.

'They found my wallet and watch in his miserable little flat.' He shook his head. 'Time and time again, these idiots like Crowfield incriminate themselves, don't they? They never learn.'

'So did Lydney ask him to attack you?'

'I should think so. Inspector Fenton is interviewing Lydney at the moment and I hope he'll be charged too. Neither he nor Crowfield liked me asking them questions. They wanted to find their treasure and reap their reward. And now they have it, of course. A box of pipes.' He laughed, then winced as the movement hurt his bruised ribs.

'I can't imagine the members of the Inveniam Society being very impressed by the pipes,' said Penny. 'They were presumably hoping for something valuable. That's what Lydney had led them to believe he would find. All that fuss over the map and it's worthless now. It's probably lying in that creepy house, forgotten about. I wonder what will happen to the society?'

'It will probably be disbanded,' said James. 'It can't really continue without Lydney, can it? He was in charge and Crowfield was his assistant. The other members put their money in and hoped for a share in the treasure.'

'I suppose that's what William was hoping for,' said Emma. 'Lydney obviously persuaded him to invest a large sum of money in his society. Presumably the monthly meetings were held so they could discuss their progress on searching for treasure. Although Lydney's an unpleasant character, I think he deserves some credit for his research skills. Do you remember all those books and maps we found in his office, Penny? He clearly took his work seriously. And he managed to identify the location of the treasure without solving all the clues.'

'So did you, Emma.'

She smiled, a little embarrassed. 'Well, it was a lucky guess.'

'So was there ever any real treasure?' said Penny. 'Or was it all just Theobald Harpole's idea of a joke?'

'According to the newspaper article, he left a note in the box explaining the pipes were the treasure,' said Emma.

'How disappointing,' said Penny. 'Although it's amusing that Stephen Lydney ended up with them.' Her eyes sparkled with sudden humour. 'To think of all our efforts – only to have Lord Theobald Harpole play one final joke from beyond the grave!'

'Francis Edwards told me he couldn't find any detail about the treasure which Sir Francis Drake gave to Lord Henry Harpole,' said Emma. 'I remember wondering then if it had actually ever existed. But the rumours it did clearly interested treasure hunters and encouraged Lord Theobald Harpole to create his puzzle. He enjoyed puzzles but he also enjoyed practical jokes.'

'And burying his pipe collection in an empty grave is an amusing joke,' said Penny with a smile. 'The story of Sir Francis Drake's hidden treasure has turned out to be a myth. But it was fun solving the clues, wasn't it?'

'Fun?' Emma exclaimed incredulously. Her hand rose unconsciously to her throat at the memory. 'Being hunted through Hampton Court maze by Mr Maitland, terrified he might do heaven knows what if he caught us?' She shook her head vehemently. 'I don't think I'll ever find mazes amusing again.'

'He never intended to harm us,' said Penny. 'He was just hopeless at following people without being noticed.'

Emma nodded. 'That's true. And poor Mr Maitland is no longer with us.'

'That's a real shame,' said James. 'He acted foolishly at times but didn't deserve to be murdered. And as for Richard Harpole, he'll have to live out the rest of his life in obscurity. Perhaps he'll make friends again with his former valet and they can share rooms together in the lodging house.' He chuckled then winced at the pain again. 'Isn't it remarkable how some people manage to orchestrate their own downfall?'

EIGHTY-NINE

A horse-drawn van stood outside the Solomons' house when Emma returned to Northampton Square.

As soon as she stepped into the entrance hall, Mr Solomon took her by the arm and led her towards the dining room. 'Don't go into the parlour, Mrs Langley.'

'Why not?' She felt concerned. 'What's happened? Is Mrs Solomon all right?'

'She's fine.'

'What's the van doing outside?'

'It's for the neighbours.'

'But it's parked outside this house.'

Mr Solomon sighed. 'You ask far too many questions, Mrs Langley. What am I supposed to say?'

'I don't know. I'm just worried.'

'Don't be worried. Everything is fine.'

'Ronald?' Emma turned as she heard Mrs Solomon's voice in the hallway. 'Where are you, Ronald?'

Mr Solomon was hard of hearing. He stood impassively, still holding Emma's arm.

'Mrs Solomon is calling you,' she said to him.

'She's what?'

'She's calling you from the hallway.'

'Oh. Stay here. And don't move!'

Emma couldn't resist a smile. She sat on a dining chair and waited. She had no idea what the Solomons were up to, but she felt reassured there was nothing to worry about.

Five minutes later, a flustered-looking Mrs Solomon opened the dining room door.

'Hello, Mrs Langley. I wasn't expecting you back so soon.'

'I'm sorry.'

'Don't apologize.' She turned and called out to her husband. 'Ronald! Bring the blindfold!'

'Blindfold?' said Emma. 'What's going on?'

Mr Solomon appeared at the door. 'What?'

'Have you got the blindfold, Ronald?'

'No. Did you ask for it?'

'Yes! Go and fetch it!'

A short while later, Emma was led blindfolded by Mr and Mrs Solomon to another room of the house.

'Take off the blindfold now, Mrs Langley,' said her landlady with an excited whisper.

Emma did so and found herself in the parlour. In front of her, an upright piano stood by the window.

She gasped.

'A piano! You didn't have to—'

'Yes, we did. And we didn't pay much for it, so don't you worry about the cost. You need a piano to practise on, don't you?'

'Yes.'

'And I would like some lessons,' said Mrs Solomon. 'I haven't played since I was a girl and I'd like you to teach me if you wouldn't mind, Mrs Langley.'

'Of course! I'd be delighted to!'

'Now go and play it,' said Mr Solomon.

Emma made her way over to the piano, but before she could get there, Laurence the cat jumped up onto the piano stool.

'Oh, Laurence! Shoo!' said Mrs Solomon.

'No, leave him,' said Emma. 'He's excited about the piano too. Let him have a look at it and I'll play once he's finished.'

NINETY

Emma told Penny about the piano when she called on her at the weekend. They shared a pot of tea in the dining room while Thomas and Florence had their afternoon sleep.

'How wonderful!' said Penny. 'You'll be able to play to your heart's content.'

'Possibly,' said Emma. 'But it's a loud instrument and I don't want to subject Mr and Mrs Solomon to it too much.'

'I don't think they'll mind at all. After all, they bought it for you.'

'On the condition I teach Mrs Solomon how to play.'

'Well, that could be fun!'

'Possibly.' Emma smiled. 'I'll let you know after her first lesson.'

'I think the piano is just what you need after this past week,' said Penny. 'That incident in Hyde Park was difficult to cope with. But you look a lot better than you did a few days ago.'

'Do I?' Emma took a sip of tea. 'That's good to know. How's James recovering?'

'He's doing very well,' said Penny. 'Almost back to his old

self. I can't believe I was so worried about him. When he wasn't waking up, I really worried that...' She took in a breath and Emma waited while she composed herself again. 'Thank you for supporting me, Emma,' she said, after a pause. 'I'm very grateful you forced me to go to that chop house. I didn't think I needed to, but I did.'

'That's what friends do,' said Emma.

Penny nodded. 'Actually, that's what I've been writing about.'

Emma felt surprised to hear this. 'You have?'

'Yes. I've written a few articles for the *Morning Express* about motherhood now. And I wrote one which Mr Fish told me wasn't jolly enough.'

Emma laughed. 'Not jolly enough?'

'No. I think he assumes ladies don't have much to get concerned about. Anyway, I rewrote the article and I'm now working on one which I believe Mr Fish would describe as jolly. Would you like to hear some of it?'

Emma nodded. 'Yes, I would.'

Penny pulled a piece of paper from her bag. 'It's an article about the importance of friendship.'

'Oh?'

'I'll read some of it to you now.' Penny cleared her throat. '"Society has us believe a woman's worth lies solely in marriage and motherhood, however I have found equal importance in the bonds between women. My dear friend Mrs L. has shown me that when ladies join forces, there is very little we can't achieve."'

'You're mentioning me in your article?' said Emma, astonished.

'Yes.' Penny smiled. 'Don't look so surprised. It's true, don't you think?'

'I suppose it is.' Emma felt her face warming. She felt flattered and a little embarrassed at the same time.

'In fact, I wonder if that last line needs altering,' said Penny. 'Perhaps it should read, "When ladies join forces, there are no mysteries we cannot solve..."'

A LETTER FROM THE AUTHOR

Thank you for reading this Emma Langley mystery. I hope you enjoyed it!

Would you like to know when I release new books? Here are some ways to stay updated:

Click here to be the first to know about my latest releases with Storm:

www.stormpublishing.co/emily-organ

Join my mailing list and receive a free short mystery, *The Belgrave Square Murder*:

emilyorgan.com/the-belgrave-square-murder

And if you have a moment, I would be very grateful if you would leave a quick review of my books online. Honest reviews of my books help other readers discover them too!

emilyorgan.com

- facebook.com/emilyorganwriter
- goodreads.com/emily_organ
- bookbub.com/authors/emily-organ

HISTORICAL NOTE

The first church on the site of St Paul's Cathedral was built in the year 604. After it was destroyed by fire, the first cathedral was constructed in the eleventh century. During the Middle Ages, pilgrims travelled there to visit the shrine of Saint Erkenwald – a seventh-century Saxon prince and Bishop of London. That cathedral was destroyed in the Great Fire of London in 1666, and the magnificent replacement we see today was designed by Sir Christopher Wren.

One of St Paul's most famous features is the Whispering Gallery – a circular walkway that runs around the base of the cathedral's dome. Thanks to its unique acoustics, a whisper spoken against the wall can be heard clearly by someone standing on the opposite side, over one hundred feet away. This extraordinary effect was not intentional – I wonder who first stumbled upon it!

Sir Christopher Wren is buried in St Paul's alongside prominent military figures such as Vice-Admiral Horatio Nelson and Arthur Wellesley, the 1st Duke of Wellington. The poets John Donne and Philip Sidney are also interred here, as are the artists J.E. Millais, Joshua Reynolds, Edwin Landseer, J.M.W.

Turner and Anthony van Dyck. The scientist Alexander Fleming and architect Edwin Lutyens are among others laid to rest in this iconic cathedral.

Hampton Court Palace, located on the River Thames in southwest London, was built in the sixteenth century for Cardinal Wolsey, who later gifted it to King Henry VIII. It soon became one of the king's favourite residences. In the seventeenth century, King William III expanded the palace. Today, Hampton Court is a popular tourist attraction. Its famous hedge maze, created in the 1690s, is the oldest surviving maze in the UK.

Ye Olde Cheshire Cheese has stood on Fleet Street since 1538. After being destroyed in the Great Fire of London in 1666, it was rebuilt the following year. Its cellars date back to a thirteenth-century monastery that once occupied the site. As one of the few surviving seventeenth-century chophouses in London, the pub is steeped in history. Notable patrons have included Dr Samuel Johnson, Charles Dickens, Arthur Conan Doyle, Mark Twain, W.B. Yeats, Alfred Lord Tennyson, P.G. Wodehouse, Winston Churchill, George Orwell, Princess Margaret and even Voltaire. The pub is referenced in several works, including *A Tale of Two Cities* by Dickens and Agatha Christie's *The Million Dollar Bond Robbery*. Inside, a warren of rooms spans multiple levels. The pub's most colourful resident was Polly the Parrot, who lived there for thirty years in the late nineteenth and early twentieth centuries, famous for her foul-mouthed outbursts. Polly's gender was never confirmed, but her death made national headlines. She is now preserved in a glass case inside the pub.

St Mary's Hospital in Paddington opened in 1851 and continues as a hospital today. Its private Lindo Wing has become well-known as the birthplace of numerous celebrity and royal babies.

The Royal Opera House in Covent Garden began life as

the Theatre Royal in the eighteenth century. The current building dates from the mid-nineteenth century, following the destruction of the earlier structure by fire. In the latter half of the nineteenth century, it was known as the Royal Italian Opera House, with all opera performances staged in Italian. Today, it serves as the home of both the Royal Opera and the Royal Ballet.

The church of St Bartholomew-the-Great dates from the twelfth century and boasts a striking timber gatehouse, built in the sixteenth century on top of a thirteenth-century arch. Once part of a priory complex alongside St Bartholomew's Hospital, the church has seen varied use over time, including commercial activity. Notably, Benjamin Franklin worked here as a typesetter in a local print shop. The church remains a beautiful and atmospheric place to visit and has featured in numerous films, including *Four Weddings and a Funeral*.

Hyde Park was established in the sixteenth century by King Henry VIII and opened to the public around a century later. Rotten Row, a broad track running almost a mile through the park, became a fashionable place to ride horses in the eighteenth century. The upper classes would flock there to see and be seen. The track is still maintained today for horse riding and is regularly used by the Household Cavalry, stationed nearby at Hyde Park Barracks. The Household Cavalry forms part of the British Army's division responsible for ceremonial duties in London and Windsor and serves as the monarch's official bodyguard.

The Serpentine, Hyde Park's picturesque lake, was created by damming the River Westbourne – one of many small rivers that once flowed through London and now run underground. Hyde Park's police station, known as the Old Police House, was built in the 1870s. It remains in use today as part of the Metropolitan Police and is considered one of London's most attractive police stations.

Printed in Dunstable, United Kingdom